THE LAUNDRYMAN

PRAISE FOR THE LAUNDRYMAN

"A fast-paced, always arresting historical mystery, Dwayne Brenna's The Laundryman *pits two Mounties as mismatched as Holmes and Watson against an array of murder suspects in pre-provincial Prince Albert during a numbingly cold winter, with a bit of love, a hint of sex, a lot of suspense—and even a dog."*

— DAVE MARGOSHES, AUTHOR OF *A SIMPLE CARPENTER*

"Dwayne Brenna's The Laundryman *is a hard one to put down, a classic murder mystery that is nothing like any whodunit I've ever read. His setting (late 19th century, Northern Saskatchewan), his characters (cops, good women, greedy bastards, Indigenous hunters, and hardscrabble farmers), and his plot are painstakingly woven together. If, like me, you begin to miss Brenna's authentic world, the only remedy is to read* The Laundryman *one more time."*

— DAVID CARPENTER, AUTHOR OF *THE EDUCATION OF ANGIE MERASTY*

"Dwayne Brenna knows his characters well, their strengths and weaknesses, and creates a compelling narrative as they struggle to solve a series of crimes in the turbulent North West. This is a novel touched by the spirit of an engrossing era, and it's a pleasure to read."

— ROBERT CURRIE, AUTHOR OF *LIVING WITH THE HAWK*

THE LAUNDRYMAN

DWAYNE BRENNA

SHADOWPAW PRESS

THE LAUNDRYMAN

Copyright © 2026 by Dwayne Brenna
All rights reserved

Shadowpaw Press
Regina, Saskatchewan, Canada
www.shadowpawpress.com

CERTIFIED CANADIAN PUBLISHER

Cover design by Shaun Stevens, Flintlock Covers

All characters and events in this book are fictitious.
Any resemblance to persons living or dead is coincidental.

The scanning, uploading, and distribution of this book via the Internet
or any other means without the permission of the publisher
is illegal and punishable by law.

Trade Paperback ISBN: 978-1-998273-52-2
Ebook ISBN: 978-1-998273-53-9
Audiobook ISBN: 978-1-998273-66-9

Made possible through Creative Saskatchewan's
Book Publishing Production Publishers' Stream Program

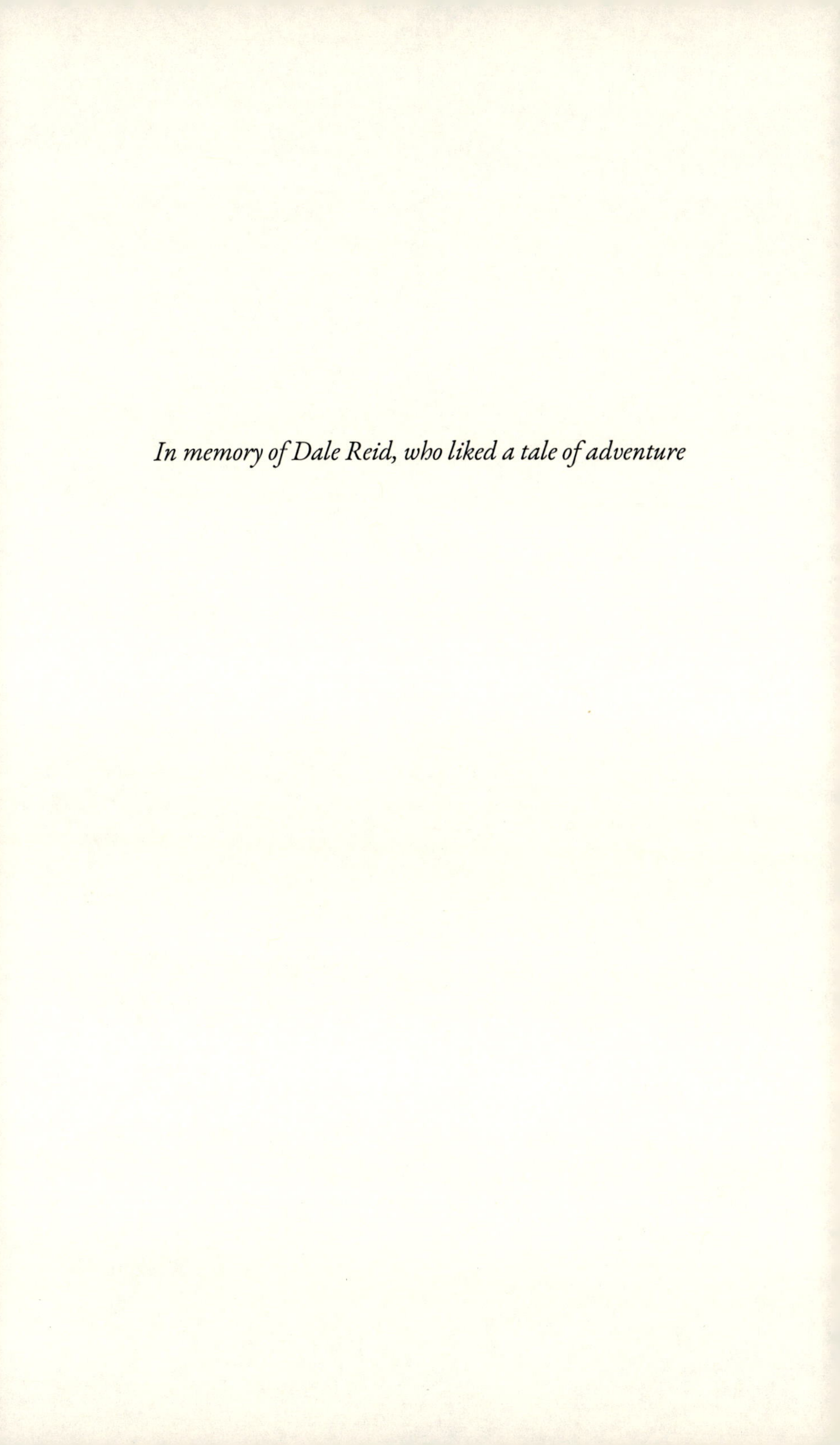

In memory of Dale Reid, who liked a tale of adventure

"He walked out in the gray light and stood and he saw for a brief moment the absolute truth of the world. The cold relentless circling of the intestate earth. Darkness implacable. The blind dogs of the sun in their running. The crushing black vacuum of the universe. And somewhere two hunted animals trembling like ground-foxes in their cover. Borrowed time and borrowed world and borrowed eyes with which to sorrow it."

— CORMAC MCCARTHY, *THE ROAD*

1

We'd been riding for half a day, and I don't believe I'd heard Belvedere utter one word. He sat on his roan like a lump, cradling his terrier in front of the saddle horn as the October sun began to wane. I wondered if the terrier even had a name. Sometimes, Belvedere would let it run in the tall grass as we traced our way along the banks of the North Saskatchewan River. When he wanted the terrier to keep up, he would whistle high and urgently, the kind of whistle you might expect as a catcall in some eastern theatre. Our horses trudged together, side by side, in the deep wheel ruts along the traders' road.

Belvedere was no picnic, and neither was the assignment Colonel Herchmer had given us. He'd briefed us two days earlier in Battleford. There'd been a murder in Prince Albert, a town of two thousand souls three days east. A laundryman had been gunned down in his own backyard. The town's sheriff had done due diligence, but no perpetrator had been found. The local garrison of the Mounted Police was at odds with the sheriff's office and had never dealt with a murder before. "I know it's not the most glamorous assignment," Herchmer had said, sitting smugly at his desk in the officers' quarters, "but I'm sure you'll make the best of it." I couldn't help but feel that the assignment was some sort of punishment, at least for Belvedere, who never bothered to demonstrate much admiration for authority. There had been a rumour about a fiasco at Fort Walsh some years before, and he was often given assignments that nobody else wanted, at least for as long as I'd known him. "There's currently no medical man in the garrison at Prince Albert," Herchmer added, not bothering to look at me while he stuffed tobacco into his meerschaum. "We'll need you there, Montgomery, to examine the body."

"How long has the man been dead, sir?" I asked.

The colonel rubbed his chin. "At least a week," he said. "It took three days for the rider to get here."

"Then there might not be much left to examine."

When Herchmer looked at me finally, it was a gaze of unhappiness at being questioned by an underling. "Well, examine what you can." He handed me an envelope containing private orders that were meant to be kept confidential.

We'd been told to keep an eye out for a farmstead thirty miles downriver where we might find food and shelter on the first night of our trek. The sky had been overcast since mid-morning. I was glad of my riding boots and woollen socks, glad of the muskrat hat and thick leather gloves. The wind came out of the north—not a good thing, I'd learned in the few short months since I'd joined the force. Cold weather emanates from the tundra and the arctic wastes above it and grips the open prairie in its steely hand. My feet grew numb as the wind blew in. Fastening the buttons on my heavy buffalo coat as I rode, with one hand and fingers that felt like sticks of wood, was an awkward procedure. I found myself looking over my shoulder, like a man hunted by a wild animal, as a darker set of clouds clamoured toward us.

It was five o'clock in the afternoon, by my pocket watch, and still no sign of the promised farmstead. Belvedere grew increasingly more sullen, if that was possible, his eyes like blackened marbles. He nudged his horse in the flank when it stopped to munch the tall, dead grass. The dog inside his bulky buffalo coat was every bit a silent as Belvedere. Maybe it was asleep.

Snow began to fall, a smattering at first. You wouldn't have known anything was out of the ordinary by the blank look on Belvedere's face. He kept riding, oblivious to the changing weather.

The wind grew more intense, hoodoos of snow swirling around us. Soon I could not see a hundred feet ahead of us. I counted on our horses to follow the trail, although, as far as I knew, the beasts had never travelled that road before. The whiteness in the air around us was something like what it is, in my imagination, to die: a vast nothingness, no coordinates, no here and no there, a swirling whiteness like the maelstrom of creation and destruction.

I had packed enough food in my saddlebag for a three-day journey, or so I thought, mostly hard tack and jerky and some bread but also a puckered apple that I'd managed to liberate from the mess hall before leaving. Whether out of hunger or fear, I found myself devouring most of that on the first day, even gnawing at the desiccated apple that had frozen like a rock during the afternoon. Belvedere ate in a more conservative fashion, allowing himself a morsel of jerky now and then and providing his dog with the same ration.

Then it got dark. Our horses lost the trail, and we found ourselves lurching over rocks and undergrowth. "Perhaps we should set up camp?" I shouted, competing with the wind.

"We'll stay the course," Belvedere snarled. His moustache and his goatee were caked with wet snow. He tucked his chin lower into the buffalo coat, like a helmsman sailing into a gale. I couldn't argue with him. A corporal with five years' service under his belt, he had much more experience of the Territories than I. Still in the first months of my contract with Her Majesty the Queen, I outranked him only by virtue of my medical degree. I had been hired as a commissioned officer, but rank means little in the face of a prairie blizzard.

My horse, Belle, trudged bravely into the storm. The wind bit at my face. It chewed on my earlobes and searched out the fingers inside my gloves. Luckily, I'd remembered to stow a woollen scarf —a parting gift from Emily—in one of my coat sleeves. That scarf was my talisman. It protected me in the same way that a gift from his damsel shielded a knight errant in olden times. Clenching the reins in my teeth, I wrapped the warm scarf over my nose and mouth.

We rode doggedly. The horses' pace had slowed to a crawl, and the only other comfort I had was the cold metal compass that assured me we were heading in a northeasterly direction. There were no stars in the whitened sky, no moon to steer by. Little more than a block of ice before long, I was ready to tumble out of the saddle and find my eternal rest in the first snow of the prairie autumn.

Belvedere did not acknowledge the cold. He spurred his horse into it, kicking the tired animal in the flank if it balked or expressed any kind of unwillingness. The corporal's jaw was set, and his hooded eyes peered fiercely into the storm.

Faintly at first, and then a trifle more clearly through the blizzard, a light appeared. Cold and tattered as I was, I could have been hallucinating, but then a rough-hewn farmstead with a few squat buildings materialized out of the darkness. The light I had seen was a coal-oil lantern blazing in the greasy window of a log shack. We were glad of any warmth and shelter, and I held the horses' reins while Belvedere knocked at the door with a gloved hand.

A sturdy-looking young man opened it. He had a Winchester rifle in his hands, clutching it tight in front of his chest as he spat some words in French and Cree at Belvedere.

"Are you McCallum?" I heard Belvedere shout over the wind.

"*Lafreniere dishinihkaashon.*"

"We are officers of the North-West Mounted Police," Belvedere declared. "We require shelter for the night."

The conversation went back and forth for a few minutes while I stood in the cold, shivering. The horses were shivering, too. It was clear that the young farmer did not trust us, but it would have been unconscionable for him to send us out again into the blizzard. He spoke partly in French, but it did not sound like the language of romance. When the negotiation ended, he reluctantly donned a thick cloth coat and escorted us out to the barn, where we stabled our horses and fed them alongside a few wizened cattle and three cats that huddled near the cows for warmth.

Then we went back to the house. It was a one-room shack with a stove and a table at one end and a bed at the other. Hides of beaver, fox, and muskrat were stretched on frames and hung from the ceiling on long hooks. Hanging on the wall near the rough bed was a silver necklace that seemed out of place with the rest of the décor. It was perhaps evidence of a wife who had succumbed to the pox or some such illness in previous years.

The young farmer studied us as we huddled over the stove for the better part of an hour. He was still sitting in a homemade chair at the table as we arranged our bedrolls on the wooden floorboards. Belvedere draped his tunic over a chair and fed his dog another morsel of jerky. When it was time to sleep, he rested on one arm on his bedroll, studying the farmer at the same time as the farmer was studying him. Then he pulled his buffalo coat over himself and closed his eyes. I wondered if we might be murdered in our sleep, but I took some comfort in the fact that Belvedere had left his holster, with the Enfield revolver at the ready, near to his right hand. He slept with the little terrier pressed against his back.

After some time, the farmer leaned his rifle against a wall and replenished the stove with wood. Seeming to give up on his animosity, he extinguished the flame in the lamp and lay down on the straw mattress of his bed, his back propped against the drafty wall. I can't remember which of us went to sleep first.

WHEN I AWOKE the next morning, the young farmer was again sitting at his rough-hewn table. He was wearing woollen trousers and a thick corduroy shirt. His feet were clad in beaded moccasins. The rifle was cradled in his arms.

The log house smelled of brain-tanning, and the smoky, meaty smell made me hungry. The stove was still hot and crackling, but there was nothing cooking on its French plate or in the oven—no porridge, not even a pot of coffee. I sat up on my bedroll and poked Belvedere gently.

The terrier was already awake and growling softly, his alert eyes trained on the farmer. Belvedere's hand was still wrapped firmly around the Enfield. He sat up and looked warily about. "Have you anything for us to eat?" he asked the farmer.

"Eat?" the farmer said.

Belvedere rubbed the stubble on his chin. "*Manger*?"

"*Maanzh?*" the farmer repeated. "Noo."

"We need sustenance," Belvedere said.

The farmer pointed toward the door with his rifle. "*Shipwaytay*."

I looked to Belvedere for guidance. "What does '*shipwaytay*' mean?"

"It means there is no breakfast here," Belvedere said. "He wants us to go away."

The morning was cold and crisp and clear as we walked toward the barn. Scattered on the thin layer of snow were a few yellow aspen leaves that might have decorated branches the day before. The sky was again clear, and the sun so bright that it almost hurt the eyes. I turned and looked toward the river and saw that the land had been cleared in a thin finger, abutting against the water.

Unlatching the barn door, the young farmer watched closely, rifle still in hand, as we entered the building. Our horses, at least, looked well-fed and replenished. They grunted and farted in their stalls, the breath from their nostrils visible in the morning air. When the horses were saddled and ready, Belvedere opened his saddlebag and produced a piece of jerky, about the size of my wallet. Offering none to me, he fed a portion to the little dog and put the rest in his own mouth. "If this witty fellow can't be bothered to feed us," he said, "we'll have to make do with our provisions." I began to lament my own stupidity at having packed so little sustenance before leaving Battleford.

We mounted our horses outside the barn. The farmer latched the door again and stood in front of the building as though he were a sentry left there to guard his last remaining possession. Sitting tall in the saddle, Belvedere stared at the man with cold, dark eyes. "You, my friend, are a scholar and a gentleman."

The farmer showed no sign of understanding. Fingering the trigger of his Winchester, he pointed with his lips toward the east. "*Shipwaytay*," he said again, and we spurred our animals out of his domain.

We headed northeast on the traders' road. The sun was still low on the horizon, and we had to be careful to steer our horses through the soft snow of the wheel ruts and not up into the uneven grass. Belvedere kept the terrier sequestered inside his coat, feeding it a scrap of jerky now and then. I was powerfully hungry, but I did not want to admit to the corporal that I had lacked the foresight to slide more than a small packet of unperishable food into my saddlebag.

It was clear that we had failed to find the McCallum farm the night before or that we had somehow overshot it. "Not a very pleasant fellow, that Lafreniere," I said, as my horse picked its way along the trail.

Belvedere shot me a desultory glance. "The *brule bois* don't love us."

"Oh?" I asked. "Why's that?"

"They know we've come to take their land."

Just then, a prairie chicken burst out of a thicket six feet away, frightening my horse into a skittery side-step. I tumbled out of the saddle into the newly fallen snow, hurting my right shoulder and my pride. The horse stopped and nosed me as I lay on my back on the ground. Belvedere had little sympathy. "For Gawd's sake,

Montgomery," he said from his saddle, looking down at me, "haven't you ever sat a horse before?"

Brushing the snow off my trousers, I climbed back into the saddle before another word was spoken. I massaged my aching shoulder as we rode, happy to find no evidence of a broken bone or a separation.

We had ridden about two miles when we heard an unearthly wheeze and squeal coming toward us from over the next hill. The concatenation grew louder and louder, sounding like an unhappy parade of wooden soldiers. When the cart crested the top of the hill, I could see a man in a brightly coloured cloth coat and baggy woollen trousers walking beside the ox that was pulling it. The fellow was of short stature, with squinty eyes and a pinched, rutted face. He'd been no stranger to the pox in his time.

Belvedere held up a gloved hand, and the cart screeched to a thankful halt. It was constructed entirely of wood, and I construed that the caterwauling I'd heard was nothing more than the friction of a rough wooden wheel on a wooden axle. The oxen's sides were heaving after the exertion of pulling the cart, laden with goods for sale or trade, up the hill.

The trader spoke up first, in a breezy, open manner. "Well, if it ain't 'er Majesty's constabulary," he said. "Fancy meetin' you out 'ere."

"You're with the English company," Belvedere replied.

"I am indeed, guv," the man said. "I sells and barters wif the natives 'ereabouts."

Belvedere dismounted and approached the cart. He ambled with a slight limp, reportedly from a wound he'd received while in military service in India. "What do you sell?"

"Blankets, clothing, beads," the man said. His demeanour was suddenly furtive.

"Whisky?"

"Well now, guv, that would be illegal, would it not?"

The trader's goods were covered by a thick canvas tarp. Belvedere toyed with the rope that fastened one corner of the tarp to the wooden frame of the cart. "I'll find no intoxicants if I look in here?"

"That's private property," the trader replied. "You've no call to dabble in't."

Belvedere untied the knot and flipped back a corner of the tarp. He rummaged through some small pelts—mostly fox and beaver from what I could see—and then some blankets and odd scraps of clothing. Underneath all of that, he found a wooden box. When he dragged the box from the cart and placed it on the ground, I could hear the unmistakable clatter of glass against glass. Kneeling over the stash of illegal whisky, Belvedere peered up at the trader. "What's this, then?"

"Fer medicinal purposes," the trader said.

"Twelve bottles," Belvedere replied. "That's a great deal of medicine." He stood up and drew the Enfield out of its holster. "I could confiscate all of this."

The man was immediately penitent. He took his cap off and pleaded with Belvedere. "Blimey, guv, can't we make a deal?"

Belvedere stared at him, steely-eyed. The heavy exhalation of the oxen was the only sound. "Have you got any food?"

"I 'ave pemmican," the trader replied.

"We'll take half your food supply," Belvedere said, "and the whisky."

"The whisky?"

"Unless you have special permission, in writing, from the Lieutenant Governor."

The trader looked from Belvedere to me and back to Belvedere. He was cornered, as he well knew. "Aw, guv," he said, "you're cutting into me profits."

"Or maybe you'd prefer the two-hundred-dollar fine and six months in prison?"

"I would not prefer that, no."

The trader marched to the rear of the cart. Under Belvedere's watchful eye, he divvied up the pemmican. He tossed the pelts and apparel back into the two-wheeled wagon and fastened the tarp over them. When he was finished and ready to go, the trader turned again to Belvedere. "It's been an education," he said. "I truly 'ope we never see each other again."

We watched as the cart creaked like a symphony of untuned violins up the next hill and disappeared into the distance. Belvedere handed the pemmican to me. "You can have this," he said.

It was a concoction of berries and animal fat, wrapped in a leather hide, and, although the presentation was none too appetizing, I picked away at it, a nibble at a time. The pemmican was not at all tasty, and it smelled like the intestines of a dead animal. I started to feel queasy after a while, and I placed the concoction back in its leather hide to save it for a rainier day.

Meanwhile, Belvedere stowed six of the whisky bottles in various saddlebags on his horse. He deposited a seventh bottle in the deep pocket of his buffalo coat and hid the remainder of his confiscation behind a large rock by a clump of trees. "We'll find it on the way back," he said. "No sense letting good whisky go to waste." He retrieved the bottle from his coat pocket, twisted off the cork, and gulped down a mouthful. Then he mounted his horse.

It was an uneventful ride for the rest of the day. I found myself wondering what sort of man I had been partnered with. He seemed equally capable of upholding the fragile new laws of the territory and of breaking them.

While we were plodding along, I draped the reins around the horn of my saddle. Then I surreptitiously fished Herchmer's envelope out of my medical bag, tore it open, and read the letter inside. Riding ahead of me on the narrow trader's road, Belvedere somehow either glimpsed the letter out of the corner of his eye or heard me rustling the paper. "What's that you're reading?" he asked.

"A letter from my fiancée." I folded the confidential letter and tucked it into my medical bag along with the envelope.

"Be careful that you don't fall off your horse again." Belvedere chuckled darkly to himself. "A letter from your fiancée?"

"Yes."

"There's no place for a married man in these environs."

By the time darkness settled in, Belvedere had consumed the entire bottle of whisky that he'd stowed in his coat pocket, but he carried his drunkenness quietly, like a man seasoned to hard liquor. If anything, he grew more silent and morose under the whisky's influence.

About twenty-five miles from Prince Albert, we stopped at a farmstead owned by a middle-aged man named Buckton. He was far friendlier than Lafreniere had been the night before, and he welcomed us into his wood-frame house for a late supper. His wife, a woman whom I guessed to be about thirty years old, looked terrified when we sat down at the long table, and his seven young children opened their mouths and bawled like newborn calves when they saw Belvedere's surly face. They had to be sent early to bed.

Belvedere and I placed our bedrolls on the floor after the master of the house and his missus had gone upstairs for the night, and the corporal and his dog were both asleep and snoring long before I managed to nod off. Staring up at the dark ceiling, I lay in my bedroll and thought of the confidential orders the colonel had given me. A gnawing ache crept in at the pit of my stomach, and I worried about the future of this investigation. More than that, I worried about my own future as a surgeon in Her Majesty's constabulary.

2

We arrived in Prince Albert the next day, tired and saddle-sore. From our vantage point on the north side of the river, I could see that the town was bustling with activity. Buckboards rattled through the long main street that ran parallel to the river. Civic buildings, many of brick construction, were straight and tall. Various shops stood sentinel over the river, their false fronts gleaming with paint. There was a mill for grinding flour and a huge sign that advertised logging and lumber. In the shadow of a steep hill, toward the south, was the residential district with its neat frame houses, all trim and neatly painted. We waited as the ferry, a rickety-looking longboat, crept across the river toward us, pulled doggedly against the current by thick ropes and winches.

A ragtag band of canines patrolled the riverbank, some looking housebroken and others looking mightily feral. They met us at the landing, whimpering for handouts of food, and followed our horses in a wide semi-circle all the way up the bank toward the detachment office. They came in all sizes. Some were sleek and small and used to gaining their advantages through wit and stealth. Others were large, hairy, and wolf-like, with protruding yellow teeth and scruffy hair that bristled around their necks when they barked. Several had the marks and scars of backstreet brawls. Belvedere's terrier growled at them from the happy confines of Belvedere's buffalo coat, and so did Belvedere.

The detachment office was situated in the Stobart and Eden store, a low building sided with unpainted shiplap, on a ridge above the settlement. The rental of the space was a temporary measure, or so we were told, which would be rectified as soon as the force was able to erect its own offices. We warmed ourselves at the pot-belly stove near the back of the store and waited for the commanding officer, Sergeant Slade, who strolled in a half hour later. He was a sturdy fellow with short-cropped hair, a scrubbed face, and a waxy moustache. His scarlet tunic was immaculate, and his boots so shiny that one might be forgiven for thinking they had never been worn before.

There seemed to have been some history between Slade and Belvedere, and not a happy history, either. Slade froze the moment we walked in the door, and he stared at our frostbitten faces for a long while. "Well, well, well," he said at last. "I ask for good men and true, and they send me Corporal Belvedere."

"I didn't want this posting," Belvedere snarled, staring like a wolf with hackles up right back at the commanding officer, "but they told me you lot of pansies couldn't find shite in a dung-heap."

Slade turned his attention to me. "Corporal Belvedere is in the habit of creating international incidents," he said. "I take it you are the medical man?"

Happily, I was not required to elaborate on my medical past or the reasons I might have left a lucrative family practice in Quebec City and parted temporarily from my beautiful fiancée for the adventurous life of a mounted policeman. I stood at attention and saluted. "Surgeon Virgil Montgomery, sir, reporting for duty."

The commanding officer didn't bother to return my salute. "I've had some dabblings in medicine myself, Montgomery, but I gave it all up for a career in the Great North-West." There was an awkward silence. "No barracks have been built yet," Sergeant

Slade continued. "We've had to lodge our men in the town. After you've stabled you horses, I'll have Sub-Constable Parry walk you over to your billet." He gave Belvedere one last withering glance. "Do me a favour," he said, "and don't start any gunfights until you're nicely settled in."

Sub-Constable Parry was a chatty Canadian-born lad. Despite a pronounced stutter, he talked our legs off all the way down to the lodging house, wanting to know about Poundmaker and "the Indian p-p-p-problem," as he called it, near Battleford. With six months under my belt as a mounted policeman, I did not feel qualified to prognosticate on anything related to Poundmaker and his band. Belvedere maintained his usual silence, cradling the terrier inside his coat. I didn't think his initial interview with Sergeant Slade had made him happy to be in that town.

The house was a wood-frame two-story building, white-washed in the usual style. It looked pleasant enough from the outside, its plain roof nicely shingled and smoke tumbling out of a tall brick chimney. There were not many windows in the building, probably out of deference to a cold winter that was to come, and I imagined that the interior would be dark. I was correct in that assumption.

We were met at the front door by our landlady, Mrs. McLaughlin. Maybe twenty-five or twenty-six years old, she was, according to Parry, the wife of an Anglican clergyman. She was a fine-looking woman, tall and lithe, although she cloaked her femininity in a drab black dress. Her auburn hair was pulled back in a severe coiffure, parted in the middle, the bulk of it resting in a hairnet behind her neck. Something about her was pinched and unhappy. It was there in the listless way she moved and in the flatness of her voice. Her husband was nowhere in sight. "Come in," she said, after the introductions had been made and Parry had departed. "Have you eaten?"

I was quick with my reply. "No, ma'am, not since yesterday evening."

She led us into a dining room that was plain and unadorned,

dimly lit by a single kerosene lamp on a plain wooden table. On a wall above the table, there was a portrait of Christ with children kneeling at his feet. There was another painting, on the wall opposite, of an old man at prayer, looking peaceful and resigned to his own imminent death. A roughly built sideboard stood, devout and immovable, along a third wall. Mrs. McLaughlin opened its doors and dutifully placed two chipped china plates on the little square table. "Please sit," she said. "We don't have much in this house, but I'll give you what we have."

Belvedere's terrier squirmed out of the folds of his coat at that moment. Mrs. McLaughlin's demeanour grew cheerier. "Oh," she said, "you have a puppy."

"Hope you don't mind," Belvedere replied. "He sleeps in my room."

"Not at all," Mrs. McLaughlin said. "I've wanted a puppy for some time." She reminded me of my sweetheart, Emily, who adored dogs of every size and breed.

Her response would have made a man smile if that man had a cheerier disposition than Belvedere. "Would there be a morsel for him to eat?"

"I'm sure I can find something." She retired to the kitchen, and Belvedere and I sat down at the table. The homey odour of the coal oil in the lamp was comforting, as was the sound of clanking pots and pans. The terrier roamed into the kitchen, having smelled the food as it was heated on the stove. He was a well-behaved mutt; he didn't bark much, only whimpered a little when the pangs of hunger were too great. Belvedere didn't say a word as we waited. He unbuttoned his coat and slung it over the back of his chair. His tunic and his boots were still muddy from the journey. There was a trail of mud behind him, all the way to the front door. I had taken my boots off in the entrance, but Belvedere hadn't followed my example.

After what seemed like a long time, Mrs. McLaughlin emerged from the kitchen, bearing a tureen of soup and setting it on the table before us. Belvedere did not wait for the advent of spoons; he poured the soup into a bowl and tipped the bowl to his lips like it was a cup. In the meantime, Mrs. McLaughlin went back into the kitchen and returned with a cold joint of ham and a few slices of dry cornbread. She was not the best of cooks. The soup was a thin beef broth that offered little nourishment. The ham was lardy and unspiced, and the corn bread had the consistency of congealed sawdust. Belvedere and I gulped down the meal, as we were hungry, and the dog received a hambone to gnaw on.

Mrs. McLaughlin apologized for her lack of culinary skill. "I'm afraid my mother taught me little," she said.

"This is delightful," I lied. "Best meal I've had in many months."

She looked at me as one looks at a child who has just chopped down an apple tree. "You're very kind."

Belvedere said nothing.

After supper, Mrs. McLaughlin escorted us up a narrow, winding staircase to the second floor, where beds were situated in two cold, dark rooms across from one another. The rafters above the narrow beds were bare and unadorned, angling down toward the eaves so that it was impossible to stand erect except where the roof peaked. Above the rafters were unpainted boards, and above the boards were presumably shingles. "I'll keep the stove going until late in the evening," Mrs. McLaughlin said from the top of the stairs. "My husband has been concerned with the cost of firewood of late, but I'm sure he will not mind the burning of a few extra sticks if it serves to keep the guests warm."

"The accommodation is perfectly lovely," I told her, although I knew I would be wearing woollen socks as I slept. At times like that, I realized how far away from Vermont I had travelled.

She bade us good night, and Belvedere closed his door. I sat at the tiny desk in my room and fished a half-written letter from my Gladstone medicine bag. I had intended to complete the letter and mail it to Emily long before that moment, but something had prevented me from doing so. I could not bring myself to mention the mistake that had threatened my reputation and that had necessitated my quick departure from the city and civilization.

Taking a deep breath, I wrote that I was sorry for the pain my sudden departure had caused her. I complained to her about the hardships of my recent journey, and I expressed my undying love. I reassured her that when my tour of duty was done, I would return to Montreal and we would wed. Having addressed the envelope and sealed it, I extinguished the lamp and staggered to my bed.

IN THE MORNING, we ate a breakfast of porridge and toast. Mrs. McLaughlin was busy in the kitchen when Belvedere and I straggled down the stairs. She was wearing the same black dress, and her hair was coiffed as severely as it had been the night before. Her husband was not at the dining room table waiting for us. We still hadn't met him. I took it he was in his bedroom and still asleep.

Mrs. McLaughlin asked us what was on our agenda for the day, and Belvedere told her that we were investigating a murder.

"Poor Mr. Chen," she said, almost involuntarily.

"You know about him?" Belvedere asked.

"There aren't too many murders in a town this size," she said.

"What do you think happened?"

"I've no idea," she replied, "but the townsfolk have all sorts of crazy suggestions.

"Like what?" asked Belvedere.

"Some blame his wife," Mrs. McLaughlin said, pouring coffee into the cups on the table before us. "Others blame the Indians hereabouts. I have no idea what to think."

We ate our breakfast, and then we donned our coats, having decided to visit the local sheriff that morning. Belvedere cursed his sore left leg as we walked down the hill toward the town hall. A cold wind had come up out of the north, and it sliced through our buffalo coats like a thrown axe. Mrs. McLaughlin had agreed to take care of Belvedere's dog while we were away from the house, so he was momentarily freed of that encumbrance.

The town hall was situated near the riverbank, a brick edifice that also housed the local jail and sheriff's office. The sky was grey and the trees were barren of leaves. The only hint of green came from across the river, where a great pine forest loomed.

I must admit that I was trepidatious about visiting the local sheriff. There were often disputes about jurisdiction between law enforcement organizations out on the plains, and I didn't know how territorial the sheriff's office might be. Even in my short time there, I'd seen arguments between Mounties and sheriffs that had ended with guns drawn.

The sheriff was a massive hulk of a fellow, clearly hired more for his size than anything else. He looked like an overgrown farm boy at a child's desk when we met him in his office. His face was a round boulder, and his hands, clasped self-consciously on the desk in front of him, were the size of baseball mitts. His name was Dan McQuaid, and he was jovial enough, as big men often are. He did not bother to stand up or to shake our hands when we entered. "So yer the fellers they sent from Battleford," he said, as Belvedere and I settled into chairs on the opposite side of the desk.

"We are," Belvedere said.

"And you must be Belvedere," the big man said. "The feller who solved that murder out near Fort Pitt."

"I am."

The sheriff took a moment to size Belvedere up, and then his face creased into a crooked grin. "And then they sent you here because a Chinaman got hisself kilt."

"They did."

"Well, I'm glad you came," the sheriff replied. "I cain't get nowhere with this one, no matter how hard I try." He didn't seem too upset.

Belvedere looked at him hard. "Where was the body found?"

"Out back behind the laundry," the sheriff said. "Musta went back there to dump his dirty water."

"Who might have wanted to kill him?"

"Beats me." The fellow didn't have a great deal of curiosity about a murder in his own town. "There ain't a lot of sympathy fer foreigners here. Coulda bin an argument over shit on a shirt-tail, for all I know."

There was a moment's pause while the sheriff twiddled his sausage-sized fingers. I decided to jump into the conversation. "Is it possible to examine the body?"

"It sure enough is," replied the sheriff. "I was instructed to postpone the burial. Although I might say that the Chinaman's widow didn't take that decision kindly."

"And where might the corpse be viewed?" I asked.

"Follow me," the sheriff said and stood up. He strode to the door and turned sideways to manoeuver his wide shoulders through.

We followed the sheriff outside and down the street. The morning was cool, and as bitter as the wind was, people were mostly indoors. Some of the same dogs I had seen the day before were huddled around a mass of feathers, probably the remnants of a magpie that had gotten too big for its britches. The sheriff led us to a squat shack sided with unpainted shiplap. "Didn't have nowhere else to keep the body," he muttered, "and it was still hot out when the Chinaman met his end, so we put him here at Old Lady Reed's place." I could see rough burlap curtains moving inside the shack, and I caught a glimpse of the old lady's face, severe and scared. When she saw me looking in at her, she snapped the curtains shut, almost as if I were a Peeping Tom.

The sheriff stopped in the backyard. He began lifting heavy two-by-sixes that served as a covering for a well, and he tossed them aside like matchsticks. From where I was standing, I caught a glimpse of the wooden cribbing that reached down deep into the earth. A rope, too thick to be used for the simple task of hauling up water, protruded from the chasm, tied off to a poplar that stood at the edge of the yard. As the sheriff began hauling up his sorry cargo from deep in the well, a shapeless mass materialized out of the darkness, identifiable as a human body when it got closer. It was apparent that the rope had been tied tightly around the man's ankles.

I was horrified by the sight of the cadaver. "Twas the onliest way we could figger to keep the body cold," the sheriff said. "Didn't git wintry here until two days ago."

When the corpse was lying in the snow before us, I could see that it was clad in thin trousers, typical of Chinese haberdashery, and a baggy shirt. The shoes had been removed. On the feet and face, the bare skin of the man was blue-white and the texture of cheese, not at all like the preserved cadavers in Doctor Osler's medical class back at McGill. An expression of horror or surprise was situated on the lips and in the open eyes. I felt repulsed by the state of the corpse and by the carelessness with which it was handled, hoisted from the well and unceremoniously pitched onto the snowy grass. I thought of Orpheus returning from the underworld.

"We had a word with the undertaker," the sheriff explained. "This is the best we could do."

The weather seemed suddenly twice as cold, and the wind twice as biting, as I observed the cadaver in the snowbound yard. I felt myself shivering. "Have you got a horse and wagon somewhere?"

Because there was no other place to conduct an autopsy, I had the body delivered to the Presbyterian mission. There was a shed behind the church, not at all suited for such business, but I had little choice. The sheriff and I laid the cadaver out on a rough wooden work bench that had formerly been used by the local minister, a man named Nesbitt, who was also—or so I was told—a fine carpenter. His tools, hammers and bits and saws, were hanging neatly on the interior walls.

Good lighting is of the utmost importance when conducting postmortems, and the lighting in the shed was atrocious. I gathered as many coal oil lamps as I could find in the mission and placed them around the body. The flames reached up into the flues of those lamps, casting garish shadows and emitting blue smoke. It wasn't long before the acrid pollution had found its way to my nose and throat, and I was choking. Even the bone handles of my scalpels were slippery from the oily residue of the lamps.

My fingers partway frozen from the inclement day outside, I cut away the shirt and trousers with a pair of scissors. An initial observation of the body revealed that no physical altercation had taken place before the shooting. There were no bruises about the face and torso, and the knuckles were not skinned. Chaoxing Chen had been shot in the back at some distance. Neither the clothing nor the epidermis showed signs of powder burn.

Having placed the body in a prone position, I made two deep incisions across the entry point of the bullet and probed the wound. The slug had entered the body at the top of the shoulder blade on a trajectory that carried it through the heart. The poor man probably did not see his attacker, and he died quickly, if not instantaneously. After no small amount of effort, I was able to retrieve the slug with a pair of forceps. It looked to be from a centre-fire cartridge, probably a .44-40 from a Winchester rifle, the same kind of rifle mounted policemen carry. I washed the slug with turpentine and placed it, for safekeeping, in an empty camphor tin in my medicine bag.

Having gleaned that much information and no more, I shifted the body to a supine position and sat vigil for some time. It seemed that the spirit of the man was somehow in the small shed with me and that he had something to tell me. The oil lamps sputtered, and the residue settled on my own skin as well as on the cadaver's. Who was this man? And what stories did he have to tell?

Belvedere was standing in the cold outside the McLaughlin house when I returned that evening. The wind had died down somewhat, but the temperature had dropped.

Belvedere's terrier was in tow, yipping at passers-by and then doing his business at one corner of a leafless caragana hedge. Belvedere and I talked for a moment before going inside for supper. I told him of my findings at the autopsy. Belvedere's face was flushed, and I could smell the demon rum on his breath, even out of doors. He said he'd spent the afternoon in the public house down at the hotel, interviewing the sheriff. I asked what he'd learned. "You'd be surprised what you might learn," he said, "over a dimpled glass or a broken bottle." After the dog had barked at one last leaf falling from an elm tree at the corner of the street, we went inside for supper. Mrs. McLaughlin was busy, gathering plates from the sideboard and placing them at four settings around the table.

A newspaper rustled in the parlour, and I became aware of the presence of Mr. McLaughlin. From where I was standing, I could see only the leg of his black woollen trousers and his high-laced black boot, a crevice worn into its sole. The reverend hadn't bothered to get out of his chair and greet us when we'd entered the house. He sat quietly in the other room while his missus was setting the table, which, I thought, was strange. The only sounds emanating from the parlour were the occasional rustling of the newspaper and the clearing of the reverend's throat.

When, at last, the meal was prepared and we were all bade to sit down, the minister appeared and stood at the head of the table. He was of average stature, with a wan face and a balding head. He studied us through grey eyes, almost as though we were unexpected guests.

Mrs. McLaughlin broke the silence. "Dear," she said, "these are the boarders that the mounted police have sent us. Mr. Belvedere and Mr. Montgomery."

The reverend's voice was low and lifeless. "Pleased to meet you, I'm sure." He didn't look pleased to meet us, and he did not offer a handshake.

We sat down at the table and joined hands while the reverend intoned a grace. It was a long prayer—longer than I had been used to—and not really a prayer of thanks. Mostly, the reverend asked God to forgive our multitude of sins and to spare us from the terror of Hell. We ate silently after that, a meal of roast venison and boiled potatoes. The venison was tough, and the potatoes were too soft, falling apart as I forked them out of the serving bowl. Mrs. McLaughlin's culinary skills had not improved in a day's time. The reverend did not look up from his plate during the entire meal, but he also did not seem to enjoy his repast. He ate sullenly, as if eating were somehow an immoral act. When he was done, he pushed his chair back wordlessly and retreated to the parlour.

After the dinner was eaten, I hastened to my room, where Colonel Herchmer's confidential letter was lying in my medical bag. I retrieved Herchmer's missive from the bag and read it again. *Aside from your duties as a medical man*, he had written, *I want you to keep a close eye on Corporal Belvedere. Report to me, at your earliest convenience, any irregularities in his behaviour and any departures from the code of conduct to which all mounted policemen must adhere.* I made a note in my personal journal of Belvedere's conduct towards the Hudson Bay man and of his confiscation and imbibement of the illegal whisky, but I thought it best not to alert the colonel of these infelicities so early in the investigation.

3

The next morning, Belvedere and I marched down toward the river for a look-around. It was another cold day. The snow that had fallen a few days earlier was still on the streets, sullied by horse manure and the wheels of buckboards. I pulled my buffalo coat tight around my neck to ward off another brisk wind coming out of the north.

The laundry was located along River Street, a mile-long roadway where most of the businesses in the settlement were located. On the east side of the laundry was a dentist's office. A shoe repair shop was immediately to the west.

There was no indication of life or commerce at the laundry. A sign on the false front above the door spelled "Chen's Laundry" in distinctly Chinese lettering, but there was no light emanating from inside the building. Belvedere tried the front door and then knocked on it, expecting the deceased man's wife to answer. He was met with silence. We ambled around to the rear of the building, where we found a large tin washing basin upturned and partially blanketed with snow. I surmised that this was the washing basin the poor man had been carrying when he suffered the gunshot wound. Belvedere kicked at the basin, flipping it over in the snow. There was nothing under it but a splotch of barren grass.

Belvedere squinted up at the dull morning sun. "You say he was shot from a high angle?"

"He was."

"From the roof of one of these buildings?" He pointed first at the dentist's office and then at the shoe repair shop.

"Perhaps," I replied.

Belvedere thought for a moment, looking south toward the ridge. "Or he might have been shot from up there." It was a distance of at least a hundred rods. "Would have to be a bit of a marksman to accomplish that."

I shuddered at the thought of such an anonymous killing. "Would have to be."

We proceeded to the back door of the laundry and found it ajar. Belvedere peered into the darkness and called out, "Anybody here?" There was no response. When he opened the door further, I heard a savage snarl and glimpsed a flash of fur hurtling toward us. Belvedere motioned toward his revolver, but it was too late. The large dog, more a wolf than a dog, was driving toward him, its canine teeth bared and ready for violence. Belvedere shouted something that resembled "Get out!" and the hound veered past us, escaping out of the laundry's backyard and disappearing down the alley. We were lucky that neither of us had been bitten. Belvedere took a deep breath and then exhaled all the air that was in him. "Fekking wild dogs run this town." He pulled his gun from its holster to ward off other intruders, canine or human, and we edged quietly inside.

It took a moment for my eyes to adjust to the semi-darkness. The place was shrouded in shadows, and there was no fire in the cookstove at the rear of the building. Near the stove were a table and chairs, and two cots. There were signs of a rapid departure. Pots and pans were still and silent on the stove. A ratty blanket was balled up and stuffed behind one of the cots. There were chopsticks and bowls on the scratched little table.

Belvedere saw these signs too, and he looked grimly at me. "Someone quit this place in a hurry," he said.

Separated from the living quarters by the flimsiest of partitions was the laundry proper, which contained a large steel vat and some laundry paddles. A rudimentary inspection revealed that there was two feet of dirty water in the vat, covered by a thin layer of ice. In front of the vat was a doorway to the public area. When I walked through the doorway, I saw several piles of clothing, neatly folded on a wooden counter. There was a small black cashbox, bereft of any money, lying open beside the clothing. On the wall near the cash box was a chalkboard with white letters scrawled across it. There was some Chinese lettering that I could not decipher, and underneath that, a sentence in an unschooled scrawl: "GO BAK TO WERE YA CAM." The writer of those final remarks was certainly no scholar.

I turned to Belvedere, who was also studying the blackboard, a bemused look on his face. "Someone didn't care for this man," I said.

"That's putting it mildly."

"This was more than a disagreement over dirty clothes."

"Clearly."

Having finished our inspection of the murder scene, we visited the shoemaker's shop next door. The shoemaker was a thin, swarthy fellow who went by the name of Silas Haggardy. His straight black hair cascaded down the sides of his face like waxed boot laces. He was busy as we entered, tacking a sole onto a leather upper. He glanced at us from his workbench. "Kin I hep you genlemen?"

"We're policemen of the North-West Mounted," Belvedere declared. "Investigating the murder of Mr. Chaoxing Chen."

The cobbler placed his hammer on the workbench and stood up tentatively. "D'ya mean Jerry?" He ventured to his side of the counter, across from us.

"Is that what they call him here?"

"Ev'ybody calls him Jerry. I din't know no Chock Sing."

I could hear footfalls on the floor above us. Belvedere heard them, too. He peered past the shoemaker at the steep stairwell leading to the second floor of the building. "You live upstairs?"

"Yeah." The shoemaker clasped his hands in front of him. I'm no expert in the language of postures, but I'm pretty sure his was defensive. His knuckles were cut and bruised with cobbling, and the skin on his fingers was permanently tattooed with dye.

"You a family man?

"I am."

It was plain that this line of questioning made the shoemaker nervous. Belvedere didn't cease and desist. "Who lives upstairs with you?"

"Jus' my wife and kids."

Belvedere paused for a moment, looking deeply into the cobbler's eyes. "Did you hear anything untoward on the day of the murder?"

"I heard the gunshot," the cobbler said. "Imagine ev'ybody did. 'Taint uncommon fer people to be firin' guns in this town."

Belvedere moved in closer, his face a few inches from the cobbler's. "At what time of day did this take place?"

"I din't look at my watch," the shoemaker said. "Was towards the end of the workday."

"Did you go outside to take a look?"

"I went outside when I heard Ruby cry out."

"Ruby?"

"His wife."

"Where is she now?"

"Don't rightly know," the shoemaker said, uncomfortable as a cat in a coyote's coven. "She vamoosed, day after the killin'. She'd be somewhere in town, though."

Belvedere turned to me and grinned. "I think that's all the questions we have for today," he said. "Unless you have any, Montgomery?"

I shook my head.

Belvedere turned abruptly and strode toward the door, hesitated, and turned back to the shoemaker. "What kind of a man was Mister Chen? In your estimation?"

The shoemaker shrugged. "He was a kind fella, I guess. Personable-like. I had no beef with him, if that's what ya mean."

When we were outside the shop, I remarked tentatively to Belvedere that the cobbler might be hiding something. Belvedere chuckled morosely. We proceeded to the dentist's office on the other side of the laundry. While also of wood frame construction, the building was much smarter looking than its neighbours. The sign in the window was professionally painted, and the exterior of the building had seen a recent coat of whitewash.

We went inside. A bell behind the door announced our entrance. There was an outer office, vacant but for a few chairs and a partition, behind which the dentist was pulling a patient's tooth. I could hear their voices. A beleaguered voice pleaded inarticulately, "Can I have a little more of that powder?"

"Certainly, sir," a plummy British voice replied. I heard footfalls across the floor. Then, after a silence and some moaning and grunting, came a caterwauling the like of which I have not heard since watching my supervisor at medical school perform a tonsillectomy without anesthetic. The cries were those of a trapped animal before the decision has been made to gnaw off its own leg. The moment was unbearable, and then the caterwauling ceased, replaced by a huffing and puffing. "All done now, Mister Adams," I heard the plummy voice say. "We will sponge it now and pack it with gauze, and then you'll be on your way. That tooth will not bother you again."

The patient replied with words I could not decipher. There were more footfalls. I heard some gargling and spitting. A few minutes later, the patient emerged from behind the partition, his face that of a man who had been beaten soundly with a croquet mallet. Splotches of blood had coagulated on the front of his shirt. I took him to be between forty and forty-five. He did not make eye contact with us as he trundled out the front door. I watched as he plodded sullenly down the street.

After a moment, the dentist entered from his hall of tortures. He was wearing a blood-spattered apron over a rather dapper woollen suit. His moustache was waxed and his short hair gleamed with pomade. He was drying his hands with a towel. His demeanour was not that of a man who had just administered sustained torture upon a hapless victim. In fact, he seemed rather joyous. I disliked him intensely.

"The mounted police have arrived!" he exclaimed. I reckoned he was no more than a year off the boat from England.

"We have," Belvedere growled.

"And glad of it we are here too," the dentist said, tossing his towel onto an empty chair. "This town has been lawless long enough."

Belvedere did not share in the man's jocularity. "Yes, well," he said, "we are here about Mister Chen next door."

A softer emotion flickered across the dentist's face. "Poor man. I didn't know him well."

"Were you on these premises when the shot was fired?"

"I was not. The office was closed that day."

Belvedere tugged at his own moustache. "Did he have any enemies that you know of?"

"My good man," the dentist replied, "I didn't know him well enough to say if he had any friends, let alone enemies."

"Where's his wife at the moment?"

"I believe you'll find her with the only other Chinese family in this town," said the dentist. "At Sam Gee's place behind the café, just down the street."

"Was Chen on good terms with his wife?" Belvedere asked. "Did you ever hear them argue?"

"They spoke Chinese," the dentist said. "It all sounded like argumentation to me."

We were about to question the dentist further, but the door swung open and another unhappy-looking customer entered. He cradled one cheek in his hand and, when asked what the trouble was, he muttered something that sounded like "bruise age." The dentist smiled at us and ushered the sad fellow behind the partition, where further acts of torture were likely to take place.

When we were outside, in front of the dentist's office, Belvedere spat on the boardwalk. "That man is a twit and a ponce," he said. "Pulls teeth for a living and thinks he's better than me."

We walked two blocks down River Street to Sam Gee's restaurant. It was a little hole-in-the-wall café, a squat building with a false front and a hand-painted sign that said "Foody Goody" in a window by the door. The place was half-full of loggers and dusty flour mill workers, there for a noon meal of chop suey, pork, and rice. The proprietor was a little man in a traditional cap and tunic. He approached us as we walked in the door. "Can I help you, officers?"

Belvedere did not mince words. "Is Ruby Chen on the premises?"

Sam Gee looked shaken by the mention of her name. His eyes darted around the room and settled again on Belvedere. "She's helping out in the back." He led us into the kitchen at the rear of the building, where two women were labouring over a hot stove. Gee spoke some words in Chinese to one of the women, and she grasped a wok that had been on the stove and placed it on a wooden countertop. Then she retreated from the kitchen into a spartan room behind a curtain, where I could see a table and chairs and one end of a bed.

The woman who remained in the kitchen with us backed into a corner, holding her wooden spoon in front of her like a weapon and looking stricken. Sam Gee introduced her. "This is Ruby Chen," he said. "She doesn't speak English."

Belvedere took a moment to appraise the woman. She was tiny, with dark hair and frightened dark eyes. She wore a shapeless grey smock, partially covered by an apron. Belvedere turned to Sam Gee. "Can you translate?"

"I can try." Gee seemed inordinately troubled by our presence.

Perhaps he had never had any dealings with Canadian police before.

"Ask her, then," Belvedere said, "how long she's been married to Chaoxing Chen."

Gee did not bother to translate the question. "She was not Chaoxing's wife," he said plainly to Belvedere. "She was his sister."

Belvedere was clearly taken aback. "His sister?"

"Yes."

"Did he have a wife?"

"Not to my knowledge," Gee replied.

Belvedere looked at the woman and then again at Gee. "And he lived with his sister at the laundry?"

"He did."

"Ask her if she knows who might have wanted to kill her brother."

Gee launched into a rather long-winded question, posed in one dialect of the Chinese or another. Ruby Chen backed farther into the corner and said a few words. I think she would have liked to be back on Chinese soil at that moment rather than being interrogated by an officer of the North-West Mounted Police.

Gee turned to Belvedere. "She says she can think of no one who might have wanted to kill her brother."

Belvedere nodded. "Were there any suspicious characters hanging about the laundry in the days preceding the murder?"

Again, Gee posed what seemed like a rather verbose question, and Ruby Chen replied with a timid sentence or two. "She mostly worked in the back," Gee told Belvedere. "She says her brother had an argument with a fellow named Lerat a few days before the murder."

"A fellow named Lerat?"

Ruby Chen said a few more words, and Gee translated them. "She thinks he was a trapper from across the river."

Belvedere extricated his notepad and pencil from his tunic pocket and wrote a few words. Both Gee and Chen seemed horrified that their words were being transcribed. "Did Chaoxing Chen own a gun?"

Gee's question was shorter this time, and Ruby Chen's response was equally brief. "No."

Belvedere leaned toward the woman and looked her in the eye. "Have you ever argued with your brother?"

Gee translated, and Ruby Chen replied. "She got along with her brother very well," Gee said to Belvedere. "Perhaps they argued about which soap to buy from time to time."

"Did her brother ever hit her or lay hands on her in any way?"

After the translation and the response, Gee said to Belvedere, "He was a good brother. He never laid hands on her."

Ruby Chen seemed on the verge of tears. Belvedere pulled back. "Very well," he said to Sam Gee. "Tell her that she is not to leave this town until our investigation has concluded."

Gee explained to the woman what Belvedere had said, and then he led us back to the dining area. "We are law-abiding people," Gee told Belvedere, speaking quietly so that his clientele would not hear. "I hope we are not in any trouble with the Canadian government."

"As long as you abide by the law," Belvedere said, "you will be in no trouble at all."

At that moment, a logger at a corner table shouted, "Here, Sammy, where's our lunch, for Chrissakes?"

Belvedere glanced at the logger witheringly, then turned and walked out the door.

"Coming! Coming!" Sam Gee said, and he scurried back into the kitchen. I followed Belvedere out into the street.

As we were huffing and puffing up the hill toward the McLaughlin house, I questioned Belvedere about Ruby Chen. "Do you really think she could be a suspect in this case?"

Belvedere smirked at me. "First thing they teach you when you become a policeman," he said, "is that the murderer is almost always somebody the victim knows. And often somebody he knows intimately."

"But a sibling?" I thought it unlikely that Ruby Chen, meek as she was, might have murdered her brother.

Belvedere stopped and kicked off the snow that had caked on his boots. "What if dear old Chaoxing Chen was fornicating with his sister when no one was looking? Do you think she might have a motive for a killing then?"

THE MINISTER WAS NOT present for supper again that evening. Mrs. McLaughlin apologized for his absence. Apparently, he was leading a prayer meeting down at the Anglican church. He seemed a devout man.

While we ate, Mrs. McLaughlin regaled us with stories of the Prince Albert Literary Society. She was a member of the Society, she said; she dabbled in poetry, although she did not want to show us any of her work. There were penny readings scheduled twice a month throughout the winter at Treston Hall, she told us, something to dull the edge of a sharp, biting winter. I asked her to remind me closer to the date when a penny reading might take place. Secretly, I was hoping that our case would be solved and we would be well on our way to Battleford before any opportunity to attend a reading of local doggerel might occur.

Belvedere was not much interested in penny readings or in conversing, for that matter. Reunited with his terrier, who had been in Mrs. McLaughlin's keeping all day, he surreptitiously fed the dog morsels from his own plate, sometimes the choicest morsels, although little of the leftover venison might have been termed choice. The dog sat obediently at Belvedere's side, his dark eyes pleading for another bite.

After supper, I went upstairs and thought about Colonel Herchmer's orders. Surely there was nothing in Belvedere's conduct on that day that might be termed reproachable. He was unconventional, to be sure, and I didn't think Ruby Chen was a prime suspect, but the interrogation was entirely justified. Perhaps it would lead to more fruitful investigations down the road.

To pass the time, as it was not a reasonable hour to go to bed, I sat at my small desk with charcoals and a sketch pad. I like to sketch directly from life, but there was little to inspire me in the darkness outside my window. The laundryman still haunted me, though, and I found myself almost involuntarily sketching the grimace on his face as I first saw it, when his corpse lay in the snow beside the well. There is a theory that the last sight a man sees before dying is imprinted on his retinas and that we might be able to discover that image, if only we had the means. Did he look up at the blue heavens in his last moments? Or did he reel about and look up at the ridge from whence the shot had come? It was not the most heartwarming of subjects for a brisk October evening.

I sketched the laundryman's face several times, from several different angles, and I could not get it right. With each successive attempt, the face came to resemble that of a dead child, mouth agape, eyes wide, the innocent features looking merely startled in death. By the evening's end, I could not bear to look at my attempts at rendering the likeness of the man. I tore the paper from my sketch pad, crumpled it in a ball, and tossed it in the small garbage can by the table. And then I went to bed.

Sometime later, I heard the front door of the house open and close. There was a muffled conversation in the front hall. When it stopped, I surmised that the reverend must have been eating his repast. Then I heard a crash, something like the sound of a plate or a glass breaking. There were vehement, hissed words. I couldn't make out much of it, but I did hear snippets, words like "debauchery" and "unforgiven," spat out like searing coals. It was the minister's voice I heard. Whether Mrs. McLaughlin made a response, I could not tell. The argument was momentary; the fire and brimstone soon subsided and resolved itself in stony silence.

4

We encountered Sub-Constable Parry in the Hobart and Eden store the next morning. Belvedere was there to buy a new straight razor; he had forgotten to pack his old razor when we left Battleford. I took advantage of the time to post my letter to Emily, feeling at the same time how inadequate it was, and also to buy a small packet of jerky. I had an inkling that the meals in our new room-and-board situation would not be of high standard, and I wanted something to tide me over in case one or more of them were inedible. Parry was standing in the canned goods aisle, looking somewhat lost. Perhaps he was waiting for Sergeant Slade to finish with his paperwork so that he could give Parry his daily orders. "Good m-m-morning, officers," he said when he saw us.

"Good morning, Parry," Belvedere replied. "What's the word of the day?"

"B-b-b-buffalo shit," Parry said quietly, with a sly grin on his face.

Belvedere was examining a razor for sharpness. He scraped it lightly against the calloused palm of his hand, then held it up to the light. Sunlight from the front windows reflected off the blade and into my eyes. "Do you know anything of a trapper named Lerat?" Belvedere asked Parry. "Lives out in the country somewhere?"

Parry did not take long to initiate a response. "I know he's a c-crazy s-s-son-of-a-bitch," he said. "Used to c-c-c-come into t-t-town quite often. Haven't s-s-s-s-seen him in a while, though."

Belvedere lowered the razor. "Crazy?" he asked. "In what way crazy?"

Sub-Constable Parry closed his eyes and tried to concentrate on whatever he was about to say. "Lerat is t-t-t-two p-p-people," he said. "A c-c-crazy m-m-m-man when he's drunk, and a shy m-m-m-man when he's s-s-sober."

"Where does he live?" asked Belvedere.

"S-s-six m-m-miles east along the r-r-river," Parry said. "L-l-l-log house that l-l-l- looks l-l-like it's about to f-f-fall down."

Belvedere looked sidelong at me. "We'll ride out there tomorrow, Montgomery." He turned and walked toward the cash counter with his razor.

"I wouldn't g-g-g-go out there unannounced," Parry called after him. "You're l-l-l- liable to g-g-g-get yourselves sh-sh-shot."

THE RIDE along the riverbank was uneven. Our horses had to pick their way through wolf willow brambles and around rocks, all lightly covered with an icing of snow. I was worried that my horse Belle would lame herself stumbling along through the treacherous landscape, but horses, I have found, are much more dexterous than we give them credit for. She was frightened, along the way, when a gang of crows suddenly wakened from their mid-morning slumber and cawed at us as if we were interlopers on private property. All that was between me staying on her back and catapulting off and into the river was my handhold on the horn of the saddle. Belvedere watched unsmilingly through hooded eyelids as I righted myself.

It was a clear day but not too cold. I was not frozen through to the marrow as I had been on our journey east from Battleford. There is something about the clarity of cold northern air that sharpens both eyesight and mental acuity. As we rambled along the riverbank, I thought about Parry and what he had said. Who was this Lerat, the two-headed monster that was one day shy and the next day insane? And what did he have against Chaoxing Chen?

We approached Lerat's house, a squat log building that seemed to have sunk farther into the ground under its own weight. It was situated among aspen trees, a short distance from the North Saskatchewan River. A soft plume of smoke issued from its tin chimney.

We were no more than twenty rods away when a fellow stepped out of the doorway of the house, aimed his rifle at us, and fired. Belvedere jumped down from his horse's back and shooed the horse away. He crouched behind the wintry skeletons of wolf willow and extracted his sidearm from its holster. I was slow to realize what was going on. "For Chrissakes, Montgomery," Belvedere shouted at me, "get down off your horse!" Following Belvedere's lead, I leapt off Belle and slapped her on the rump. She charged off after Belvedere's horse into a stand of aspens. Another shot was fired. I scurried behind a rock and took as much cover there as I could find.

Peering over the rock, I could see that the man who was shooting at us was still in his shirt sleeves on that cool morning, not having had time, apparently, to don a coat for the occasion. Not a young man, he had a mop of curly grey hair pasted close to his head. He was wielding an ancient flintlock, laboriously tearing the cartridges open by biting them and filling the flash pan with powder. I noted that when Lerat opened his mouth to chew on the cartridges, there were no teeth in sight. He munched on the cartridges as though he were chewing on a vulcanized rubber ball.

Standing the rifle on its stock, he poured powder down the muzzle and stuffed the cartridge in with a ramrod. When he fired the weapon, flames shot out of the flash pan, and a puff of smoke momentarily clouded the man's vision. It was a slow process, and one that would not have served the man well if Belvedere had a Winchester in his hands. "Get on out of it, redcoats!" the fellow yelled at us. "None of your sort is wanted here!"

Belvedere poked his head up out of the tangle of wolf willows. "Is your name Lerat?"

"That's what my mama calls me." Having finished the involved reloading process, Lerat shouldered his weapon and squeezed off another shot with a flurry of fire and smoke. The recoil of the muzzleloader nearly knocked him off his feet.

Still with his Enfield in his hand, Belvedere called out from behind the wolf willows, "Mister Lerat, we need to talk."

Lerat was busy ramrodding another cartridge down the barrel of his musket. "Ain't nothin to talk about except yer leavin." He raised his weapon again and fired at the bush where Belvedere was hiding, but without hitting his mark.

Belvedere stepped out into the clearing to get a better look at his assailant. Lerat was tearing at another paper cartridge with his toothless gums, spitting the excess paper onto the snowy ground at his feet. "It's time to put the gun down now, Mister Lerat," Belvedere said in a low, calm voice.

From where I was stationed, behind the rock, I could see that Lerat was growing quite frantic. He was hurriedly pouring gunpowder from a leather pouch into the flash pan of his antiquated weapon. "It's time fer you to git on out of here!" he shouted back. I could see the whites of his eyes as he glanced wildly about.

Belvedere strode through the soft covering of snow toward Lerat's house. "You know you're not going to hit anything with that blunderbuss of yours."

"You might be surprised what I can hit!" Lerat was busily closing the frizzen of his weapon.

"Why don't we call it a day," Belvedere said, "and leave off shooting at one another for a happier time?" Fifty feet away from the man, Belvedere broke into a run. It was an awkward run, not a fast gait, but as fast as Belvedere's habitual limp would allow.

Frantically, Lerat poured powder down the muzzle of his flintlock. He was in the act of stuffing in the cartridge with the ramrod when Belvedere arrived at his side and grabbed the barrel of Lerat's weapon with his strong left hand. Lerat tried to wrest the rifle away from Belvedere and, when that failed, he took a closed-fist swing at my partner, delivering a blow that glanced off Belvedere's forehead. Not to be outdone, Belvedere drove the stock of the muzzleloader into Lerat's chin, sending the old man sprawling into the snow in front of his house.

He was still lying in the snow, unconscious, when I emerged from my hiding place behind the rock. When I arrived at Belvedere's side, he was standing over Lerat. The flintlock was cradled in Belvedere's arms. "We'd best get him inside," I said. "He'll catch his death of pneumonia if we leave him out here in the snow."

On the floor of Lerat's cabin was a maze of whisky bottles, some broken, some lying on their sides, some still upright. All were empty. The place smelled of brain-tanning. Hanging on the walls and over the exposed rafters below the ceiling were hides of almost any animal one could imagine. A few large beaver pelts were stretched on frames and leaning against the walls. Lerat had dug a tunnel in the dirt floor along the foundation line at the back of the house, spacious enough for a man to crawl through for an emergency escape from the building, but also susceptible to a north wind and drafty. There were various ancient rifles and fowling pieces hanging from spikes on the walls, but I could not see a Winchester anywhere.

When the old man came to, a few minutes later, he was lying on his tick mattress. Rather angry when he noticed that his hands had been manacled, he thrashed about incoherently and then opened his mouth with a deep, guttural snarl. His chin was bleeding. There was something about the man that was otherworldly;

he peered not at us but into the vacant air and addressed us in a hollow voice. He seemed quite insane.

Belvedere pushed him back into his bed and told Lerat to calm down. Still, the old man thrashed about, spouting some nonsense about the phases of the moon and the world's end. Only after Belvedere clenched a fist and offered to punch him in the face did the man calm down slightly. "You've taken a shot at a police officer," Belvedere explained to the man. "That, in itself, is a hanging offence."

Lerat bared his angry gums. "I bow to no man and to no earthly law," he growled. "You can shove your earthly law where the sun don't shine."

Belvedere sighed deeply. I could see that he was at the end of his patience. "I'm going to need some answers," he said. "Do you live here alone?"

"I live with my son," Lerat said. "He's out on the trapline at the moment, but I can tell you he ain't gonna be happy when he sees what you done to me."

"Have you ever heard of a man named Chaoxing Chen?"

Lerat breathed hoarsely. His face became a mask of fear. "Never heard of the fellow. Is he some kind of a Chinese junk peddler?"

"He was the laundryman in Prince Albert settlement," said Belvedere, "before someone saw fit to shoot him."

Lerat seemed to calm down somewhat, but his eyes still darted about. "Musta bin a shitey-arsed bamboozler livin' in a shitey-arsed town if he was deemed fit fer killin'."

"Did you shoot the man?"

"I wouldn't go into that town," Lerat said, "if they offered me a roast beef supper and a welcoming parade."

Belvedere bent low and peered into the madman's eyes. "Did you shoot the man?"

Lerat's only response was to spit directly into Belvedere's face. Belvedere leaned back and smashed an elbow into the old man's nose, nearly flattening it. I pulled Belvedere away as forcefully as I could. "He's clearly mad," I said, "and he can't be held responsible for his own actions." Surely Herchmer would want to hear about this, although I did think that Belvedere had been provoked. Perhaps this was all in the line of duty. I resolved not to say anything to the colonel, at least for now.

Because he did not possess a horse, we fastened Lerat like a dead man sideways over the back of his donkey, a stubborn animal that we found tied to a tree near the river. Led by a rope tethered to the horn of Belvedere's saddle, the donkey balked and hee-hawed at every rock and stump in its way, and there were many. At one point, we were stalled in mud by the river, and Belvedere's horse was made to pull mightily in order to budge the unhappy animal. Lerat lifted his blood-smeared face and shouted at us. "Where in tarnation are you taking me?"

"We're taking you to a jail cell in Prince Albert settlement," Belvedere shouted back. "You've been arrested for the murder of Chaoxing Chen."

"I din't murder no Chaoxing or no Chen neither," the old man protested, "and I don't wanna go to Prince Albert settlement."

"Nevertheless, that's where you're going."

The Mounted Police jailhouse was little more than a lean-to attached to the rear of the stables. It boasted a single window and a low slanted roof with a latticework of four conjoined cells, set against the back wall. In each cell was a bed and a commode. There was a potbelly stove in one corner and a stovepipe snaking up the wall and through the low roof, creating just enough heat to keep the room above freezing temperature. Every night when prisoners were being kept, one unlucky sub-constable was given the duty of guarding them. His chair was situated near the stove, and he huddled there all the night long, marginally warmer than anybody else in the place.

Lerat did not like his new confines, and he was not shy about letting us know that fact. "This cage is neither fit for man nor beast," he muttered as Belvedere removed the manacles from his wrists.

"You'd do well to get used to it," Belvedere told the man.

WE ENCOUNTERED SERGEANT SLADE, scrubbed and polished, as we were leaving the jailhouse that evening. He pretended that he was merely out for an evening walk and had happened upon us by sheer happenstance, but I suspected that the meeting was not accidental. He feigned surprise at seeing us. "So you've made an arrest," Slade said, "and you have your man."

"We've made an arrest," Belvedere responded. "Whether it holds up in court or not is another matter."

Slade breathed deeply, as if the cold northern air was just what his lungs needed. I could see his exhalation in the moonlight. "I'm sure that if you've made the arrest, Belvedere, you've had reasonable grounds to do so."

Belvedere looked disdainfully at the sergeant. "We have had reasonable grounds."

The sergeant smiled. "And so you'll be leaving town in short order?"

Belvedere spat a sickly wad of green phlegm into the snow. "We'll be leaving when we're certain of our quarry."

He turned and walked down the hill toward the McLaughlin house. I said good evening to the sergeant and followed. When we were out of range of Slade's hearing, I asked Belvedere if he thought Lerat was Chen's murderer.

"We have a witness," Belvedere said, "who has claimed that Lerat threatened to kill Chen."

"Chen was shot with a slug from a Winchester rifle," I replied. "I didn't see a Winchester rifle on the old man's wall."

"It's common for folks to bury their rifles after they've done something wrong with them."

We walked the rest of the way in silence. It didn't seem to me that Lerat had motive or opportunity to commit the murder. There was no sign of a Winchester at his house. And I knew that the poor man's mental state would lead to a non-conviction by reason of insanity, whether he was guilty or not.

LERAT MALINGERED in his jail cell for two weeks. In that time, his foothold on reality grew more and more precarious. I visited him occasionally with a view to seeing how I might help the infirm man on his journey, wherever that journey was taking him.

On one occasion, he refused to speak English to me. He mimicked a pair of wings with his arms and cawed, high and loud, like a magpie teasing a dog. I asked the attending guard how long this had been going on. The guard's posture was a semaphore of fatigue and unhappiness. "He's been going on like this for three days now. One day he's a bird, and the next day he's an angry moose. I can't bear it much longer."

On a second occasion, three days later, Lerat was crouched on all fours and barking like a dog. When I asked him how he was feeling, he leapt up on his bed and howled at the ceiling. His mental state had deteriorated, and I could see that the old man was also not doing well physically. He had lost a considerable amount of weight since his incarceration, and there were scratch welts on his face, neck, and arms. It was almost as though he was trying to excoriate the skin from his own bones. There was little I could do but admonish Lerat for doing harm to himself. And I told the guard to make sure his prisoner was given good rations, three times daily.

Lerat's son arrived at the end of those two weeks. He was a tall, open, broad-shouldered fellow, wearing a corduroy jacket and a toque. I met him on the road near the jailhouse as I was walking there for a visit. He did not mince words. "You're a mounted policeman," the son observed as I strolled toward him.

Sensing that a question or some violence was in the offing, I stopped in front of the man and readied myself for the onslaught. "I am."

His eyes were like cold, dark marbles. "Why is my pappy in jail?"

I was quickly putting two and two together. "Your father is—"

"Stephane Lerat."

Surreptitiously balling my right hand into a fist, in case fisticuffs were offered, I said, as resolutely as I could, "Your father has been arrested for the murder of Chaoxing Chen."

As Lerat's son registered this information, his face became a map of perplexity. "Who the hell is Chaoxing Chen?"

"He was the laundryman in this town," I replied, "until he was shot and killed some weeks ago."

"And when exactly did this murder take place?"

"October third of this year," I told him.

He placed his mittened hands on his hips and looked me in the eye. "There are two reasons my pappy couldn't have done this murder," he said. "He was with me on the trapline on October third. I remember because we trapped a cross fox on that day. And the other reason my pappy couldn't have done this murder is that I don't let him go into town no more. Not since he got weak in the head."

Lerat's son was confirming my suspicions about his father. "Would you be willing to swear an affidavit to that effect?"

"I'll swear on anything you like," he replied. "My pappy is a madman and a drunk, but he ain't no murderer."

When I told Belvedere of my meeting with Lerat's son, and of the son's insistence that his father was not guilty of Chen's murder, he was at first wary of jumping to conclusions. We were eating supper at Mrs. McLaughlin's table. "That's his kith and kin talking," Belvedere said over a hard crust of bread, "and kith and kin are notoriously unreliable." He chewed a rubbery morsel of salted pork for some time. "But maybe it's time to bring Ruby Chen back into the picture."

We strolled down to Sam Gee's restaurant early the next morning. The usual clutch of coffee drinkers and breakfast eaters were in the café. Sam Gee always seemed excited, but he got even more excited when Belvedere and I entered the premises. He approached us quickly. "Coffee for you, gentlemen? Green tea?"

Belvedere was blowing on his fingers to ward off the cold. "We're here to see Ruby Chen," he said. "Is she in the kitchen?"

"She is." Gee looked at us apprehensively, as though he thought his own arrest was imminent, and then led us into his kitchen for a second time. Gee's wife and Ruby Chen were busy with their hands and with their voices. One was pouring coffee grinds into a tin pot. The other was at the stove, cracking eggs and frying them. They were speaking to each other a mile a minute.

Belvedere stood before Ruby Chen, and the incongruity of a tall man towering over a small woman was not lost on me. Terror was evident in Ruby's eyes. "I'm afraid she'll have to come with me," he said to Sam Gee.

The restaurateur looked crestfallen. "She has done nothing wrong."

"I'm quite aware of that," Belvedere replied, "but I will need her to identify a suspect so that we can proceed with the case. And I will need you to come along with her."

Sam Gee said some words in Chinese to Ruby Chen, and tears immediately began to stream down her face. Gee turned to Belvedere. "She is afraid," he said, "that the murderer will kill her too."

"She needn't fear," Belvedere told Gee. "If the man is convicted of murder, he will be hung by the neck until dead."

The poor lady was quietly weeping as Gee led her into the living quarters at the back of the café. The two of them emerged a few moments later, dressed in their winter garb. Gee said some words to his wife, and she nodded back at him. She would serve as chief cook, waitress, and bottle washer while her husband was away on police business. Gee and Chen followed us up the hill toward the jail.

It was an apprehensive Ruby Chen who ventured into the jailhouse behind Belvedere later that morning. She was wearing a short, quilted coat and a hat. Her colourful scarf was pulled tight around her face, partly to fend off the cold of the brisk morning walk and partly, I think, because she did not want Lerat to recognize her. Lerat's son had been sitting with his father before our arrival. Belvedere asked him to leave, an act which sent the elder Lerat into a fit of howling. It was an off-putting display. I could see tears in Ruby Chen's eyes again. Belvedere exhorted the elder Lerat to be quiet, and then he turned to Ruby. "Look closely at the man," he said. "Is this the fellow who threatened to kill your brother?"

Through misty eyes, Ruby peered at the prisoner Lerat. He was perched on his bed, howling like a timber wolf, eyes wide, mouth open. I'm not sure I would have recognized the man; his face was distorted like an animal's. Ruby turned to Sam Gee and said some words, quietly, almost confidentially. Gee was dismayed, and there was disbelief in his voice when he told Belvedere, "She says this is not the man."

It was Belvedere's turn to be incredulous. "Not the man?"

Sam Gee shook his head.

"Tell her to look again."

The prisoner arched his back and snarled. Upon hearing from Gee, Ruby Chen scrutinized Lerat's countenance one more time. I was standing directly behind her. Lerat hissed at her, and she almost swooned, retreating backward against me. "Do not be afraid," I said, although I'm certain that she did not understand any of my words.

She turned to Gee again and spoke quietly. "This is not the man," Gee translated. "She is sure of it."

Belvedere looked sternly at Gee. "She's not saying this out of a fear of reprisal?"

Gee uttered some words to Chen. She shook her head.

"And she's sure of it?"

"Yes."

Belvedere sighed deeply. "But this is the trapper Lerat."

"Perhaps there are other trappers named Lerat," Gee offered, "or perhaps she had gotten the name wrong."

Belvedere looked out the one greasy window that adorned the jailhouse. "Well," he said, "she's led us on a merry chase."

"I know she is sorry to have done so," Gee replied.

Maintaining his gaze out the window, Belvedere said, "Montgomery, would you be so kind as to let the man's son know that this was a case of mistaken identity and that we will release Lerat into his son's care and custody forthwith?"

"Certainly." I went out into the cold and conferred with the younger Lerat, explaining as best I could how events had led to the arrest of his father.

"I told you he wasn't guilty," the younger Lerat said. "And look at the state you've brought him to now. He thinks he's a goddamned dog!"

"Sometimes people behave erratically when they are imprisoned." There wasn't much comfort in my words, but I could think of little else to say.

"And I'm supposed to take him home like this?"

"Unless you can think of someplace else you'd rather take him." As far as I knew, the nearest insane asylum was in British Columbia, and that alternative was likely out of the question for a poverty-stricken trapper and his son.

By the time I was finished conferring with Lerat the younger, Sam Gee was already escorting Ruby Chen down the hill toward his café. His arm was around her shoulder, and she was leaning heavily against him, almost as if the tension of the morning's activities had been too much for her.

The guard had released the prisoner from his cell. Belvedere and I watched as the son escorted his father down the snowy road toward the public livery stables. The father refused to stand. He was on all fours, scurrying through the snow, as his son admonished him to walk like a man. Even the local dogs, ever vigilant for one of their kind, steered clear of the elder Lerat. He was a rare beast, perhaps even more rare a human than he was a canine.

"So we got the wrong Lerat," Belvedere said to me as he watched the curious spectacle.

"Do you suppose Ruby Chen got the name wrong?"

"That's possible," he replied, "maybe even likely, given that she doesn't speak English."

"So what do we do now?" I asked.

"We keep looking."

5

Parry was at our door again the next morning. We were enjoying a repast of salt pork, stale bread, and gruel when he knocked. Mrs. McLaughlin had been even more reserved than usual all morning, hardly saying a word and keeping to herself in the kitchen. The reverend had not crawled out of bed yet. No one had mentioned the set-to of that October night three weeks earlier when a plate was broken and cruel words were uttered, but it had been in the air like fog since then.

When Mrs. McLaughlin answered the door, Parry stepped in out of the cold and made his oration. "C-C-C-Corporal B-B-Belvedere," he stuttered, "the S-S-"

Belvedere was in no mood to be patient early in the day. "Come on, man, spit it out." I don't know why Belvedere was so impatient with a speech impediment that Parry could not overcome. Belvedere was an impatient man, sometimes to the point of rudeness.

The sub-constable grasped the doorjamb to steady himself. "S-S-Sergeant S-Slade would like the s-s-s-see you, s-sir."

"Oh, is that all?" Belvedere replied. "When we're done eating."

"Sh-Sh-Shall I wait, C-corporal?"

"If you must."

Twenty minutes later, we were marching up the ridge toward the Stobart and Eden store, where Slade kept his office. Belvedere grumbled all the way. The temperature had dropped overnight, and the cold was exacerbating his bad leg. "What does that silly son-of-a-bitch want?" he asked Parry.

"He d-d-d-didn't s-say, s-sir." Parry's breath was freezing in the crisp air in front of him. "Only w-wanted me to c-c-collect you."

We paused at the top of the hill. Belvedere peered down toward the laundryman's backyard for some time, and then he turned to me. "You say it was a rim-shot cartridge, .44-40?"

"Yes." I knew what he was thinking, and I did not like the smell of it. "You'd have to be a crack shot to hit a target from up here."

I was glad to be inside the store on such a day. The stove was crackling hot, and the distinctive aroma of brain-tanned beaver and fox hides gave the place a roundness that I liked. When at last we stood in front of Slade's desk at the rear of the store, the sergeant looked up from his paperwork. "Belvedere," he muttered as though the name were synonymous with sphincter. "Shot anyone yet?"

"Not recently."

"And I hear that your arrest of Lerat was unwarranted after all."

Belvedere's face, red with the cold, looked like it might crack. "What do you want?"

The sergeant studied him as one might study a barn that had just burned down. "It did not take you long to find the local purveyor of spirits," he said. "I have a report that you were frequenting the hotel pub some weeks ago with Sheriff McQuaid."

Belvedere grinned at him, but his grin looked like a death mask. "Are you spying on me?"

"I have eyes all over this town," replied Slade.

"Yes, well, I was conducting an investigation."

"In a public house?"

"Sometimes, Slade, you have to get your hands dirty." Belvedere plopped himself down in a chair opposite the sergeant and sat like an insolent schoolboy. "But you wouldn't know about that, would you?"

Slade straightened up in his chair. "You were seen staggering from the pub at four in the afternoon. While in uniform."

Belvedere chuckled darkly. "I have a war wound. It causes me to limp sometimes. Maybe you hadn't noticed."

The sergeant cleared his throat and looked squarely at Belvedere. "I could make your life here miserable, Belvedere."

"You could try."

There was a long pause in the conversation, during which Slade pretended to be interested in a piece of paper on his desk. "Rest assured that I will write a report about this."

"You do that," Belvedere said. "You're good at writing reports."

"And the report will be sent to Superintendent Herchmer."

There was a frosty pause. Belvedere broke the silence. "Will that be all?"

"That will be all." Sergeant Slade returned to his paperwork as if we were no longer present.

Belvedere stood up and manoeuvred toward the door. He exited without another word. I lingered for a moment, hoping to catch the sergeant's eye and silently apologize for Belvedere's behaviour, but the sergeant did not look up from his paperwork. My fear was that I would be tarred with the same brush as the surly corporal through my close association with him.

WE INTERVIEWED a local newspaperman that afternoon. His name was Sylvester O'Rourke, and he was hard at work, with a leather typesetter's apron tied over his tweed suit. He wore a large, ink-stained silver ring, embossed with something that looked like a triangle, on his right hand.

It turned out there were two newspapers in the town, which was odd for so small a settlement, but which was also evidence of a town divided. O'Rourke's conservative paper was called *The Herald*. His competition, more liberal and with offices down the street, was known as *The Saskatchewanian*.

Mr. O'Rourke was a well-fed fellow, tending toward fat, but he was mentally nimble. He carried on a conversation with us in a back room, over the printing press, all the while selecting typesetting characters from wooden boxes in front of him and slotting them squarely into his composing stick. Sorting the characters rapidly and setting the type, he never missed a beat in our conversation. Occasionally, he would scrutinize an M, wipe the ink off its face, turn it clockwise and scrutinize it again. O'Rourke was clearly practised in his technique; he found the letters often without looking for them and composed with speed and accuracy. From where I was standing, I could see that he was reading the type backwards and upside down. He apologized for his own busyness. "It's Thursday," he said, "and I have a paper to circulate."

Belvedere seemed unimpressed. I knew enough about my colleague to surmise that he had little respect for men who pushed pencils for a living. "We read your report of the laundryman's murder," he said. "Were you at the scene?"

"No. I interviewed the sheriff, and that's all."

"Did you interview anybody else?"

"Nobody else knows anything."

Belvedere watched him for a moment. "You have your ear to the ground in this town?"

"I try."

"Any idea who might have wanted to kill Mr. Chen?"

The newspaperman gently lifted the lines of type from his composing stick and placed them on the galley. He wrapped a dirty string three or four times around the type. "There's plenty of acrimony in this town," he said. "The settlers are afraid of the Indians, and the Indians are afraid of the settlers. And the Métis are afraid that their land is going to be taken from them."

Belvedere scrubbed his face with one hand. "So where does a Chinese laundryman fit in with all of that?"

"I've no idea," O'Rourke said. "I'm just telling you that the town has some unhappy citizens."

"Ever heard of a fellow named Lerat?" asked Belvedere. "We've been told that he threatened Mr. Chen some time ago."

O'Rourke shook his head. "Only Lerat I know is that crazed trapper who lives west of here."

I was busy, all that while, trying to decipher the article O'Rourke was typesetting. After some time, I was able to make out the headline. "LAND MEETING AT TRESTON HALL THIS FRIDAY NIGHT."

AFTER SUPPER THE NEXT EVENING, I sat down at my writing desk and began again to tell Emily the whole truth of what had happened in my medical practice back east. A few lines in, I tore the letter up and resolved to wait. I was unsure of how much sympathy she would have for me after hearing of my shortcomings, and I did not want to tell her that I was contemplating giving up medicine completely. From the moment I met her, I had been striving to become a doctor.

With little else to do, I wandered over to Treston Hall to view the proceedings. The hall was filled to its rafters with townsmen and farmers. There were delegations from Groschen and Pochaville, Métis communities on either side of Prince Albert settlement. They were men in moccasins and colourful sashes, and buckskin coats beaded in a flowery style. A man named Isbister seemed to be their principal spokesman. He was a farmer from the western edge of the settlement, near the Hudson Bay Company store. Mr. O'Rourke was also in attendance, no doubt planning to report on the proceedings in the next issue of *The Herald*. A meek land office agent sat off to one side near the front of the hall. I could see the sheriff leaning against a wall near the coat room at the entrance.

First, the land agent shuffled to the lectern and said a few words of apology. He understood that there was discontent in the settlement and in the surrounding area, he said, but was handcuffed by the provisions of the Dominion Lands Act, which required three years' residence after the filing of claims. There were shouts and catcalls from the floor, mostly from white settlers who said they had filed their claims in good faith and had returned to Ontario for provisions, only to find, upon returning, that their claims had been jumped.

Then Isbister spoke. He was eloquent. "I've lived on this land for fifteen years," he said, "and now I'm told I have to file for a patent?"

"That's correct," the land agent replied.

"In Manitoba," Isbister continued, "there is an act which has set aside a million acres for the benefit of the Métis. When will that happen here?"

"There's no timeline," the agent replied.

"Perhaps," said Isbister, "we will have to secure the services of Monsieur Riel to do for us what he did for the people of Manitoba."

There was further shouting and cheering, after which the land agent opined that he would not recommend such an action. A better way, he said, and a less inflammatory route, would be to have an elected official speaking for the territory in the national parliament in Ottawa.

Isbister was incredulous. "And when will that happen?"

The shouting had reached a crescendo, and I feared that physical violence might ensue, but the burly sheriff sauntered to the front of the hall and stood, with his arms folded, behind the land agent. The shouting soon subsided, and after a few choice words from shopkeepers who said they didn't even know who owned title to the lots they were on, the meeting came to an end. As we were let out into the cold blue evening, I noticed O'Rourke and the sheriff still in earnest conversation at the front of the hall.

In a spare moment, on that Saturday, I strolled over to the Hudson Bay store in Groschen and found, to my delight, some canvas and a small selection of charcoals and oil paints. I had brought a brush with me from Battleford—I always carry one with me—but my painting supplies were running low. It was good to see that the town was not entirely devoid of artistic sentiment.

A well-spoken man by the name of Lawrence Clarke ran the store. He had seen me at the land meeting the night before, so there was an air of familiarity about him as he sidled over and asked what business I had in the town. I told him I was there to help with the investigation into the laundryman's murder. "You're a Mountie?" he asked. His bemused stare made it apparent that he did not see in me the stature or demeanour of a policeman.

"I'm a surgeon," I told him, "and an officer."

He was suddenly quite apologetic. "Forgive me," he said. "I didn't mean to imply—"

"Quite all right," I told him. "I don't imagine you have many mounted policemen in here looking for oils and canvas."

"Not many, no," he replied. "But it's good to see a new surgeon in this town, by gawd. That old sawbones Williamson is just one step up from a veterinarian."

EARLY THE NEXT WEEK, a dapper-looking man in a tweed overcoat appeared at the front door of the McLaughlin house. Mrs. McLaughlin had been busy dusting lampshades and bookshelves all morning, but she managed to get to the door before Belvedere and I had got up from our places at the dining room table. The man asked to speak to Corporal Belvedere. He was brought into the vestibule. Belvedere stood at the entrance to the dining room and asked the fellow what he wanted. "My name is Lerat," the dapper gentleman said. "I understand you've been looking for me."

Belvedere almost fell over. "Your name's Lerat?"

"August Lerat."

I was watching from the dining room. The man did not look the least bit nervous.

Belvedere took a moment to digest the man and his name. "What do you do for a living, Mr. Lerat?"

"I'm a purveyor of patent medicines," the man declared. "Some might call me a drummer or a peddler, but I prefer the more dignified title. I travel from town to town selling my wares."

"Selling medicines?"

Lerat looked over Belvedere's shoulder at me and Mrs. McLaughlin. "Perhaps this house could benefit from a bracing snake oil tonic or a lovely camphor lineament. I have some fine lineaments."

Belvedere did not bite at Lerat's sales pitch. "How did you know that I've been looking for you?"

"Joe Scriver, the liveryman," August Lerat said, "seems to have his finger on the pulse of this town."

"And you've had some past dealings with the local laundryman, as well?"

Lerat exhaled audibly and searched the ceiling for a proper phraseology. "I had an unfortunate argument with the man, middle of last summer. He'd managed to lose two of my handsomest long-sleeved shirts and a very expensive scalloped vest. And now I understand there's been a murder."

Belvedere's voice was suddenly dry as last week's tinder. "You argued about some shirts that were lost?"

"And a fancy scalloped vest."

Belvedere took a step forward. "Witnesses say that you threatened to kill the laundryman."

"An unfortunate choice of words," said Lerat. "I was speaking euphemistically."

"So you've come to turn yourself in?"

"On the contrary," Lerat said, "I've come to declare my innocence, and to prove it, too."

"And how might you prove your innocence?"

"If you'll be kind enough to accompany me to my wagon," Lerat said, "I will be only too happy to give you all the proof you need."

Thinking that the salesman's wagon and the subsequent conversation might be of interest, I donned my coat and went out into the street with Belvedere. Lerat's wagon was a sturdy four-wheeled conveyance, painted black, with a lettering on its side that read "Patent Medicines." It was drawn by a single dappled dray horse, shaggy-haired and looking like it was in bad need of a hoof trimming.

Lerat opened a compartment on the side of the wagon and produced a leather-bound ledger book that detailed his operation over the past several months. He opened the book to a certain page. "When did this murder take place?" he asked.

"The third of October."

He handed the book to Belvedere. "You will see by the ledger statements there, signed and dated, that I was in Winnipeg on the third of October this year."

Belvedere perused the book, turning pages in an effort to determine its authenticity. "Could you produce a witness who would attest to your being there?" He closed the book and handed it back to Lerat.

"I could produce a hundred witnesses, sir," the salesman said. "Anyone whose name you see there is a possible witness."

There was one last test that Belvedere wanted to administer. Later that afternoon, we walked into Sam Gee's café with the salesman. He was brought before Ruby Chen, and she quietly admitted that this was the Lerat she had heard and seen threatening her brother. Belvedere asked Gee to explain to her that this particular Lerat was nowhere near Prince Albert settlement at the time of the murder and that he could not have been responsible.

We left the café, but not before Lerat apologized profusely to Ruby. "I'm sorry for your loss," he said, and I think he meant it. "I did argue with your brother, but I never would have committed an act so vile as his murder."

We accompanied the salesman out into the street, where he climbed up into his wagon. "Where will you be, in case I need to find you?" Belvedere asked the man.

Lerat pulled his coat collar tight around his neck. "Winter's coming on," he said. "I reckon I'll be at home in Regina before the next snowfall." He peered deeply into Belvedere's eyes. "I noticed you have a limp. An old war wound, perhaps?"

"Yes."

"My camphor lineament works wonders."

Belvedere looked sidelong at me. "How much does it cost?"

"Four bits for the maximum-strength bottle."

"I'll take it at that price." He reached into his pocket, found fifty cents, and handed it to Lerat.

The salesman opened a valise on the seat beside him and produced a bottle of the lineament. He gave the bottle to Belvedere. "You won't be sorry," he said. "This stuff is good for everything from coughs to colds to sore holes." He hawed his horse down River Street, where he would no doubt make many similar sales before his departure to Regina and his winter's hibernation.

ON THE FOLLOWING SUNDAY, there was an early breakfast because Mrs. McLaughlin was expected to accompany her husband to church. I heard her downstairs early, lighting the stove and clanking pots and pans. By the time I had staggered out of bed and negotiated the steep stairs, there was a bowl of gruel steaming on the dining room table and weak coffee brewing on the stove. I sat down and began to eat. Belvedere had not yet graced us with his presence.

Mrs. McLaughlin asked if I was planning to attend the church service. I told her no. I was hoping to commune with Nature instead, to go out into the countryside and sketch a landscape.

"I thought you might be an artist," she said. "I couldn't help but notice your sketches when I was changing the bed linens yesterday."

At that moment, the reverend appeared in the hall portico. He looked sombre in his suit of black, and his face was ashen. I wondered if he was perhaps suffering from some ailment or other. Standing stiff as a slab of planed lumber, he looked at me morosely and said good morning.

"Are you feeling quite well, sir?" I inquired.

"Do I not look well?" Before I could answer his question, he turned to his wife. "Are you ready?"

She always looked ready for something. Her hair was coiffed in the same severe style as before, and she was wearing the same black dress. She stammered out a yes.

Belvedere still hadn't come downstairs by the time I finished eating. Not wanting to wake him, I crept as quietly as I could up the creaky stairs. I heard his little terrier growl, soft and low, as I stole into my room. After retrieving my notepad and charcoals, I padded softly down the stairs again. I donned my coat and cap in the front vestibule and made my escape.

The morning was clear and cool, but there was little wind to speak of. I walked up the hill toward the police stable with a saddlebag of charcoals and paper slung over my shoulder. My horse, Belle, was looking chipper and well-fed in her stall. I fancied that she was as happy to see me as I was to see her. She took the bit gracefully in her mouth and stood expectantly as I cinched the saddle. I led her out of the barn, climbed gingerly into the saddle, and, in almost no time, we were traversing through scrub brush in a southerly direction. To be truthful, I was grateful for the opportunity to practice my riding skills.

About a mile from the village, I dismounted and tied Belle to a tree. She dug with her hooves until she found grass, still green under the new-fallen snow, and then she munched away happily. I sat on a rock and sketched into a notepad while Belle ate her fill. Rolling hills and stands of poplar and spruce had managed to compose themselves into an attractive autumnal landscape before my eyes. When my fingertips got cold, I blew on them and deposited them into my mittens, marvelling at the vast expanse before me. It was an enormous empty land that had never known the scythe or the furrow plow. After a moment's respite, I got back to sketching.

When I tired of the spot, I mounted Belle again and headed farther south. Along the way, I discovered a trail, covered with snow but deeply rutted from the traffic of wagons and Red River carts. I followed the trail for another mile, and then I saw in the distance a line of telegraph poles stretching as far as the eye could see.

As I rode closer, I saw a gaggle of ragged labourers. They were digging postholes in the almost frozen ground. Some wielded spades and crowbars. Others had in their hands long-handled spoon shovels. Their work was arduous; the postholes must have been six feet deep. When the workers became aware of my presence, one of them, a short, wide man, walked over to a grey tent and picked up a rifle. The others ceased their labours. I reined Belle toward them cautiously, with my free hand in the air. Thankfully, I didn't fall off the horse.

"You can stop right there," the man with the rifle shouted. The gun was at his shoulder, and he had me in his sights. I pulled on the reins, and Belle came to a standstill. "What's yer business in these parts?"

"I'm an officer of the North-West Mounted Police," I called back. "I'm out here on patrol."

He was suspicious, but he lowered his rifle and strode toward me. When he was ten feet away, he asked to see my badge. Luckily,

I had it with me. His demeanour changed. "I'm glad to see you," he said. "Folks out here ain't always friendly."

"Oh?" I dismounted my horse and shook the man's hand. "Why's that?"

"The half-breeds don't trust us," the man said. "We've had to appropriate a bit of land to build this line."

"Are they violent in their protestations?"

The worker nodded his toqued head. "One of our fellas was shot at a coupla miles back. And we've had poles pried out of the ground and burned."

"They don't want the benefits of long-distance communication?"

"They don't want anything the white man brings."

The man escorted me to the encampment where some of the other workers were readying a pot of tea over a fire. Together we drank and ate hardtack, and they told me about their work. They were building a line between Wolverine Creek and the Prince Albert settlement, they said, but there was apparently some confusion about where the telegraph office would be situated in the settlement. The workers had been told to extend the line to the edge of town, but not a step farther until a location for the office had been settled upon.

"Does no one in the town want the telegraph?" I asked.

"Sounds to me like everyone in the town wants the telegraph office," the man with the rifle said. "They all figger the railway is gonna be attached to it somehow, and they want the railway near to them."

When it was time for the men to get back to work, I asked one of them, a fresh-faced young Scotsman, if he needed any supplies. "I could use a wee sack o' tobakky," he replied. I reached into my coat pocket and handed him what was left of my pipe tobacco. He took a wad and stowed it in one corner of his mouth, savouring the sweetness of the nicotine, and then he thanked me and joined his comrades. I took one last look at the line of poles that stretched back toward civilization, and then I mounted my horse and headed to the settlement.

THE SUN WAS low in the sky by four o'clock when I returned to the McLaughlin house. I found Belvedere outside in the street with his mutt. It was getting colder, and our breath seemed to solidify in the air. He asked me where I'd been, and I told him. "Drawing pictures," he harumphed. "Fine work for a policeman." He tugged his buffalo coat tight around his neck and snatched his little dog from the snow drift it had just shat upon. "Best get ready for some sleuthing. There's been another murder."

"Another murder?"

"A farmer. Fellow named McKay. North across the river. I saw Parry this afternoon during my perambulations." Belvedere smiled wryly and stroked the terrier's fur. "He managed to stammer out the initial facts of the case."

"When are we riding out there?"

"First light tomorrow."

6

The ferry began running as an orange sun peeked over the horizon. We rode our horses onto the rickety wooden skiff and dismounted for the brief journey across the river. Shards of ice drifted by us, and I knew it would not be long before the river was frozen over for the winter, rendering it impassable for a time until the ice had thickened.

A forest of coniferous trees on the north side of the river felt like an impenetrable wall when we first encountered it, but loggers had made some labyrinthine and seemingly haphazard inroads. It would have been possible to lose oneself in that maze of stump-laden roads, and I remarked how different the north side of the river was from the open light of the town. We met one of the loggers as we headed north, a fellow in a Mackinaw jacket and a fur hat. He was geeing and hawing a pair of dray horses as they struggled to pull a wagon loaded with five or six fat spruce trees that had been shorn of their branches. We stopped him and asked where the McKay farm was.

"Up this here road about two miles," the fellow hollered, and he geed his horses again.

We carried on, picking our way past rocks and tree stumps until we arrived at the farm. It was a well-cared-for homestead with a house and barn of log construction. There was a clothesline in the yard, denuded of any clothes. The clothesline posts looked like two of the three crosses at Gethsemane. Beyond the barn, I could see a quarter-section of open field that had been meticulously carved out of the forest. Snow covered everything.

Belvedere and I were tying our horses to one of the clothesline poles when we saw a man exiting the house. The man walked briskly toward the loggers' road, carrying a wooden chair in one hand and a banjo in the other. Belvedere broke into a run, partially impeded by his own injured leg, and I followed. The stranger did not bother to run from us. Either he did not see us, or he was unconcerned with our presence. He carried on as though it was his God-given right to scavenge a dead man's property.

Nearing him, I could see that the man had a shapeless felt hat pulled low around his ears and the collar of his coat pulled high above his neck. He was maybe forty years old. It was difficult to tell. "Hold on there!" Belvedere shouted.

The man stopped, turned, and looked at us. He had a pug nose and a dash for a mouth. "Hullo, officers!" he shouted back.

"Is this the McKay farm?" the corporal asked.

"It is."

Belvedere fingered his handgun in its holster. "What's your business here?"

"Just takin what's rightfully mine." The man put the chair down on the snow-encrusted grass and sat on it.

"That's called theft in most jurisdictions," Belvedere replied. "And who might you be?"

The man scratched his stubbly chin and grinned. "No need to get trigger-happy here, officer. You can see I'm unarmed."

Belvedere stared a hole right through the man. "What's your name?"

"Cantrell," the man said. "Herman Cantrell. I'm his neighbour, up the road a piece."

"And what business have you with McKay's belongings?"

Cantrell smiled wryly, shook his head. “I lent young Alexander twenty dollars to get him started out here. Reckon I won’t never see that twenty dollars back now.”

“Got anything on paper to prove that?”

“It was a gentleman’s agreement.”

Belvedere unhanded his weapon and approached the man more closely. “Then I’ll have to ask you to return those goods to the house.”

Cantrell remained sitting on the chair as though to sit outdoors on a cold November day was customary in the Canadian north. He began strumming the banjo, quite tunelessly. The vibration of the cold metal strings echoed through the forest around us like a blacksmith’s hammer on an anvil. “You plan on stationing a man at this house for the next month or so?”

“No.”

“Well, then, there’s gonna be looters. And I think it best to get what’s rightfully mine before the Injuns take it, don’t you?”

Belvedere considered the man’s words for a moment. “Tell you what,” he said. “If you answer a question or two, I’ll let you take the banjo and the chair.”

“Deal.” Cantrell plunked a simple but unrecognizable tune on the banjo.

“How was McKay killed?”

“Shot, far as I could tell.”

“Did you witness the shooting?”

Cantrell shook his head. “There’s a half-mile of bush betwixt me and Alexander.”

“Did you find the body?”

“Yessir. I heard the shots. I waited until I thought it was safe, and then I come a-lookin’.” The banjo tune morphed itself into something resembling “Buffalo Gals,” but it sounded metallic and otherworldly against the echo and the coldness of the day.

Belvedere pulled his notepad from his pocket, bit off a mitt, and began writing. “Where did you find him?”

“Out there in the pasture. Had a pail beside him. Was likely feedin' the cows." Cantrell's face creased at the recollection; he seemed fond of the deceased McKay.

"Any of his cows missing?"

"He only had but two cows. I put 'em in the barn after I took care of the body."

"Was he dead when you found him?"

"Yeah."

"You're certain?"

"He weren't breathin'." Cantrell was playing full throttle on the banjo now; the tune gathered speed like a railway engine leaving the station.

"And you dragged him back here to the yard?"

"Yeah."

"Where's the body now?"

"There in the barn," Cantrell said, nodding in that direction. "I didn't want to bloody up the house."

Belvedere wrote some more, and then he looked up at Cantrell. "Does Mister McKay have any next-of-kin?"

Cantrell shook his head. He ceased playing, grasping the banjo tight with both hands. "Young Alexander come up here from Ontario two summers ago. He had no wife and no childers. And he never went back East, far as I know. Some days, he was lonesome as a four-peckered owl in a windstorm."

"Know of anybody who might have wanted Mister McKay dead?"

"Alexander was a cheerful fella. Played the banjo. Didn't have no enemies."

"And yet, he's lying dead in the barn."

"The Injuns ain't too happy with us farmers north of the river." Cantrell spat in the snow. "Seem to think everything north of the river belongs to them."

Belvedere squinted at the man. "What Indians are you talking about?"

"The Teton Sioux," Cantrell replied. "They shot four of my cattle last winter. Can I go now? My ass is gettin' frostbit."

Belvedere wrote some more in his notepad. "You can go," he said at last, "but don't be coming back to this house." Cantrell sprang to his feet and headed across the yard, chair and banjo in hand.

Belvedere and I went in the other direction, toward the barn. The hinges creaked as I opened the door. It was gloomy inside and without much natural light, as barns often are. There were two cows tethered in the stalls, munching hay, oblivious to what else was in there with them. Steam rose off their backs, and straw dust filled the air.

In the tack room, across from the stalls, there were two sawhorses placed six feet apart. Three two-by-tens were lying side by side on the sawhorses, and on top of them was the body of the murdered man. The corpse was still completely dressed in woollen trousers and a woollen coat, and sturdy leather boots. His face was frozen in a deep snarl like an animal that had died trying to free itself from a leg-hold trap. It was hard to tell, but the man appeared to be about the same age as I was.

Belvedere peered at the body for a moment, then turned to me. "What do you make of this, Montgomery?"

"I don't see a wound," I said. "Do you?"

It took some doing, but we managed to turn the body over. Rigor mortis had set in, and the corpse was cold through and through. Having noticed rough and bloodied holes in the back of the dead man's coat, I tugged it over his shoulders with some difficulty. Two gaping bullet holes were evident between the shoulder blades. One of them had powder burns at its periphery. "Two gunshot wounds," I told the corporal. "One of them fired at close range."

"At close range?" Belvedere repeated. "The murderer walked right up to the man?"

"He was probably six feet away," I said. "Do you think it was the same fellow who shot the laundryman?"

"Hard to say," Belvedere replied. "The Chinaman could have been shot for any number of reasons, not least of which is the fact that he was a Chinaman. I don't rightly know what the motive would be for this killing here. A grudge of some sort, maybe. Or maybe someone wanted his homestead."

"Well," I said, "whoever did this had time and leisure out here to finish his man off properly."

"That he did," Belvedere muttered. "Let's take a look around."

There was a trail of footprints leading out to the pasture. We could see an indentation in the dirty snow where McKay must have fallen. Frozen globules of blood decorated the snow in a sombre fashion. There was a tin pail lying on the ground nearby. Belvedere caught sight of something gleaming in the afternoon sun. He picked the gleaming article out of the snow and showed it to me. It was a shell casing from a Winchester.

More footprints led to the woods at the edge of the pasture. We followed the footprints into the dark coniferous forest to a place where the murderer must have lain in wait. There was less snow in the forest, but one could plainly see where the man must have knelt on one knee while taking aim. We didn't find another shell casing, but as we were preparing to leave, Belvedere stepped on something. I saw him kicking at the leaves and snow, an act which eventually uncovered a thin pewter hip flask. From where I was standing, I could see the letter "G" embossed in the pewter. "Seems like we have an initial, at least," I remarked. "Could be a George or a Gordon or some such."

"Perhaps," Belvedere replied. "Odd, though, that there'd just be one initial." He picked up the flask and examined it, eventually unscrewing the cork. He smelled the contents of the flask, then unceremoniously took a drink. "Hudson Bay rum," he said appreciatively. "Believe I'll confiscate this as evidence."

As we were making our way back to the yard, I saw Sergeant Slade and Sub-Constable Parry riding in from the loggers' road. The sergeant didn't bother to dismount. He trotted quite near to us before reining in his horse. Looking down at Belvedere, he said, "What are you doing here, Corporal?"

"I heard there'd been a shooting." Belvedere looked back at the sergeant unwaveringly. Parry studied the ground.

"What goes on outside the settlement falls in my purview," the sergeant barked. "Not yours."

Belvedere took a deep breath and exhaled the cold air. "Two murders in a town this size within a couple of months," he said. "You don't think they're connected?"

"There's no reason to believe that," the sergeant sputtered. "They are two separate incidents."

"Well, I'm duty-bound to investigate." Belvedere cleared his throat and spat on the ground.

Slade sat there looking at Belvedere for quite some time. Parry became even more engaged with the ground in front of him. I pretended that a magpie up in a tree was suddenly of great interest. "Good luck with that, then," Slade said at last. "Whoever murdered this man is long gone and likely never to be found. And you'd better make haste. We're sending a drayman out to gather the body this afternoon."

"We've already completed our investigation." Belvedere did not mention the flask or the shell casing. "The body's in the barn. In case you have the stomach to look at it."

The sergeant's posture was a hieroglyph for a curse word as he dismounted and handed his horse's reins to Parry. We stood and watched. The sergeant strode into the barn. Parry trailed behind him.

Belvedere turned to me and grinned. "Are you quite satisfied with what you've seen here, Montgomery?"

"I am."

"Then we'd best be on our way."

We rode toward the Sioux encampment that same day. I hadn't had much experience of the Sioux until then. The Indians near Battleford were mostly Cree. I knew of the warlike history of the Sioux. These were the brothers and sisters of Sitting Bull, who had annihilated George Custer and his men eight years earlier. They had not been party to any treaty; while their allies had mostly accepted the terms offered by the government of Canada, the Sioux were still living a migratory life, hunting what was left of the buffalo and the deer, fishing and trapping, moving their encampments to suit the seasons. I wondered aloud whether it might be advisable to arrive in the Sioux camp with some reinforcements.

"The danger's overstated," Belvedere told me. "They aren't eager to harm officers of the law after what happened down south."

It was late in the afternoon by the time we approached the encampment. There was no wind to speak of. The sun was drooping in the east, and the day had got somewhat colder, a deep chill that made my bones feel like matchsticks. Winter had not yet entirely come, but its promise was in the air.

Before us lay a circle of perhaps thirty tipis, tall and sturdy and covered with the hides of buffalo. Smoke curled up from the chimney folds. There was little evidence of activity outside, and I took comfort in the notion that we were approaching a domestic scene. I imagined that, inside the tipis, women were preparing meals; men were conferring about the hunt; children were playing.

Belvedere broke the silence. "Hullo, the tipis!" he shouted with such force that my horse side-stepped and bucked. I slid out of the saddle and toppled into the snow.

Belvedere's face darkened. "For gawd's sake, Montgomery, get up off the ground. You'll make us a laughingstock."

I got to my feet and brushed myself off. After a moment, men began to emerge from the tents. They had blankets and buffalo hides draped around their shoulders for warmth. A few of them carried rifles. Women and children also appeared, ragged and malnourished, silent witnesses to what was about to occur.

One man stepped forward. He was of short stature, but with an interesting face that was furrowed deep with much care and worry. His black hair was parted in the middle and braided on both sides. He spoke in unadorned English. "Mounted policemen," he said. "Why are you here?"

Belvedere dismounted. "We come in peace."

The Indian showed us the palms of both hands. "Do not come closer," he said. "We want no more of the White Man's disease."

"We have no disease to bring you." He ventured a few steps closer to the man. "You can see we are in good health."

"Do not come closer," the Indian warned again. "We have sickness here already."

Belvedere studiously avoided touching his handgun. He turned and looked at me and then shouted to the man, "My friend here is a medicine man. He has white cures for white diseases. Let him see your people who are suffering."

The Indian appraised me with a long, cool gaze. "You have white medicine?"

I unfastened my saddlebag and held it above my head to show him.

He turned again to Belvedere. "Your medicine man is young."

"He has the best medicine," Belvedere replied.

The man appraised me for a long time. His face softened. "Then you may come."

Uncertain as to whether I was walking into a trap, I made my way nervously, saddlebag in hand, toward the tipis. Another fellow, a tall, sturdy brave, led me toward one particular tipi separated from the others by a distance of fifty feet. He opened the flap at the entrance of the dwelling, and I peered into the darkness of a world that was new and strange to me. There was a fire smouldering in the middle of the tipi and a prone body, off to one side, swaddled in buffalo hides. After my eyes adjusted to the lack of light, I could see through the gloom that the prone body was that of a young boy. He was sweating profusely, perhaps from the warming effect of the fire, perhaps from his illness. His cough was like the bark of a timber wolf.

There was another presence in the tipi, not noticed at my

entrance, a woman who had pasted herself against the buffalo-hide wall. She looked afraid. I could not tell whether she was afraid of me or of the disease.

It all came flooding back to me at that moment. I had seen that look in a mother's face before. That wintry night in Quebec City, only one year earlier, I had been galloping from home to home, trying to quell an epidemic of the flu, or so I thought. The first child I saw that day had a fever and a rash, but no stiffness of the neck. I prescribed plenty of fluids and moved on, seeing seven more children before nightfall. Little did I know that the first child I had seen was suffering from meningitis and that I was unwittingly bringing the disease into the homes of seven other children.

The Sioux child before me looked frightened. Perhaps I looked frightened, too. I spoke to him, soothing words I'm sure he did not understand, placing my hand on his fevered brow. Tugging aside the buffalo hide that was warming him, I could see none of the tell-tale marks of the pox, no blisters or scars from blisters. I checked his neck for stiffness. His little chest heaved painfully with each breath.

Overwhelmed by sad memory as I was, I knew pneumonia when I saw it, and although a foolproof cure for the disease was not possible, I administered what medicines I could. First, I applied camphor to the boy's chest. Then, I motioned to the woman—his mother, I thought—to find a receptacle of some sort. She exited the tipi and came back, moments later, with a tin pail that was probably traded from the Hudson Bay store across the river.

I brought the child to a sitting position and placed the pail in front of him. There was a tin cup nearby, half-full of water. I gave the boy antimony in pill form, which he accepted with hesitancy, and brought the water to his lips. Moments later, he was vomiting, ridding himself of the excess fluids in his body. When that was done, I gave the child a grain of morphine to induce sleep.

Through all of this, the woman looked on with apprehension.

She must have wondered if I was murdering her son or saving him. In truth, I could not take credit for the cure if a cure was in the cards. In my limited experience, a slim majority of patients survived with or without treatment. I only hoped to expedite the process.

When I came outside again, Belvedere and the man who had spoken earlier were in close conference. Belvedere had the reins of both our horses in his hands, and the two men were speaking in hushed tones. I washed my hands as best I could in the cold snow that lay outside the tipi, wiping them dry on my trousers and reinserting them in my mitts. As I approached them, the Indian turned and asked, "How is the boy?"

"He's comfortable," I said. "I would like to come back and see him whenever possible."

"Yes," the man said. He nodded at Belvedere, and then he padded back to his tent, his moccasins barely making an imprint in the snow.

We mounted our horses again. Belle was still skittery, and I almost fell off a second time. Belvedere watched with bemusement. When we were out of sight of the Sioux encampment, I asked Belvedere, "Who was that man?"

"Good Voice," Belvedere replied. "He speaks for his people."

"What did he tell you?"

"That his braves haven't left the encampment these last three days."

"And you believe him?"

Belvedere thought for a moment, surveying the uneven road in front of him. "If they were killing for food, they would have taken McKay's cattle."

I had come to the territories partly to escape something, but I had also been lured by adventure. An Easterner born and bred, I viewed the West as a place to be tamed, teeming with savage Indians in need of the saving graces of Christianity and modern medicine. What I saw that day in the Sioux encampment was not a coven of savages but a community of families that had learned to co-exist with nature, not to tame it. Mothers and fathers loved their sons as much as white people do. Old men were wise and articulate. As we rode toward Prince Albert settlement, I couldn't help comparing the peaceful existence of the Sioux to the violence of the white men who had come to settle the area, feral as the dogs who roamed their town at will, and I began to wonder who the real savages were.

7

It was dark by the time we arrived at the ferry crossing. Luckily, the ferryman had not shut down operations for the night. He was somewhat inebriated, but he managed to transport us to the other side, where gangs of dogs waited, their hackles bristling. Belvedere fired his handgun into the air, and they scattered.

After we had stabled our horses, we trudged down the hill toward the McLaughlin house. Even a hundred feet away, we could hear raised voices coming from inside the residence. There was a woman's scream and the sound of something breaking.

Belvedere winced as he limped toward the commotion. I got to the door first and threw it open. From the front entrance, I witnessed a horrifying tableau: the minister was standing over his kneeling wife. He was wielding a broom handle. "Bitch!" he shouted. "Whore!" He brought the handle down hard on her back, and Mrs. McLaughlin collapsed to the floor.

Belvedere leaped into action. Seizing the end of the broomstick in one hand, he administered a series of blows to the reverend, knocking him to the floor and then kicking him once in the side of the head for good measure. I knelt beside the man's unfortunate wife and cradled her in my arms. She could not find words to speak. Her eyes were wide and beseeching. Her mouth agape, she seemed to be recovering her breath; the wind was knocked out of her. "Do not be alarmed," I reassured her. "The danger is passed."

A few moments later, Mrs. McLaughlin seemed to regain some of her composure and was able to sit up on her own. Her husband was groggily coming to, as well, and weeping piteously. Belvedere stood in the middle of the dining room, surveying the upheaval. Chairs had been knocked over, and the flue of the coal-oil lamp had shattered. "Is there a stove in the church?" he asked Mrs. McLaughlin.

She nodded.

"Then that's where this one will spend the night." Belvedere grabbed the minister by the collar, bringing him to a standing position. He marched the unhappy preacher to the front door, threw a coat over the man's shoulders, and escorted him outside.

"Please," I heard his wife murmur as they exited, "please don't hurt him further."

Belvedere was gone for over an hour. In the meantime, I looked to Mrs. McLaughlin's wounds. She had a gash on her scalp that required sutures, but she had managed to avoid being hit in the face. Wincing as I inserted the needle in her scalp, she nevertheless found excuses for her husband. "He's been under such pressure," she said, almost inaudibly. "He's not himself at all." I checked her for a concussion and, satisfied that there was none, gave her a drink of water and sent her off to bed. By the time Belvedere returned, the house was quiet again.

Mrs. McLaughlin did not get out of bed the next morning. Downstairs early, I stoked the fire in the cookstove and boiled some water. Having found a bag of rolled oats in the cupboard, I poured its contents into the saucepan and enjoyed the musty smell of the gruel. Belvedere had smelled the coffee I was brewing in another pot, and he was downstairs at the table by the time it was ready. His little dog stared wide-eyed and beseechingly at him, but there was no shard of bacon or ham to offer the mutt.

Belvedere sat like a sullen lump at the table, nursing his coffee. "Is the missus up yet?"

"No," I said between spoonfuls of porridge.

He looked up at the ceiling. I could tell that domestic disturbances were not within his usual purview. "Perhaps you'll look in on her then, Montgomery?"

"I surely will."

He finished his coffee in one long slurp. "In the meantime, we must keep this investigation going," he said. "I'll have a word with the people down at the lumber mill."

At the end of this rudimentary breakfast, I prepared a bowl of gruel and hot milk for Mrs. McLaughlin. In the sideboard, I found a tray on which to convey the bowl and a cup of steaming coffee. I thought about Emily and her love of flowers, and it occurred to me to adorn the tray with a trinket that would provide a little colour, but no such adornment was in sight. The best I could do was to place the spoon, once silver but now blackened with time, in a prominent position on the tray.

I carried the tray through the parlour on the way to the bedroom. Having never set foot in the parlour before, I was instantly aware of its austerity. There was one large wooden chair, straight-backed, upholstered only on its seat, in front of the fireplace, and a divan along another wall. An ancient upright piano that looked like it hadn't been played in a very long time sat quietly under a window. Portraits of Christ Jesus in various poses —at the Last Supper and walking on the water—adorned the walls at regular intervals. The busy wallpaper was the only thing in the room that felt homey; if you stood in front of it long enough, I thought, perhaps you could imagine that you saw a cloud formation or a portrait of the Devil in its patterns.

The door to Mrs. McLaughlin's bedroom was shut. I approached with trepidation, listened for a while, and then tapped on it lightly. There was no response from inside the room.

I tapped again, louder. "Mrs. McLaughlin? Are you in?" Still, there was no answer. I turned the glass knob and pushed the door open slightly. The room was dark; the blinds on the windows must have been drawn. "Mrs. McLaughlin?"

I heard a dry voice from somewhere in the room. "Go away."

While I am not so brazen as to enter a woman's boudoir without her permission, the doctor in me would permit no obstacles. "I've brought you something to eat," I said. "Are you decent?"

"Leave me alone."

"Forgive me." I opened the door farther, and a column of light fell over the bed.

Mrs. McLaughlin's face was blotchy from crying. She was sitting up, head and shoulders against the plain wooden headboard. The blankets were pulled high around her neck. Not at all like the severe minister's wife now, she looked like a waif in a Dickens novel. Her hair was not swept tight around the back of her head, as it once had been. Wavy and long, it cascaded down the sides of her face. I could tell that she had once been considered beautiful and could be again.

"Mister Montgomery," she said, her voice sterner now, "I have asked you to leave me alone."

"I am duty-bound," I replied, "to see that you are well." Having moved forward into the room, I placed the tray gently on the side of the bed. "And to see that you are nourished."

Her eyes grew darker. "Has my husband returned?"

"He has not." I found a chair and sat beside the bed. "Is your head aching?"

"No."

"And you're seeing well?"

"Yes."

"How is your back?"

"Sore," she said, as though I were the thickest person on the planet.

"Are you able to walk?"

"I could walk if I wished," she said, "but right now, I wish to remain in this room, alone."

"Certainly." Satisfied that she was suffering no serious and permanent effects of the beating she had been given, I resolved to vacate the room. I stood up and said, "I'll leave you some food. In case you feel like eating later."

When I was at the door and ready to leave, Mrs. McLaughlin spoke again. "Mr. Montgomery?"

I stopped and turned. "Yes?"

"Would you make certain that my husband receives some sustenance? He will have no food at the church."

"I will, of course."

"And Mr. Montgomery?"

"Yes?"

"Thank you."

LATER THAT MORNING, I packed some cheese sandwiches into a wicker basket and walked over to the church. It was another cold day, but the sky was clear and blue, the kind of day that reminds you of biting into a crisp soda biscuit. I pulled my coat close around me as I walked.

The large front door opened with a creak. It was cold inside the church. I surmised that the fire in the stove had gone out in the night. Shafts of light cascaded in through the arched windows at the sides of the nave.

I found the reverend sitting rigid and upright on a long pew near the entrance. He had dispensed with his coat and was shivering in his trousers and white shirt. His face was ashen. One of his eyes was blackened. I approached him warily and sat down some distance away from him, but on the same pew. Concentrating with his entire being on the cross on the wall above the altar, he did not bother to look at me. When at last he spoke, his voice was lifeless. "I have sinned egregiously," he murmured. "I have sinned."

"I've brought you some food." I pushed the basket gently in his direction.

Still, he did not look at me. "I don't want your food," he said. "I don't want to live."

"Don't want to live?"

He shook his head. "I hate myself."

"You must learn not to do so."

"I am jaded. I have jaded others. I will not achieve a life eternal. Nor will any of us. When the Day of Judgment comes, we will be left standing by the River of Fire."

I pushed the basket of sandwiches further toward him. "You should eat something."

"Thank you. No."

Although he would not eat, I thought it best to leave the basket behind. Before I left the church, I inspected the stove near the altar. There were some newspapers, firewood, and matches in a box nearby. I stuffed the firebox with newspaper and piled it full of wood. It wasn't long before a fire was crackling. I stopped near the preacher on the way out. "If you stoke that fire now and then, it'll keep you warm throughout the day." His gaze remained fixed on the cross, and he didn't respond. I turned and left without another word.

BELVEDERE RETURNED from his interview at the lumber mill early that afternoon. Having baked some bread and found some saskatoon berry preserve, I invited him to the table. Not much worse than Mrs. McLaughlin as a cook, I found myself serving as head chef in her absence. My mother had taught me to bake bread when I was just a child, and my years as a bachelor had provided me with some culinary practice, as well. I had to cook because I liked to eat.

Still wearing his buffalo coat, Belvedere sat at the table and gorged himself with fresh bread. He spooned preserves directly from the bowl into his own mouth, not bothering to slather them on the bread. I asked him how his meeting at the lumber mill had gone. Apparently, it had not gone well. The mill boss was uncooperative. "I asked the silly feck if there was antagonism between the lumberjacks and the farmers," Belvedere said. "He told me to mind my own business."

"Do you think they'd murder a man for his trees?"

Belvedere wolfed down another hunk of bread. "Entirely possible," he said. "I wouldn't put it past 'em."

At that moment, I heard some rustling out in the parlour, and then Mrs. McLaughlin appeared in the foyer. Her hair had not been done up in the usual fashion, but she was wearing her customary black dress. Her face was drawn and white. She stood still for a moment, apprehensive about what we might think of her. "I smelled bread baking," she said at last.

I got up from the table. "Come and eat."

Her voice was soft as a mouse's voice, if a mouse could talk. "If I could take a little back to my room with me?"

"Of course." I carved a thick slice from the loaf with a bread knife. "And I took the liberty of opening a jar of your preserves."

"Yes, thank you," she said, scooping the bread and a small dab of preserve onto a cracked china plate. She retreated into the foyer. "I want to apologize for what occurred here last night," she added. "And I want to thank you for stepping in so bravely."

"It was nothing, ma'am," I replied. "Please don't think twice about it."

"Please don't think poorly of my husband," she said. "He's been very unhappy lately."

"We don't think poorly of him." I looked sidelong at Belvedere, but he was silent.

"Is he all right at the church?"

"Yes." I knew he was not all right, but I didn't want to trouble her further.

"And you fed him?"

"Yes."

Belvedere remained at the table. He did not look at the poor woman or acknowledge her. Instead, he focused on the act of feeding a morsel of bread to his little dog. Mrs. McLaughlin's dark eyes rested on him for some time, and then she turned like a ghost and glided back toward her bedroom.

IN THE AFTERNOON, I walked to the butcher's shop on River Street and purchased a roast of beef. Circumstances had made me chief cook and bottle washer in the McLaughlin household for the time being, and I thought it best to bring a hearty meal to the table that evening. I fired up the oven and slipped cloves of garlic into the fat of the roast. In another pot, on top of the stove, I boiled some potatoes I'd found in the cold cellar. They were still fairly fresh. The plates I set around the table in an orderly fashion. There were no flowers for a centrepiece, but I discovered a small plaster casting of Shakespeare's birthplace in Mrs. McLaughlin's china cabinet and placed it, for decoration, near the coal-oil lamp on the table.

Supper was served at seven o'clock. It was already dark outside, and Belvedere had been in his room for some time. Having smelled the roast, he clomped down the stairs early and sat on a dining room chair, the terrier in his lap. "Smells good in here," he said, and then in a whisper, "I hope you're a better cook than the missus." The dog scampered off his lap occasionally and stood before the oven, out in the kitchen, with his tongue hanging out. He was a smart little cuss; he knew better than to touch his nose to the hot exterior of the stove.

When the meal was ready, I knocked on Mrs. McLaughlin's door. Her reply was immediate, although her voice was still somewhat listless. "Yes?"

"Dinner is served," I announced.

There was a moment's pause, and then she replied. "I'll be there shortly."

I was carving the roast on the sideboard when Mrs. McLaughlin appeared in the foyer. She was wearing her black dress, but her hair was still free of its customary tight braid. Fragile and lovely are the best words to describe how she looked. Her complexion was ashen, but one felt that the natural beauty she had been hiding away was finally beginning to emerge. She stood there, looking at us, for some time. "Have you cooked a roast beef?"

"Yes," I replied. "Procured from the local butcher this afternoon."

"Has my husband been fed?"

I continued carving as if nothing was out of the ordinary. "I delivered sandwiches this morning," I said. "Tonight, after we've eaten, I'll take him some supper."

"When will he be coming home?" It seemed an odd question, given that the set-to had only happened on the previous evening. The gash in her scalp had not yet healed; it was hidden beneath her unkempt hair.

"That will depend on Reverend McLaughlin," I said. "When he is ready."

"He's not a villain." The poor lady seemed close to tears.

"Of course not." I forked the roast onto a plate, not wanting to tell her how sullen and uncommunicative he had been that morning. "But you must eat."

Having ferried the roast beef to the table, I took Mrs. McLaughlin gently by the elbow and led her to a chair. Belvedere was already conveying roast beef to his plate when I pronounced my intention to say grace. He looked at me as if I'd lost my mind, and then he placed his fork quite deliberately on the table and bowed his head.

"For what we are about to receive," I said, "the Lord make us truly thankful."

We ate the meal mostly in silence. Belvedere fed his terrier the grizzled portions of the roast. Mrs. McLaughlin picked at her food for some time, ingesting only a little of it, and then she excused herself and returned to her bedroom.

I marched over to the church at nine o'clock with a covered pot filled with meat and mashed potatoes. It was a moonless night, the darkness pouring in around me. I was grateful to be holding in my hands a warm receptacle for the food. A pack of dogs followed me at a respectful distance. They must have smelled the beef inside the pot.

The church was cold and dark when I entered. The reverend was not sitting in a pew near the back of the church, where I had seen him earlier. In the gloom, I noticed that the basket I had left on the pew was now empty, save for a few crumbs and morsels. The minister had at least eaten something.

There was a rhythmic percussion like an axe chopping wet wood, and I followed the sound to the altar. There, even in the darkness, I could see that the reverend was kneeling. I moved closer. He was shirtless, and he was scourging himself with a leather belt. Two sentences he intoned over and over. "If we say we have no sin, we deceive ourselves, and the truth is not in us," he growled hoarsely. "But if we confess our sins, God, who is faithful and just, will forgive us." As I arrived at the steps of the altar, I could see through the gloom that the flagellation had produced welts and open cuts on the man's back. Apparently, his pilgrimage on the path toward penance had been going on for quite some time.

He must have heard me when I placed the pot of victuals on a pew near the front of the church because he ceased in his deliberations and turned to look at me. His voice was still harsh and pained. "Go away."

"I've brought some more food."

"I don't want any." With a dismissive glance, he returned to his prayer but refrained from whipping himself further.

There was little use trying to reason with him. I cannot say he was mad, but he was clearly fevered with religious devotion. The best I could do was to try and provide some comfort. I examined the firebox of the stove and, finding only smouldering embers, proceeded to throw in some crumpled newspaper and firewood. Within minutes, the fire was blazing again, and the place began to warm.

I was uncertain whether the preacher's practice of scourging himself in prayer was a customary one or whether he had newly acquired this technique. As he had desisted from flagellating himself upon becoming aware of my presence, I thought it best to leave him to his religious observances. I negotiated my way down the aisle toward the back of the church. Before I left, I turned to him and said, "Your wife has been asking for you. She is curious as to when you might be coming home." I thought this knowledge might bestow on him some measure of solace.

He did not turn to look at me. Gazing up at the cross above the altar, he said, in a clear voice, "I will never go back to that house of iniquity."

"Your wife longs to see you again."

"I do not long to see her." He returned to his fervent prayers.

I stood at the back of the church for some time, listening to his quiet rant, and then I retreated from the Lord's House. I thought about the reverend and Mrs. McLaughlin, divided as they were, although they had everything in place to live in wedded bliss. My dearest Emily came to mind then, and I knew that I had erred in our parting. I had been less than truthful with her, and I wondered how Emily would take that news if and when I could summon up the courage to tell her.

8

We were awakened early the next morning by a loud knocking at the front door. I fumbled for my pocket watch on the bedside table, and saw through sleep-encrusted eyes that it was not yet seven o'clock. Half-dressed and unkempt, Belvedere was already on the landing at the top of the stairs when I came out of my room. "Fecking noise," he grumbled. "Is nothing in this house normal?" Wearing only trousers over my long johns, I clumped down the stairs. Belvedere followed. Mrs. McLaughlin was standing in the foyer, but she retreated modestly to the parlour and out of sight, not wanting to be seen in her nightgown.

The knocking continued. I opened the door and was surprised to find an elderly gentleman, in coveralls and an overcoat, standing on the veranda, his knocking fist still in the air above his plaid woollen cap. He was a short, wiry fellow with no teeth and with stubble on his chin. "Yes, my good man," I said. "Why are you knocking at this ungodly hour?"

"I'm the janitor at the church," he replied breathlessly. "You must come quick!"

"What's your name?"

"Sandaker," the man blurted. "I'm the janitor at the church."

"And what seems to be the problem?"

The man's face was made red by the cold or by the urgency of his message. "Come and see!" he exclaimed. "He's a danger to hisself and others!"

"Go back to the church," I told the man. "We'll be there momentarily."

"But you must come quick!"

"We will."

He hesitated for a moment, then retreated from the veranda and hurried down the street. When I turned around, Mrs. McLaughlin was again standing in the entrance to the foyer. "Is John all right?" she asked, her eyes wide and frantic.

"I'm sure he is," I responded. "We'll check on him right now."

Belvedere led the charge upstairs. We quickly dressed and scrambled back down toward the foyer. Mrs. McLaughlin came out of the bedroom with an overcoat that she threw over her shoulders. "I'm going with you."

I shook my head. "It would be best if you did not."

Her eyes were imploring. "I must come with you."

Belvedere was already out the door and sprinting down the street toward the church. Running to catch up, I could hear him grunting against the impact of his injured leg on the icy roadway. Mrs. McLaughlin followed as best she could.

First light had just broken. I saw the janitor pacing back and forth outside the church's portico. In the early morning stillness, I could hear a caterwauling from some indeterminate place. A hundred feet from the church, Belvedere stopped running. He stood there, panting in the cold. I followed his gaze upward to the roof of the steepleless church. My eyes were greeted with a sight I hope never to see again.

Belvedere turned to me. "Look to the woman."

I walked back to where Mrs. McLaughlin was standing, also transfixed. She had seen the horrendous sight and witnessed the commotion. Tears were streaming down her face, almost freezing before they cascaded into the snow at her feet. "John," she whispered. "John."

Grasping her by the shoulders and turning her away from the spectacle, I said, "You must not look, Mrs. McLaughlin. You must not look."

High at the peak of the church's steep roof, the minister balanced precariously, stepping like a circus performer along its length. He had divested himself of all his clothing, some articles of which were lying in the snow near the foundation. There was no telling how long he had been up there. As he picked his way like a mountain goat across the cedar shingles, he recited some passages from the Bible in a loud, high-pitched voice. "It is said," he shouted clearly, for all to hear, "thou shalt not tempt the Lord thy God!" And then, in another voice altogether uncharacteristic of the preacher and more guttural, he responded, "If thou be the Son of God, cast thyself down from hence!" Occasionally, he would seem to lose his footing and be about to fall, but somehow he would manage to right himself.

There was a ladder propped against the eave of the church. It had probably been discovered in the janitor's lean-to and used as a method of climbing to the roof. Belvedere sprang toward the ladder and began to climb. After he'd reached the eave, I heard him urging the minister to come down. "Reverend," he implored, "it's time to stop this foolishness."

The minister pointed at Belvedere and shouted, again in a high-pitched voice, "Get thee behind me!"

"I'm not the devil, sir," Belvedere replied, as calm as the preacher was perturbed. "Now come on down."

The minister repeated his scripture. "Thou shalt not tempt the Lord thy God!" He stepped unsteadily to the gable end of the roof.

I heard Belvedere mutter a profanity to himself. Then he climbed over the top of the ladder onto the steep roof. He was on all fours, trying to get a purchase on the cold shingles with his bare hands and the toes of his service boots. After struggling to get halfway up, he slipped and slid nearly to the eave again. More profane words issued from his mouth, and then he proceeded to claw his way up through sheer willfulness. At last, he knelt at the peak, not more than fifteen feet away from the minister. Belvedere held out his hand. "Here, take it," he said. "I'll help you down."

The minister almost lost his footing again. He pointed toward Belvedere, shouting, "Get thee behind me, Satan!" And then he turned and peered at the ground some forty feet below him. I cannot say whether this was a moment of insanity or a moment of clarity. He seemed to be gathering his resolve.

Belvedere made no sudden move toward him. He simply knelt at the peak of the roof. Quietly, he said, "Don't."

It was too late. The minister leaned into the cold morning air and hurled his body earthward. All I could think to do was shield Mrs. McLaughlin's eyes with my hand as her husband tumbled toward his fate. She said no words, but an ancient keening moan began deep in her belly and issued from her mouth in breathless sobs. I did not witness the impact, but I heard the dull thud, like a bag of sand being thrown across a boxcar, as the body struck the earth.

For the expanse of time during which I held Mrs. McLaughlin in my arms, neither of us breathed. There was silence all around, interrupted only by the clamour of Belvedere as he negotiated his way down the steep roof toward the ladder. When Mrs. McLaughlin was at last able to exhale, the keening started again in her belly and was released into the frigid morning air without reservation. I held her for a good long time, and I had never known a body more shaken and wracked with grief. Belvedere had descended the ladder by this time, and he was striding toward what surely must be the reverend's corpse. "Montgomery," he shouted, "You're needed!"

I handed Mrs. McLaughlin over to the janitor, who was standing motionless nearby. "Please take her home," I said. Peering at me, wide-eyed, the janitor did not reply. "Do it, man!"

Regaining his senses, the man put an arm around the minister's wife and escorted her up the street toward her house.

Belvedere was kneeling beside the body when I arrived at the scene of the impact. He had covered the unfortunate man's nakedness with his own buffalo coat. The body was face down on the ground, blood issuing from the mouth and nose, making the snow a rusty brown. Judging by the awkward angle of the head, I surmised that the neck had been broken. I felt for a pulse. There was none.

Belvedere stood up. "Poor bastard."

Observing the man's twisted face, I said, "Death would have been instantaneous."

"That's a mercy," Belvedere muttered. "A quick death is all we can hope for."

MRS. MCLAUGHLIN WAS NOT HERSELF, understandably, by the time we arrived home that afternoon. I had been to see the undertaker shortly after the minister's death occurred, and the undertaker had transported the body, in his horse-drawn carriage, to the funeral home. I assured Mrs. McLaughlin that all the necessary arrangements had been made. Her eyes never met mine as we talked in her parlour. She seemed miles away, only managing a weak "yes, thank you" when I said something that seemed to demand a response. At about four o'clock, I brought her a sandwich and a cup of water from the kitchen, which she ate absent-mindedly. She was still sitting in the same chair as darkness fell. I asked her if she was ready for sleep, and she said, "Yes, thank you." I diluted valerian drops in a cup of hot tea, and she drank the mixture before retiring.

When Mrs. McLaughlin was safely in her room and hopefully asleep, I climbed the stairs again to my own room. I did not have the opportunity to undress before there was a knock on the door. Belvedere entered and stood in the doorway, looking disparagingly at my easel and the charcoal drawing that rested on it. Finally, he said, “What do you make of this, Montgomery?”

“Make of what?”

“This unhappy minister and his suicide.”

“I think he was a troubled man.” We kept our voices low in case Mrs. McLaughlin was still awake.

Belvedere took another step into my room and closed the door behind him. “Yes, but troubled with what?”

“With his own fanaticism.”

He shook his head. “I think there’s more to it than that.”

“Oh?”

The corporal lowered his voice to ensure that Mrs. McLaughlin would not hear. “I think he knew something about these murders.”

I was tired and irritable. Nothing of what Belvedere said added up in my mind. “What would he know? And how?”

Belvedere shrugged. “Perhaps one of his parishioners made a confession.”

“If that were the case,” I said, “why wouldn’t he have turned the fellow in?”

“Maybe the minister was involved somehow.”

I still couldn’t quite believe in Belvedere’s theory, but I found myself saying, “Maybe.”

“Something smells fishy here, Montgomery,” he said at last, “and I don’t like the smell of fish.”

THE FUNERAL, three days later, was poorly attended. The pain and hopelessness of such a death was too immense, I think, to be comprehended. Why would a man of God throw himself headlong from the roof of his own church? What demons must have possessed him? The human mind is a complicated thing. Sometimes, it defies analysis. In the aftermath, I found myself wondering what more I could have done to save the poor man’s life. Not having been trained in the subtle art of dealing with the insane, I did not recognize the signposts that pointed toward the reverend's destruction. Yet I should have done more.

It also occurred to me that Belvedere, in recent days, had been entirely unreproachable. Such bravery had he shown! Anything I might have reported to Colonel Herchmer about his bad behaviour would be trumped by Belvedere's brave actions on the roof of that church three days earlier.

Mrs. McLaughlin had barely been out of her bedroom those three days, but she appeared in the foyer, in her customary black dress, as Belvedere and I were preparing to leave for the ceremony. In my opinion, she was still in a much too fragile state to attend the funeral, but she insisted upon coming nonetheless. She held on to my arm for support as we walked. Poor thing! I think she was still in shock over the events she had witnessed. She seemed unsteady; her hand trembled on my elbow. She reminded me of a small bird that had fallen from its nest into the unwelcoming snow.

At ten in the morning, after the church service, we marched up the hill toward the graveyard. The church's janitor had been up there in the days previous, lighting fires over the burial plot to thaw the ground, and then digging the grave with a spade. Our small cortege of mourners included Belvedere and me, Mrs. McLaughlin, the janitor, and perhaps ten of the former minister's congregants. The morning was cold and crisp. We trudged up the hill like sailors bracing against a storm.

In the absence of the church's minister, a male parishioner had volunteered to read verses from the Bible. He was a corpulent fellow, and his stubby fingers fumbled awkwardly through the pages in the cold. The wind almost blew his cap off. At last, he found the intended passage and read, "To everything, there is a season, and a time to every purpose under heaven: a time to be born, and a time to die; a time to plant, and a time to pluck up that which has been planted." The words struck a chord in me. Perhaps there was something in those words that might help me if

I gave them a chance. When he had finished his recitation, the parishioner sifted some dirt through his fingers onto the coffin. Mrs. McLaughlin held on to my arm and did not move. I think she had already shed all the tears she was capable of shedding.

After the ceremony at the graveyard, we walked down the hill to another parishioner's house, where a small repast of cheese and buns and cold meat was waiting for us. Mrs. McLaughlin sat on a chair in the living room and did not eat. She asked me to walk her home when a half hour had passed, and I did so.

Belvedere returned to the McLaughlin house a few minutes later. Mrs. McLaughlin and I were seated at the dining room table, but we were not conversing. I was at a loss for anything to say that might be of comfort. Belvedere stood before us. "You'll probably want us out of the house now," he said. "We can pack and be gone by nightfall."

Mrs. McLaughlin looked at him as if she didn't quite comprehend. She shook her head. "I would be grateful if you stayed."

IN THE WEEK following the funeral, Mrs. McLaughlin retired to her bedroom, coming out only for the meals that I prepared. Belvedere's dog roamed the house at will. I suspect he spent most of his time, while Belvedere and I were out on investigation, lying at the foot of Mrs. McLaughlin's bed. She seemed to have grown quite fond of the mutt, even adopting Belvedere's habit of feeding him surreptitiously from the table at mealtimes. While Belvedere had chosen not to provide the animal with a name, Mrs. McLaughlin insisted on giving him one. She called him Mufti, and Belvedere rolled his eyes whenever she referred to the dog using that epithet. I don't know where she'd heard that name before or what it meant. I only knew that Belvedere found the name ridiculous and demeaning.

The days grew colder as November was almost on its last legs. A heavy snow had fallen by the bucketsful, four feet deep around the hedges. The streets had turned white, and a thin pane of ice stretched across the river. Because the ferry could no longer run, our major waterway was impassable. I would have to wait until the serious frosts of December to walk my horse across and visit the Sioux child as I had promised in the week before the reverend's suicide. I thought of the child often, hoping that a miracle might have happened for us both.

Belvedere and I continued with our investigation, but the trail had gone as cold as the wintry days. Whoever had murdered the laundryman and the young settler, if they were the same person, had vanished like the green grass of summer. We spent our time rehashing possible motives for the killings. Was greed the reason for these crimes? Personal animosity? Political gain?

In the evenings, I would return to the McLaughlin house and prepare a supper for Mrs. McLaughlin and myself. Belvedere would remain on River Street into the wee hours. It was not difficult to surmise that he had been drinking at the local establishment by the smell of alcohol he exuded and by his ambling footfalls as he climbed the stairs to his room while the rest of the household slumbered.

I took advantage of one of those evenings to question Mrs. McLaughlin about her husband's misgivings. We were enjoying cups of tea after supper, and Mrs. McLaughlin had Belvedere's terrier on her lap. She petted the dog incessantly. "Forgive me if this is impertinent," I began, "but I wanted to ask you about your husband."

She stopped what she was doing and stared at me for a long moment. It was as if all the cold of the out-of-doors had suddenly entered the room. "What did you want to know?"

I instantly regretted having begun a conversation on this topic, but I had ventured in, and it was too late to retreat. "I was wondering," I said, "if his conscience was troubling him somehow."

Mrs. McLaughlin's voice was dry as tinder. "He did not feel worthy of his job."

"Did he ever confide in you?"

She laughed at this notion, but without much humour. "Does a husband ever confide in his wife? Ever *truly* confide?"

Her words struck me to the heart as I had not had the decency to be completely honest with Emily, in my letters, about past misgivings and hopes for the future. I placed my teacup gently on the table. "I thought he might have told you something about his sorrows."

Mrs. McLaughlin looked at me archly. "My husband was a very private man."

I took a breath and charged in full steam. "This might seem indelicate," I said, "but I must ask. Do you think he might have known anything about these murders that have occurred recently?"

Suddenly, her back was upright and her eyes blazed. "How would he know anything about that? Are you insinuating—"

"I'm not insinuating anything," I quickly added. "I only thought that he might have learned something from one or another of his congregants."

"My husband was an unhappy man." Her voice was jagged with anger. "And he did a very foolish thing. But that does not mean that he was in any way involved in a crime so heinous as the murder of another man. Really, Mr. Montgomery!" Tears stood in her eyes. She rose from the table and, taking the dog under her arm, marched through the parlour and back into her bedroom. I decided never to speak to her of the subject again.

Having lost my equilibrium in the midst of recent events, I began to wonder what kind of town this was. It had witnessed two murders in two months, and now a suicide, and the suicide of a minister at that! I concluded then that Prince Albert was a settlement savagely ripped apart by the politics of the age, a town full of prejudice and secrecy and violence. Where would it all end? How would its mysteries be solved? And would they be solved by a man so sudden and quick to anger as Belvedere?

9

We went back to the church the day after my failed conversation with Mrs. McLaughlin. The building seemed somehow to have lost its holiness. It was cold inside, the fire in the stove having been left to burn itself out, and even in daylight, there was a gloom that had settled over the place. We made our way into the sacristy, where the minister's vestments still hung and where his plain wooden desk sat like a dog waiting for its master. This was where the minister had probably composed his sermons only days before. There was a sheaf of paper on the desk, fanned about haphazardly, a pen, and an inkwell. On some of the papers, words and phrases had been scrawled in a desperate hand. "NO USE," I read on one and "ALL IS LOST!" on another.

While I was focused on the papers, Belvedere nosed around to the other side of the desk. His attention was suddenly diverted to the wall behind me. There was a look of horror on his face. "Would you look at that!"

I turned to see rough lettering carved into the plaster wall, probably by a knife or letter opener or some such instrument. The printing was jagged but unmistakable. "I AM SORRY FOR WHAT I HAVE DONE."

Belvedere sat in the chair behind the minister's desk and pondered this last testament. "For what he's done," he muttered. "He should be sorry if what he's done is murder."

At that moment, we were startled by a gruff voice coming from the church's nave. "Who's in there?"

Belvedere sprang to his feet, and together we entered the nave, where the caretaker was brandishing a stove poker. "Oh, it's you," he said, lowering the poker. "I was worried there for a minute. We've had squatters in here from time to time."

"Mr. Sandaker, fancy seeing you here." Belvedere jerked a thumb in the direction of the room behind him. "Have you seen what's written on the wall in that room?"

"I have." Sandaker looked suddenly quite miserable. "I was meaning to plaster over it right away soon."

Belvedere approached him. "What had the minister done, do you think, that he should be so sorry?"

The caretaker exhaled and looked up at the tall ceiling, as if he was seeking God's help to answer the question. "The minister was a complicated man."

"We're quite aware of that." Belvedere peered at him expectantly, looking for a clearer response.

Sandaker behaved as though he would rather crawl through a crack in the church's hardwood floor than say a blaspheming word about the minister. "It's not my way to speak ill of the dead," he said. "Especially of a man of the cloth."

Belvedere took another step toward him. "It's a felony to harbour secrets that might impede a murder investigation."

Sandaker thought again for a moment, then shook his head. "Maybe I'm not the one you should be askin'."

"Oh? Why's that?"

"There are others in the congregation who knew him better." He gave us a knowing look. "If you know what I mean."

"And who might that be?" Belvedere wondered.

"Well, Mrs. Morley for one."

"Mrs. Morley?"

"She was the organist in the church," Sandaker explained, "until she had to quit. She was closer to the minister than most."

Belvedere's face was only inches away from Sandaker's. "I'll have a word with her."

The caretaker showed his palms to Belvedere in a gesture of submission. "I don't believe the reverend would murder any livin' soul, if that's what you think."

"But he might know somebody who did."

"I don't know a damn thing about it," Sandaker sputtered. "Alls I'm sayin' is that the reverend might've done a thing or two in his time on this earth that he regretted. But he din't have nothin' to do with no murder."

After it became apparent that he would get no more information from the caretaker, Belvedere gave him leave to depart, and the two of us returned to the sacristy. I resumed looking through the sheaf of papers that was fanned across the minister's desk. Belvedere busied himself studying a small, leatherbound journal that had also been left on the desk. In the journal was a list of the congregants of the parish, not a long list, perhaps some thirty-five or forty names. "What do you make of this, Montgomery?" he asked, thrusting the book toward me. He pointed a frost-bitten finger at one particular entry. "Silas Haggardy" was written there in a very precise cursive, and beside the name, "Lost Soul."

I scanned the rest of the list. There were no similar epithets attached to any other name. "Haggardy," I said, "that's the shoemaker."

"It most certainly is."

"A lost soul."

"Yes."

WE VISITED the shoemaker again that afternoon. There was a frenzy of hammering as we entered his shop on River Street. Greasy-haired and sallow-faced, he looked up at us as we stood before him at the counter. He seemed apprehensive, like he was ready to make a run for it if he had to. "Kin I help?"

"You can," Belvedere said. "You've heard of the minister, McLaughlin?"

Haggardy wiped some boot black from under his eye. "I was one of his parishioners."

Belvedere looked at him squarely. "A remarkable one, it seems."

"I don't rightly know what yer talkin' about." The shoemaker's discomfort at this line of questioning was palpable in his shifty eyes and the way he rocked sideways from foot to foot.

"He had a special designation for you in his congregational list," Belvedere said. "'Lost Soul' is what he called you."

Haggardy breathed a sigh of relief, and then he smirked at us. "He liked to call me that. Cuz of my profession."

Belvedere did not waver; he searched the man's eyes for evidence of a lie. "Is that the only reason?"

The shoemaker glanced at me and then back at Belvedere. "Far as I know."

"We'd like to have a look upstairs," Belvedere said. "With your permission."

Haggardy was hesitant. "My family's up there," he said. "I'll see if they're decent."

We followed him up the rickety stairs and waited on the landing as he conversed with his wife. "The Mounties is here," we heard him say, a quiver in his voice.

His wife sounded even more frightened than he. "I knew you'd bring trouble down upon us."

There was some muffled conversation that I didn't hear, and then Haggardy came back to the landing and invited us inside. The living quarters were bare except for a few homemade chairs and a table, but there was a fire in the stove and the place was warm, at least. Haggardy's wife, skinny and dark-eyed, sat rigidly in one of the chairs. Two small urchins were at her side, a boy and a girl, wide-eyed and afraid. The mother's fear was contagious, and the children seemed to have caught it. They hung on to her dressing gown as if for dear life.

Oblivious to the worries of the inhabitants, Belvedere searched about the place. "Do you have any firearms here?"

"Jus' my ol' Winchester," Haggardy admitted. "I use it for huntin' game."

"May I see the weapon?"

The shoemaker went into his bedroom and returned with the rifle under his arm. Its stock was weathered and free of varnish, and the barrel was rusty. Belvedere examined the gun and gave me a knowing glance. It was a Winchester, the make that had killed both the laundryman and the homesteader. I still had the slug from the laundryman's body, tucked away in the folds of my medical bag, and Belvedere had kept the shell casings found at the farm. Belvedere did not return the gun to the cobbler. "I'll have to confiscate this for the time being."

"But I need the gun for—"

"For the time being," Belvedere reiterated. "May I see into the other room?"

The shoemaker looked at his wife, who was staring down at the floor. "If you must."

I escorted Belvedere into the bedroom, where two rustic beds were located. On top of each bed were thick, patchwork quilts that had, no doubt, been painstakingly created by the shoemaker's wife. There were no curtains on the windows, and Belvedere stood before the grimy pane that overlooked the laundryman's backyard. "Is this roughly the angle at which the laundryman was shot?" he asked me in a harsh whisper.

"Hard to tell," I whispered back, "without knowing exactly how the laundryman was standing at the time. But yes, it could have been."

We were at the dentist's office early the next day. A mother and her little boy were in the waiting room, both of them as white as the institutional paint upon the walls. The boy, it seemed, had a rotten tooth, but he balked at going to the dentist's chair. The dentist offered a subterfuge. "We're going to play a little game called Bang." He produced a length of string from his trouser pocket and tied it around the offending tooth. The other end of the string he tied to the knob on his office door. He asked the unhappy child to close his eyes and smile, and when a smile was finally coaxed out of the boy, the dentist shouted "Bang!" and kicked the door shut.

There was screaming—oh yes, there was screaming— but the tooth had been extracted before the child knew it. When mother and child had departed, the dentist finally turned his attention to us. "Yes, good men and true, of what service can I be?"

Belvedere spoke up immediately. "We have more questions," he said. "We want to ask you about Silas Haggardy."

The dentist's face whitened. "About Mister Haggardy?"

"Was there any acrimony between Haggardy and the laundryman?"

The dentist studied the knots in the floorboard for a moment, then looked up at Belvedere again. "There was acrimony between the laundryman and just about everyone."

Belvedere exhaled loudly, studying the man. "You never mentioned that in our last interview."

"I didn't think it appropriate," the dentist replied, "speaking badly of the dead and all that."

Belvedere's eyes narrowed. I could tell he was rapidly losing his patience. "Or perhaps you were hiding something?"

"I have nothing to hide, sir."

"To return to my original question, then: was there an argument between Haggardy and the laundryman?"

The dentist thought for a moment, again studying the floorboards. "There was one argument I witnessed. The two of them were standing outside Mr. Chen's door."

"What were they arguing about?"

"The cost of Silas Haggardy's laundry bill, from what I could make of it."

"Was it a physical altercation?"

Confronted with this line of questioning, the dentist showed signs of losing his composure or, at least, his eloquence. His plummy accent seemed less plummy to me then. "No."

"Any threats made?"

"None that I heard."

Belvedere looked the dentist up and down. "When did this occur?"

"About a week before the murder," the dentist said. "But I don't think it was Haggardy who killed the man."

"Thank you for being forthright at last."

Belvedere nodded at me, and we headed toward the door. When we were out in the street and on our way back to the McLaughlin house, Belvedere nudged me in the ribs. "The plot thickens, eh, Montgomery?"

Something about it didn't sit right with me. "Do you think Haggardy killed the farmer, too?"

"Not sure about that," he said, "but he's looking like a prime suspect in the laundryman case."

IT WAS a chance meeting with Sub-Constable Parry the next morning that provided all the proof Belvedere needed. Parry had been sent down to the Hudson Bay store to buy supplies that could not be purchased at Hobart and Eden. Belvedere and I walked with him part of the way. "H-h-h-how's the inv-v-vestigation g-going?" the sub-constable asked.

"Swimmingly," Belvedere replied. "But tell me—what do you know about Silas Haggardy, the shoemaker?"

"I know he's a m-m-man with a p-p-p-past," Parry said. You

could almost see the consonants forming in the frozen air in front of him as he walked.

"Oh? How's that?"

Parry was suddenly the proud purveyor of some secret knowledge. "He s-spent some t-t-time in Stony M-M-Mountain."

Belvedere stopped in his tracks as the cold wind whistled around him. "For what crime?"

"For th-th-thievery, I th-think."

With that much news, Belvedere and I took our leave of Parry, wending our way back to River Street and the shoemaker's shop. We were surprised to see the local liveryman, Joe Scriver, with a half-loaded dray wagon in front of the shop. Silas Haggardy was carting a slew of cowhides from his shop to the wagon. His wife and children, dressed for winter travel, were standing amongst some cardboard suitcases, ready to climb aboard the dray cart.

Belvedere was quick to act, blocking Haggardy's path to the wagon. "Hold on there, maestro," he shouted. "Where do you think you're going?"

"We're shuttin' up shop," Haggardy replied. "Movin' back to Winnipeg."

"In this dray wagon?"

"If need be."

Belvedere grabbed the cowhides from Haggardy and threw them haphazardly on the boardwalk. "You're currently the subject of an investigation, sir."

The shoemaker was suddenly petulant. "Far as I know, it's a free country." He sidestepped to get by Belvedere, which prompted the corporal to lash out and strike Haggardy in the side of the head.

Haggardy fell to the boardwalk with a thud. His wife emitted a high-pitched cry that, if it had been of more duration, might have become a scream. The two children commenced weeping. Belvedere picked Haggardy up by the collar of his coat. "I'm arresting you for the murder of Chaoxing Chen, sir. I'm afraid

Winnipeg is out of the question. You'll spend the rest of this day in jail."

Without bothering to wait for me, Belvedere began frog-marching the unhappy shoemaker up the hill toward the Mounted Police jail. I stood with Haggardy's wife and children for some time, asking them if there was still food in the apartment above the shop. The comestibles had been packed, but I was assured that they could be got off the cart in time for supper. I gave the woman two dollars, a goodly portion of my weekly salary, to tide her over in case of emergencies. "I'm sure this will all be sorted out in a day or two," I told her.

Tears of rage, not gratitude, creased her cheeks. "My husband is many things," she hissed, "but he ain't no murderer."

At that moment, Joe Scriver jumped down from the seat of the dray. "Now, lookee what you done with yer damn fool investigatin'," he said to me. "You've cost us the onliest shoemaker we had in this here town. And you also done cost me a shitload of drayin' fees."

THERE WAS a disturbance on the eastern edge of the settlement at the end of November. Belvedere and I were buying food and supplies at the Hudson Bay store in Groschen when we heard the news. A telegraph worker rushed into the store and approached us. I recognized him from my artistic excursion south of the settlement a few weeks earlier, and he, apparently, recognized me. "You've got to come quickly," he blurted. "There's been a kidnapping!"

We followed him out to the street and climbed into his cutter. The telegraph worker lashed his horse with a whip, and soon we were galloping down the snowbound lane. "It's Evert Sinclair!" the telegraph worker shouted breathlessly. "He's taken one of our men hostage!" Snow sprayed from the runners of the cutter as he whipped his horse. Shop owners came out of their stores, wondering what all the geeing and hawing was about. Soon we were out of the business district and into the residential area.

"Where does Sinclair live?" I heard Belvedere ask the telegraph man over the din of the galloping horse and the creaking cutter.

"A river lot," the man shouted back. "Just out of town."

We skidded around a bend in the river and sped out of town. Houses were farther apart, and the properties, obviously broken into a patchwork of fields, were agricultural. Plumes of smoke cascaded from chimneys. Near a woodlot at the edge of one of the properties, out of sight of any of the houses, a gaggle of men was standing in nervous anticipation. As we drew closer, I recognized the foreman of the telegraph crew, the man I had spoken to some weeks earlier. Our driver pulled on the reins and brought his horses to a skittery stop. He turned to Belvedere. "I dare go no further," he said, his voice hoarse from all the yelling. "I understand Sinclair is a crack shot with a rifle."

Belvedere sprang out of the cutter, and I followed him. The telegraph foreman approached us. "This silly bastard is angry because the line runs acrost his land."

"He's got a hostage?" Belvedere eyed him in an unfriendly manner.

"He does," the foreman replied. "He took a shot at the rest of us, and then he escorted young Angus Kerr toward the house."

"They're in the house now?"

"I believe so."

Belvedere did not hesitate. He strolled around the edge of the woodlot and out into the clearing like he was there for a Sunday walk. A shot rang out, and I could tell by the way Belvedere ducked his head that the bullet had come close to hitting him. He stood his ground. "Mr. Sinclair," he shouted. "I'm an officer of the North-West Mounted Police."

I could not see the house from where I was standing, but I could hear the occupant's voice, guttural and angry. "Go away! We do not want any of your police or your telegraph, either."

"I will go away," Belvedere shouted back, "but not until you hand over your hostage."

"This man stays with me!" Sinclair replied. "If your land agent gives me my patent, you can have the hostage back."

"That's not going to happen," Belvedere said. "Not without a ruling from the Dominion government." He took a few more steps toward the house. Another shot was fired. I could see the bullet crease the snow a few feet in front of Belvedere. "Think about this," Belvedere shouted. "Shoot me, and you've got ten Mounties riding in here." He stepped forward again.

Wanting a better view of the proceedings, I scrambled through the woodlot toward the clearing. Denuded of their leaves, the aspens stood like skeletons in the forest, but the broad evergreen branches provided some cover. Kneeling behind one of the spruce trees at the edge of the clearing, I could see the house well enough. Sinclair was standing on his front porch, training his rifle's sights on Belvedere. Not dressed for the weather, the farmer was wearing only a checked shirt, trousers, and boots. "Don't come closer!" I heard him shout.

Belvedere halted again. "I need to know if your hostage is in good health."

"He is!"

"Let me see him," Belvedere said, "so I can be sure."

The two men were only a hundred feet apart now. If he had a mind to do so, Sinclair might surely have shot Belvedere between the eyes. "Is this a white man's trick?"

"No trick," Belvedere replied. "I want to see that he is unharmed."

Sinclair headed into the house and returned, a moment later, with his hostage. I could see, as soon as he stepped onto the porch, that the hostage was none other than the young man I had shared tobacco with a month earlier. He did not look like he had been harmed, but his hands were tied behind his back by a length of rope. He was still wearing his woollen overcoat.

"Angus Kerr," Belvedere called to him, "are you in good health?"

"I am," said young Angus, "but I think this man will shoot me if he's pushed." There was fear in his voice.

"Nobody's pushing." Belvedere walked closer to the porch. Sinclair raised his gun again and fired. I could see the buffalo fur on Belvedere's coat roil as the bullet whizzed past his arm. Belvedere stopped and examined his sleeve. "By Gawd, you are a good shot," he said calmly. "I believe you have creased my nice winter coat." He chuckled and reached into his pocket.

Sinclair cried, "Don't!"

"I only want to offer you a cigar." Belvedere gently pulled a silver cigar case from his pocket. He opened the case and chose a nice, fat cigar. Fumbling in another pocket, he found a small box of matches. As Sinclair and his hostage watched, he lit the cigar and puffed on it gratefully. "No one wants this to end badly." Belvedere moved to the bottom of the front step.

"Don't come any closer." Sinclair turned his rifle on the hostage, pointing it at the young man's chest. Kerr cowered backward, shielding his torso with his arms.

Belvedere proceeded up the steps. "I only want to offer you a cigar." Sinclair tensed for a moment, his finger on the trigger. Young Angus's eyes were squeezed shut against the oncoming horror. "Let's just smoke a cigar and talk this over."

Taken aback, I think, by Belvedere's brazenness, Sinclair lowered his rifle. Angus Kerr opened his eyes again and watched in disbelief as Belvedere handed Sinclair his lit cigar. The farmer took a long puff and exhaled the smoke in a drawl of breath, then handed the cigar back to Belvedere.

The conversation grew quiet. Belvedere said some words I could not hear, and Sinclair answered him, also in hushed tones. Then Belvedere reached out his hand, and the farmer relinquished his rifle. They talked for some moments and, at last, Belvedere shook Sinclair's hand. After a few more words, Belvedere escorted young Angus down the porch steps, and they strolled nonchalantly back toward the edge of the woodlot.

The telegraph foreman was waiting for them. His face was crimson with anger. "Are you not taking that man into custody?" he asked Belvedere.

"It was a simple misunderstanding," Belvedere replied. "No harm, no foul."

"Will charges not be laid?"

Belvedere shook his head. "You'll have to take that up with Sergeant Slade," he replied, "but I think you should be happy that you've got your man back in one piece." Belvedere marched over to the telegraph worker's cutter and climbed aboard. "Are you coming, Montgomery?"

I must admit that I was developing an admiration for Belvedere. His brazenness in the face of fire was something I had rarely seen before. I climbed into the cutter and sat next to him. The worker conferred quietly with the foreman for some moments, and then he returned to the cutter.

As we were traversing the icy roads toward town, I turned to Belvedere. "A crack shot with a rifle, that man."

"We'll keep an eye on Farmer Sinclair," he whispered, "but he doesn't comport himself like a man who would shoot his adversary in the back."

The telegraph worker's horse trotted lazily into the settlement, where we saw Sergeant Slade and Sub-Constable Parry spurring their horses in the direction of Sinclair's farm. They did not stop to confer with us. Sitting comfortably in the cutter, Belvedere nudged me in the ribs and chuckled. "Sergeant Slade to the rescue."

10

I prepared supper again that evening. The fare was not spectacular, but I recalled some of my mother's household hints from my childhood home in Bennington. "You should find a good wife," she had said, "but if that's not possible, you'll have to learn how to cook." Thankfully, she taught me a few culinary skills, including how to boil a ham and how to scallop potatoes. Armed with those recipes, I was able to prepare a nutritious meal in a little over an hour.

Mrs. McLaughlin came to the table in her widow's weeds. She picked at her food and did not seem to enjoy it. Wishing to raise her spirits, I regaled her with a tale of Belvedere's heroism on that day. "Sinclair fired three rounds," I said, "and still Belvedere approached him. And then, do you know what he did? He offered the man a cigar. A cigar! It was a stroke of genius!"

She turned her gaze upon Belvedere. "You are a brave man."

"Not so brave," he growled, poking a forkful of potatoes into his mouth. "Montgomery, here, is a teller of tales."

"You also tried to rescue my husband," she said. "I saw what you did."

"Let's not talk about that now." Belvedere tucked into his ham and potatoes with great fervour.

Mrs. McLaughlin's eyes did not waver. "I never had a chance to say thank you."

Belvedere spoke with a mouthful of food. "No thank-yous necessary." Bits of potato were spilling onto his goatee.

At that moment, there was a loud knocking at the front door. "My goodness," Mrs. McLaughlin said. "Who might be knocking at this hour?"

I went to the door and opened it. There, in the snow on the veranda, stood a congregation of young men, Cree by their dress, some of them carrying rifles. There were eight or nine of them, with angular faces and equally angular bodies. Some were wearing deer hide. Others were in European jackets, woollen coats that were better suited to summer than to winter. One young man spoke while the rest stood like silent sentinels in the night. "We need food." He raised a gaunt hand to his mouth, the fingers puckered together, in the manner of someone who wants to eat.

Not used to so brazen a request, I replied that they should come back in the daylight when I would be better prepared to help them.

"Now," the young man declared.

"Surely you can get by until tomorrow."

"No."

The young man's belligerence offended me. I attempted to shut the door on him, but he pushed his rifle barrel between the door and the jamb. Belvedere's hand was on my shoulder at that moment. He pulled the door open again and confronted the men. "Hullo," he said, "what is it you want?"

"Food," the fellow replied. "We need food."

Belvedere peered at the young man. "Where are you from?"

"West of here." He jerked his thumb in a direction that approximated west.

"There is no need for force," Belvedere said. "We haven't much, but you are welcome to what we have." He went into the dining room and returned, a few moments later, with a packet of sliced ham on parchment.

The fellow observed the meat and smelled it. He ate none and offered none to his compatriots. Instead, he placed the packet into a birchbark basket that was at his side. He did not say thank you. The severe tension in his face dissolved for a moment, and he nodded slightly at Belvedere. Then he motioned his companions away with a jerk of his neck, and they moved down the street, no doubt to assail another householder.

I looked at Belvedere. "They were very rude."

"They were hungry." He turned on his heels and went back to the table, where his plate of ham and potatoes awaited. I followed him back to the table but could not eat. Instead, I sat there ruminating on what had just occurred.

Later, alone in my room, I spent the rest of the evening reflecting on my own poor behaviour. Who was I, an interloper in this land, to deny sustenance to the people who rightfully owned it? Why was I instantly so afraid and so defensive? They had made no attempt to point their rifles, which, I later thought, were probably bereft of ammunition. Would I have refused a beggar on the streets of Bennington in so forthright a manner? Probably not. It seemed to me then that every society creates an Other, a people who are lesser than, more frightening for their otherness, less deserving of one's generosity. I quietly resolved to do better toward my fellow inhabitants of this earth from that day forth.

JUSTICE WAS a slow process in the North-West at that time. We learned that a judge would have to be brought in from Regina, and that doing so might take as long as a month. Meanwhile, Haggardy malingered in his cold jail cell. At least he ate well. Slade had contracted a local lady to cook the prisoners' food whenever the cells were occupied. The fare was perhaps not to the standards of a restaurant in France, but from what I saw, it was no worse than what Mrs. McLaughlin managed to put on the table.

I went to visit Haggardy a week or two after his incarceration.

His initial denials, forceful and sincere, had led me to believe that he might not be guilty of the laundryman's murder, and I was eager to question him about it. He slumped in his cell like a broken man, his head bowed. After some initial pleasantries, I asked him outright, "Did you kill that man?"

He raised his head to look at me in the gloom. His eyes were like burning coals. He spoke almost in sobs. "No, sir, I did not."

"Have you any way of proving that you didn't do it?"

"What do you mean?" He looked at me as though the thought of proving his innocence had never occurred to him.

"Any witnesses to prove that you were elsewhere at the time of the shooting?"

"I was downstairs workin' when I heard the shot. If you don't believe me, you kin ask my wife." He took a deep breath, and then he said, "Lookee, I know I done some bad things in my life, but that's all behind me now."

"You'll get a fair trial," I told him. "But in the meantime, I would advise you to think carefully about the day of the murder. You will need to marshal your arguments if you are going to prove yourself innocent." I turned to go, but the cobbler had more to say.

"Mister," he pleaded, "will you see to it that my wife and kids has food to eat? Will you see to that?"

"I'll do what I can." I took one last look at the poor fellow, and then I stepped outside and felt the cold bite of my own freedom on my skin.

I VISITED Haggardy's wife the next day. When I arrived at the shop door, I was surprised to be greeted by her young son, who had evidently been playing with some of the tools of his father's trade. Standing at the door with a shoemaker's last in his hands, he looked at me as though I were an emissary from Hell itself. His sister was pounding on some scrap of leather with a small hammer, but she turned to see me, mouth agape, as I entered. "Is your mother home?" I asked the boy.

He looked as if he was about to cry. "She said not to bother her."

"Oh, well, then, I'll come back another day." I smiled at the boy in a consoling way.

Just then, I heard the door at the top of the staircase open, and a burly fellow came tramping down the stairs, buttoning his mackinaw. He was the lumberjack I'd seen during my first foray north of the river. He said nothing, but offered me a wry smile as he pushed past me and headed out the door.

I waited a few moments until Haggardy's wife also appeared at the top of the staircase. She was wearing a flimsy cotton nightshirt, and her hair was dishevelled. Not seeing me at first, she called to her children, "You can come back upstairs now."

The boy ran to the foot of the stairs. "There's a policeman here!"

Mrs. Haggardy came down a few steps until I was in her line of vision. "What do you want?"

I composed myself and began. "I promised your husband that I'd look in on you."

"I don't need you, or any man, looking in on me." Her face was hard as granite.

Immediately regretful that I had found her in such a situation, I stammered out the next few words. "He told me that he was downstairs in this shop at the time of the shooting. He said you could attest to that."

"I already told you he ain't no murderer."

"Were you upstairs at the time?"

"Yes."

The little boy ran up the stairs toward his mother. "Mama," he said, "is the man going to put you in jail, too?"

Cradling the boy's head against her stomach, she said, "No, Calvin, nobody else is going to jail. Now, you and your sister run along upstairs. I'll be there in a minute." The boy charged up the stairs, and the little girl scurried behind him. Mrs. Haggardy turned her attention to me. "Is there anything else you wanted?"

"I'm looking for a way to exonerate your husband," I said.

"Look all you want," she replied. "In the meantime, I got to put bread on the table."

With that much justification for her own behaviour, she turned and headed up the stairs. I began to realize then that we, who are on the side of the law, have little understanding of the havoc our so-called justice produces. Justice, I have found, is a hoped-for state of being, something akin to love, and law is its poor cousin. I ruminated on the cobbler and his family as I trudged up the street toward the McLaughlin house.

A LETTER ARRIVED from Emily a few days later. The envelope was smeared with the handprints of many mail carriers; it was coated with the dust of the road. It had been sent first to Winnipeg, then to Fort Battleford and then, belatedly, to me in Prince Albert. In the letter, Emily told me about her grand life in Montreal, the fancy parties she had attended with her mother and father. She provided me with some details of her life as a teacher in a private school, the misbehaviours of the children, the advances made upon her by the headmaster. All of this brought me into a blue funk.

"Oh, when will my darling return?" she asked. "When will he rescue me from my boring life?" I had not explained to Emily that when I enlisted in Her Majesty's police force, I had contracted myself to five years in the great North-West. There were many things she didn't know.

She expressed sympathy about my cold journey from Battleford to Prince Albert settlement. "How are you able to keep yourself warm in such a climate?" she asked. "And what is your landlady like? I hope she is not beautiful." And finally, she wrote, "I look forward to your return come summer."

In truth, I had no more fervent wish than to return to Emily post-haste and to habituate myself again in civilized life. I was stuck in a northern town with little to recommend it but a Hudson Bay store, two scrawny newspapers, and a landlady who dabbled in poetry. I thought of the lovely parties Emily would be attending with her father and mother in the days leading up to Christmas—the bowls full of wassail, the canapés, the soft grind of the violin and the dancing. I daydreamed about desertion, about trekking across the frozen wastes until I would at last be in the arms of my beautiful Emily again. I thought of going back, and knew that there were many reasons why I could not.

I WATCHED THE RIVER ICE, still too thin to support horse travel. The fate of the young Sioux child, whom I had treated for pneumonia, rested heavily upon my conscience. I wondered if he had survived. It seemed to me that my own absolution was tied up in his recovery. If I could manage his cure, I might somehow restore a semblance of self-respect and make amends for my own past errors. Perhaps my priorities were askew, but the well-being of the child seemed somehow more important to me than my own life. There was no way of knowing if he was alive or dead, and I knew the coming winter might be a danger to his scarred lungs. His encampment was only three miles away, but the impassable river made those three miles feel like five hundred. I watched and waited.

The McLaughlin house had been sombre for so long that I could hardly remember what laughter sounded like. It was the fifth of December. I remembered Christmases in Vermont with carolers strolling door-to-door, plum pudding, roasted leg of lamb, and sweet liqueurs. No such celebration was likely to happen in the great North-West unless I became the instigator. Mrs. McLaughlin was in no condition to enjoy the holiday and, judging by his demeanour, Belvedere did not know what

Christmas was. I resolved to beautify the house as best I could and to draw its inhabitants out of their momentary exile from happiness.

As it was a Saturday, and as the prime suspect for the murder was already in jail, I found an axe in the woodpile behind the house and went south in search of an evergreen. I must have walked at least two miles. A woodlot on the edge of a farmstead offered a choice of white spruce trees of all lengths and girths. I did not know who owned the land upon which the woodlot stood, but I reckoned that the absence of a single tree would not be noteworthy.

In the middle of the forest, I found a sweet specimen, six feet high, its branches full, although caked with snow. I whisked the snow away from the base of the tree and felled it with a few brisk strokes of the axe. When I had dragged the tree through the soft snow to the forest's edge, I encountered Sheriff Dan McQuaid. He was poised in a clearing, fifty feet away from me, his legs apart and his rifle aimed squarely at my chest. "Hang on there, sheriff!" I shouted. "I'm only poaching a Christmas tree."

He kept his sights trained on me for a few more seconds, and then he raised his head. "You the surgeon?" He looked like an overgrown child who'd been caught with his hand in the cookie jar.

"Yes," I replied. "Out looking for a tree to decorate the McLaughlin house."

He lowered his rifle and ambled toward me. "You oughta be more careful," he said. "A fella could git hisself shot out here." He bit one mitten off and shook my hand, but it was an odd handshake. McQuaid didn't grasp my hand firmly as you might expect a big man to do. Instead, he clasped my fingers with his own, resting his huge, stubby thumb on top of my forefinger. There was a moment of awkwardness between us. He looked expectantly into my eyes.

"I thought your jurisdiction was in town?" I said, more to rid the occasion of its strangeness than to learn anything new about the man.

His face creased into a grin. "Just doin' a little huntin'," he said. "Thought to kill some venison fer me and the wife."

"Who owns this land?"

"Feller name of Johnson," the sheriff replied. "He gave me permission to hunt out here."

I didn't bother mentioning that I had not been given permission to chop down evergreens. "Happy hunting," I said. "A little venison would taste fine this time of year."

"And a good day to you, sir!" The sheriff clapped me heartily between the shoulder blades and went his merry way into the bush.

The tree in tow, I trudged back toward town, leaving a tell-tale trail of pine needles along the way. As I neared the McLaughlin house, I heard a single gunshot that reverberated from a southerly direction, and I surmised that the sheriff had bagged his quarry.

MRS. MCLAUGHLIN CAME out of her bedroom when she heard me rummaging about in the parlour. I had already found a tin pail and filled it with sand. Having buried the base of the evergreen in the sand, I was attempting to make the tree stand upright, or as nearly upright as I could manage.

As the spruce tree thawed, the room began to smell like a forest. The sharp, sweet assault on my nostrils reminded me, as nothing else could have, of Christmases past. Mrs. McLaughlin's spirits were also lifted. She fingered the pinecones near the top of the tree, exclaiming "Oh! Look!" when she spotted a vacant sparrow's nest that had somehow survived the journey home. "How sweet!" No more than two inches in circumference, the nest had been attached with mud to one of the branches. Mrs. McLaughlin was beaming. "A promise that spring will come again!"

She went back into the bedroom and returned with a small stack of coloured paper. We spent the rest of the afternoon, scissors in hand, cutting squares and triangles of red, blue, and gold, folding them and placing them over the branches. I was reminded of my earlier days, back in Bennington after my father had been killed in the war, when my sister, June, and I would decorate trees in just such a fashion.

Mrs. McLaughlin seemed suddenly drawn into the irresistible charm of the season. At one point, while she was in the act of creating a crimson snowflake with her scissors, I heard her humming the tune of "Buffalo Gals"—not a religious tune, and nothing I would have expected from a minister's widow. When I glanced up at her, she was quite lost in thought and smiling, yes, smiling! Aware of my gaze, she ceased humming, but the smile did not altogether disappear from her face.

BELVEDERE'S EYES were more glazed than usual the next morning, and I reckoned that the pain in his injured leg had got unbearable in the wintry cold. He was no stranger to the laudanum bottle all that time, and his thinking seemed particularly jumbled. When I came down the stairs, he was sitting at the dining room table, rubbing his face as if to wear away the skin. Noticing me, he muttered, "When's supper ready, Montgomery?"

"Supper?" I said. "You mean breakfast."

"Yes, yes, yes. Breakfast, of course." He slapped his own face lightly, with both hands, trying to wake himself up.

"In two shakes of a dog's tail," I replied. Belvedere's mutt was standing four feet away, peering uncertainly at his master.

While I was kindling the stove, a knocking came at the door. I could tell by its erratic rhythm and intensity that the knocking belonged to Sub-Constable Parry. Opening the door, I felt a rush of cold air entering the room. Parry didn't offer a greeting but proceeded instead with his statement. "S-S-S-Sergeant S-S-Slade would like—"

I heard Belvedere clearing his throat behind me. "I know what Sergeant Slade would like," he growled. "You may save your breath, Parry. We'll meet him at his office forthwith."

A half hour later, after ingesting our bowls of gruel, we were shuffling from foot to foot in Slade's chilly office at the Hobart and Eden store. The sergeant was sitting red-faced at his desk, a pile of papers neatly stacked in front of him. "I understand that you were both at the Sinclair farm some days ago?"

"Correct," Belvedere replied. His eyes were still shiny with the drug, but he was managing to stand up straight.

"Where a hostage-taking incident had occurred," Slade continued, "and where you disarmed the perpetrator and freed the hostage."

"Correct on both counts."

"Then perhaps you could tell me," the sergeant said, getting more agitated by the minute, "why you failed to take the perpetrator into custody and why charges were not laid."

"A judgment call," Belvedere replied. "No one was hurt—"

"I understand that shots were fired!"

"No one was hurt," Belvedere repeated. "It was a misunderstanding. I thought it best to leave well enough alone."

"Well enough alone?" sputtered Slade. "A man with a rifle takes a telegraph worker hostage, and you thought it best to leave well enough alone?"

"The Métis are on edge over their land claims," Belvedere replied. "Would you prefer that I take the man into custody and that his friends burn down your jail?"

"I would have preferred that, yes!" Slade was nearly shouting. "In fact, I took the man into custody myself, just yesterday, and he sits rightfully in a jail cell at this moment."

Belvedere coughed up some phlegm and spat it on the sergeant's floor. "That's brave of you, Slade, but I fear you will one day regret having done so."

Sergeant Slade was in a fury. He vibrated in his chair like a man suffering from chilblains. "I will be sending a message to the colonel, and I will be advocating for your return to Battleford at his earliest convenience." His eyes settled on me for a brief, deprecating minute. "That goes for both of you."

Belvedere's face was twisted into a surly smile. "Fine by me," he said, "but until that time, I've got two murders to investigate."

BY THE TENTH OF DECEMBER, the ice on the Saskatchewan River was deemed thick enough to warrant horse travel. With a view to continuing our investigation, we mounted our trusty steeds and traversed through pockets of knee-deep snow to the north side of the river. Belvedere had decided to visit the Sturgeon Lake Cree. The journey would take us a distance of nearly thirty miles, which meant that we could not expect to arrive after a single day's ride. We were fortified against starvation with plenty of rations—I had learned my lesson well on the trip from Battleford two months earlier. We munched jerky as we rode and conversed about the band and their leader. Belvedere did not know much about them. "From what I hear," he said, "their chief is a force to be reckoned with."

I had persuaded Belvedere to stop first at the Sioux encampment three miles north of the river. A white mist issued from the smoke flaps of the tipis as we arrived. Snow had drifted against the faded hides that covered the tipi poles. All was quiet that morning. As Belvedere and I were dismounting, we saw Good Voice stooping to fold back the leather door of his abode. He did not look happy to see us.

Belvedere shook the chief's hand. "We're here about the boy."

Good Voice sized me up with a look that might have been called disparaging. "The boy is not yet well."

"May I see him?" I asked.

The chief seemed hesitant to grant me that permission. He

was on the fence about the efficacy of the solutions in my medicine bag. "It seems your medicines have not worked."

"Medicines take time," I said.

Good Voice thought about my words for a moment. "Our own medicine has not worked either," he admitted at last. "Perhaps it would do no harm for you to see him again."

He escorted me to the tipi where I had first treated the boy, and what I saw there made me fearful for the boy's life. A buffalo hide pulled close around him, the child was lying near the fire on the floor of the tipi. His brow was soaked with perspiration. One could easily see that he was weak and fatigued. His skin was sallow, and he appeared to have lost what little body fat was on him at my last visit. The child's mother was bent over him, stroking the boy's long, dark hair.

I asked for permission to examine the boy, but I am quite sure that the mother did not understand me. She did, however, pull open the buffalo hide that covered the boy so that I could see the pounding of the heart inside his scrawny chest.

The boy's breathing was more than laboured. It sounded like the death rattle of a sixty-year-old man. I smeared camphor on the boy's chest and back, smeared some more on a length of cloth that I had in my medicine bag and wrapped it around the boy's neck. It was precious little, but it was all I could do. The child was too weak for antimony. I administered another grain of morphine so that the boy would rest.

The boy's mother had a face that one might read as a book, and she could not hide her apprehension. I tried to reassure her with a confident glance, but I was fearful as well, and I'm sure my fear was evident. I took one last look at the boy, said a silent prayer, and then I went outside.

Belvedere and the chief were standing near the horses. Good Voice asked me about the prognosis. "I've done what I can," I told him, "but the boy is very ill. We must hope for the best."

When Belvedere and I were on our horses again, and out of

earshot of the chief, I told my compatriot that I thought the boy might die. "If only I could spend another night here."

Belvedere's jaw was set, and he spurred his horse forward through the thick snow. "They do not want you to spend a night with them," he said. "They have little trust in your medicine. And I will need you when we meet the Cree at Sturgeon Lake." As we rode, I thought again about the verse that was read at Reverend McLaughlin's funeral, and I took some comfort in the words. *"To everything there is a season, a time to live and a time to die."* Against the onslaught of Time, a man can only do his best, and I had done my best, both with this Sioux child and with the children back at home.

We stopped at the McKay farmstead along the way. Two feet of snow blanketed the roof of the house. The barn door was open, and the animals were gone, probably ferried to a butcher's shop in Prince Albert settlement. There were no tracks in the snow that had fallen in the pasture since our last arrival there. House and barn seemed faded and almost to blend in with the forest that surrounded them. They were going back to nature.

It was four o'clock, by my pocket watch, when Belvedere suggested we stop in for a visit with McKay's neighbour, Cantrell. His farm was a half mile farther north, up the logging road. The buildings were ramshackle and low to the ground, clearly not the work of a man who knew anything about carpentry. There were scruffy cattle in a barbed wire pasture, and a mangy dog guarded the house. He growled at us as we approached the door. "Shut up, ya mutt," Belvedere growled back. He fingered his sidearm in its holster.

At that instant, the door swung open, and Cantrell was standing there in his long johns, a clay pipe hanging out of his mouth. "No need to shoot my dog, Captain." He grinned at Belvedere. "Seems to me yer a tad trigger-happy."

"I'm not willing to be bitten," Belvedere replied, "unless I first put a bullet through the cur."

Cantrell gave the dog a kick. "Go lay down, Harold." The dog sauntered nonchalantly to a haystack near the barn and burrowed inside. The farmer turned his gaze on Belvedere and me. "You can come into the house," he said, "but leave yer handguns in their holsters, please and thank ya."

"We'll need to bed these horses down first."

Cantrell went back inside the house and donned a pair of trousers and a coat. Then he showed us to a stall in the barn and, when the horses were bedded and fed, we returned to the house. Belvedere had to duck to get inside the door. The ceiling was low, and the floor was nothing but dirt. Knotholes permeated the rough lumber walls in places where they had not been plugged with straw or cow manure. A fire was burning feverishly inside the potbelly stove, fighting a losing battle against the knotholes and the weather.

Belvedere and I perched on roughhewn benches while Cantrell sat like a king on the factory-built chair he had liberated from McKay's farm six weeks earlier. "So what kin I do ya fer?"

"We're on our way north," Belvedere replied. "We'll need a place to stay tonight and also for tomorrow night, when we're on our way home."

"I only got but one bed." Cantrell pointed with his stubbled chin at a home-made bed, of two-by-four construction, in a dark corner. "But yer welcome to lay down on a bedroll on this ballroom floor." I surveyed the dirt below my feet one more time, imagining the biting insects and the infectious rodents that had probably burrowed into that same dirt floor at the onset of winter.

"That'll do for us," Belvedere said. "Any suspicious activity out here since the killing?"

Cantrell scratched his stubble with a greasy paw. "Haven't seen much," he said, "unless you consider a horny elk tryin' to mount my heifer suspicious." He chuckled outrageously at his own joke. Clearly, he'd been alone in the forest for too long.

"No strangers hanging about?"

Cantrell thought for a moment. "They're all strangers to me. Just logging men and you."

"Nobody else?"

"I had a feller come through here just after the murder," Cantrell added. "Tryin' to buy this farm offa me."

Belvedere leaned forward and looked Cantrell in the eye. "Who was that?"

"Name of Screever or Scribang or somethin'. Told him I wasn't interested."

"What did he look like, this fellow?"

"Kind of a brown-noser. Suit and a pair of glasses. That sorta thing. Not very tall." Cantrell got up out of his posh chair and threw another log into the firebox. I was amazed that the cast-iron stove had not cracked from the heat. "Would you boys care fer a drink?" He retrieved a bottle of hooch from a rough shelf along the wall.

"Suppose I could," Belvedere said. "Something to fortify me against the cold."

Cantrell poured each of us a shot glass full of rotgut. I could hardly get it past my lips, but Belvedere threw the home-made liquor back in one gulp. "I imagine you'll be needin' supper, too?" Cantrell continued.

I stepped into the conversation at that moment. "What have you got in the pantry?"

"Just butchered a pig three days ago," Cantrell said. "You'll be eatin' high off the hog, as they say in aristocratic circles."

We waited while Cantrell prepared the meal. It was tolerable, although the meat had been hacked unprofessionally and there were no vegetables. We ate while Cantrell jabbered on about his farm and the low offer he had received for it from a man he did not know. "Thought he was gonna walk away with this homestead in his back pocket," he intoned. "I showed him where the bear shat in the buckwheat, yessir, I did."

After supper, Cantrell found McKay's old banjo by the side of his majestic bed and began strumming away. There is little that is more annoying than a badly played banjo, and Cantrell was as bad a banjo player as I have heard. I could faintly make out the tunes. He started with something like "Haul the Woodpile Down," and then proceeded to murder "Never Done Anything Since." When he delved into "Rove Riley Rove," and started to warble, I began to understand why toothless men should not sing. Thankfully, his little concert was finished by bedtime, and Belvedere and I covered ourselves with our bedrolls, happy that the banjo had been silenced.

11

We awoke before daybreak. Belvedere placed a fifty-cent piece on the table, and we took our leave while Cantrell was still snoring in his bed. I was cold, riding in the dark, but warmed up gradually as the sun began to rise. The snow was deep in the forest, and our horses waded through it as though they were trudging through a sea of molasses. We were only about ten miles from Sturgeon Lake, but we arrived there just after noon.

The encampment, nestled along the lake's edge, bustled with activity. Men were returning from traplines with their catch of muskrat and beaver. Women busied themselves around a fire, skinning the animals, retaining the meat and fur, and throwing the offal into a steaming iron cauldron. Their hands and arms were red with blood and gore, but they worked cheerily, chattering amongst themselves in a language I could not understand. They did not look as impoverished or famine-stricken as the Sioux had looked in their encampment along the Saskatchewan River.

A tall man approached us. I could tell by his dress and demeanour that he was chief of the band. He went by the unfortunate name of William Twatt—something in which the locals back in Prince Albert took much delight—but his name did not represent him well. He was poised and intelligent, and he spoke

English in a thoughtful rhythm. "To what do we owe the pleasure?" he asked.

Standing in the packed snow beside his horse, Belvedere shook the man's hand. "Routine visit," he said. "Wondering how you must be faring."

"As you can see," the chief replied, "my men are among the best trappers in the north."

"No need of food?"

"Nor of land, neither." The chief gestured away from the encampment with an outstretched arm. We followed him as he walked, the snow crunching under his thick moccasins. "We have heard about the settler who was killed. No one here would do such a rash thing."

Belvedere peered at the snow-covered lake. A dog sled, with a man at its rear, was speeding across the ice. "Are you quite sure of that?"

The chief's face turned serious. "I know why you came. I was expecting you."

"Yes?"

"That farm is a half-day's ride from here. And I can promise you that none of my men have been gone that long. Not even to manage their own traplines." The chief looked back at the encampment and the women cooking. "Would you like to join us for a meal," he asked, "before you make the long journey home?"

"We would," Belvedere said, and I was glad of his reply.

The chief ushered us back to the fire, where we were offered tin Hudson Bay bowls heaped full of steaming stew and sweet bannock fried in suet. We sat around a smaller fire in the chief's tipi and consumed the food. The tipi was surprisingly warm on such a cold day. I divested myself of many layers of clothing as I ate.

When the meal was finished, it was time to take our leave. Outside the tipi, Belvedere shook the chief's hand. "It was a pleasure meeting you."

"Perhaps when we meet again," the chief replied, "it will be in more favourable circumstances."

As we approached the Cantrell homestead that evening, I could tell something was amiss. There was no smoke billowing from the tin chimney of the house, and the door was open. The dog was nowhere in sight. Belvedere also sensed that something was wrong, and he broke his horse into a gallop. I followed him. Belvedere called Cantrell's name, but there was no response. We left our horses untied in the yard and ventured to the open door of the house. Belvedere drew his gun.

The interior of the house was dark, but there was a full moon outside and moonbeams flooded through a window. I nearly tripped over the body of Cantrell. It was slumped face down on the floor. The dog stood whimpering by his side. I found a coal-oil lamp on the rustic table and lit it with a match. The dog growled at us and bared its teeth. "Get out of it, ya whelp!" Belvedere muttered. The mutt retreated to a corner of the house, and Belvedere and I turned over the corpse, which was clad in nothing but a ragged pair of long johns. There was a gunshot wound in the man's forehead, from a weapon fired point-blank, as the powder burns attested. The body was cold, but rigor mortis had not set in. There was no need to feel for a pulse.

Belvedere looked up at me. "When did it happen?"

"Sometime today."

"Poor man." Belvedere took the coal-oil lamp from the table and headed outside. Not wanting to be alone with the mangy dog, I straggled after the corporal. Belvedere dropped to his knees in the snow and placed the lamp on the ground. "The horse was shod that brought the killer in here," he shouted. "That's something to think about." He picked up the lantern and followed the horse tracks out to the logging road. When he came back into the yard, Belvedere told me, "The man was heading south at a full gallop."

"Maybe we could track him tomorrow?"

"Doubtful," Belvedere replied. "The foresters have been through with a skidder."

It was a macabre evening. We dragged Cantrell's body out into the snow and covered it with a thick woollen blanket. I hauled wood from the woodpile, and Belvedere lit a fire in the stove inside the house. After chasing Cantrell's mutt out to the barn, we huddled around the table until the cabin was tolerably heated, and then we readied ourselves for sleep.

Belvedere claimed Cantrell's bed without hesitation, bunking down on its thick straw mattress. Left with no other choice but the dirt floor, I was careful to avoid the spot where Cantrell's blood had seeped into the ground. Sleep, when it came, came fitfully, and I found myself dreaming mayhem and murder all the livelong night.

In the morning, Belvedere busied himself fashioning a travois out of two poplar saplings, tying a blanket between them. We rolled Cantrell's body onto the makeshift contraption, and Belvedere lashed the body securely between the poles with a length of hemp rope he'd found in the barn. He tied the travois to the horn on his saddle, and we commenced the long ride home, Belvedere's horse skittery from the dead weight behind him. Cantrell's last ride to the settlement was not a smooth one, I'm afraid, as the travois bumped and jarred against every rock and stump on the trail.

Word travels fast in a small town. We dropped the body off at the local undertaker's and headed up the hill toward the police stables. By the time we got there, Sergeant Slade and Sub-Constable Parry were standing at the large barn door, waiting for us. We dismounted and walked our horses into the barn. Sergeant Slade followed us inside. "So, Belvedere, have you shot another one?"

Belvedere didn't bother to look at him. "This one got shot by other means."

"And what were you doing out there?"

"Investigating the murder of his neighbour." Belvedere tied his horse to a railing in the stall. He found a bundle of oats and threw it into the manger. "Body's at the undertaker if you have the stomach for looking at it."

"Oh, I have the stomach for it," Slade replied. "I have the stomach for a lot of things."

"I'm sure you do." Belvedere unsaddled his horse and curried its wet back as Slade watched. "How's your report to Herchmer coming along?"

Slade was instantly red in the face. "It's already sent."

"That's good," Belvedere replied. "You keep writing your reports. That's what you're good at." He hung the curry comb on a nail on the wall and went to the open barn door. "Let's go have some supper, Montgomery." He left without a salute to his superior or even a goodbye.

I shrugged and smiled as if in apology for my compatriot. Slade didn't smile back. He turned militarily on one heel and marched back toward his office, with Parry tagging along behind him.

THE NEXT MORNING, Belvedere and I visited the sheriff once again in his office at the town hall. It was a chillier office than it had hitherto been. McQuaid sat in his creaky chair like a felled buffalo, woollen coat draped over his massive shoulders. A bottle of whisky graced the desk in front of him. He told us that vandals had smashed one of the windows in another part of the building and that a carpenter was busy covering the gaping hole with boards. We could hear the erratic pounding of a hammer on nails.

Snorting with laughter, McQuaid said, "Whoever's the

goddamn sheriff in this town should kick the asses of the hoodlums that done it." He offered us a drink of whisky.

Belvedere accepted his offer, but I was put off by the time of day. "C'mon," the sheriff exhorted, "it's a Christmas tradition in this town to drink to the season. Every office up and down River Street has a bottle hidden away somewhere in the back room."

I declined again, but with a thank-you.

Belvedere sipped his whisky. "We're interested in finding a fellow by the name of Screever or Scribang or some such. Ever heard of him?"

The sheriff rubbed his nose in thought. "Scribang?"

"Or some such."

McQuaid shook his head. "Don't know any Scribangs livin around these parts. There's old Joe Scriver, who runs the livery up the street. But he ain't no Scribang."

"Thanks." Belvedere swallowed the remainder of his whisky in one gulp. "We'll pay Mister Scriver a visit."

River Street was unusually busy as we walked toward the livery stable. Men were in the butcher's shop, purchasing Christmas roasts. The general store was crowded, as well, with people looking for odds and ends to put under the tree.

The stable doors were shut against the cold when we arrived. Belvedere pried one of the doors open, and we ventured into the gloom. There was no artificial light to illuminate the stalls and pens, probably because of the abundance of flammable straw that covered the dirt floor. The sun's light shone through a few panes of glass that dotted the walls in an irregular fashion. In one of the stalls, Joe Scriver was huffing and puffing as he forked manure onto a stone boat. In another stall, a younger man was also forking manure. He was a slender fellow, and his eyes had the vacant look of an incompetent, but he sang a tuneless song merrily as he wielded the fork. It was not entirely warm inside the stable, but Scriver's coat was unbuttoned, and I could see sweat running down his bald head.

"Mr. Scriver!" Belvedere shouted.

The old man turned to us and leaned on his manure fork. He didn't look much like a murderer. "Well, la-di-da," the old man said, over the din of his acolyte's singing, "the mounted policemen is here. Come to whip this town into shape, have you? Or maybe just to git rid of the only shoemaker in the territory?"

Belvedere grinned at me. He clearly admired the old man's bravado. "Just have a few questions."

"Go ahead and ask 'em," Scriver replied. "I ain't got all day."

"Have you been away from the settlement at any time in the past week?"

"Nope."

"Not even to hunt or to visit someone?"

"Nope."

Belvedere stared at Joe Scriver for a long moment. "Happen to know a man named Cantrell?"

The concert in the background ceased. Scriver stared back at Belvedere. "I knew Herman Cantrell. I understand he ain't livin' no more."

"That's correct," Belvedere replied. "How did you know him?"

"He came into town about once a year."

"You ever visited his farm?"

"No."

Belvedere directed his attention to the young man in the other stall. The young man did not return Belvedere's gaze; instead, he became completely engrossed in the manure he was moving. "And who might this fine fellow be?"

Scriver edged closer to Belvedere and spoke quietly. "That fine fella is my sister's son. His name's Abel Dickson, and he's two bricks short of a load. And now, if you don't mind, we got some shit to shovel before it freezes."

Belvedere grinned at me again and shook his head, and we turned and walked out of the stable. When we were outside and on our way to the McLaughlin house, he was chuckling to himself.

"What do you think of old Joe Scriver?" I asked.

"I think he's too damn cantankerous to kill anybody."

Word came down through Sub-Constable Parry that the promised magistrate would be arriving by the end of the month. "I sus-sus-suspect there's g-gonna be a hangin'," Parry said. "C-c-can't say it hurts my f-f-feelings. I'm tired of f-f-feeding and b-b-boarding the b-b-bastard."

Thinking to hear the cobbler out one last time, I visited the jail the next day. Evert Sinclair sat, a study in dejection, in the drafty cell next to Haggardy's. When Sinclair looked up at me, I saw in his face a menacing anger. He clearly had lost his trust in mounted policemen over the past weeks.

Haggardy was no happier. He leaped to his feet when he saw me approaching. "Have you looked in on my wife and kids?" I told him that I had but offered little further information. His eyes were miserable. "Do they have food to eat?"

"Yes," I said, "they're eating well. Still living above the shop."

"That's good," he replied. "Thank you for looking in on them."

I sat down on a wooden bench opposite the cell. "The magistrate will be coming to town in the next weeks to hear your case."

"I know."

"Have you given any thought to your defence?"

He grasped the lattice of metal bars with his slender fingers. Those fingers had got whiter over the course of his stay in jail. "I told you before," he said. "My wife knows where I was at the time of the shooting."

"Her testimony would not likely be believed," I said. "Is there anything else? We have your rifle, but we were unable to find a box of cartridges in the house."

"That's because there ain't no box of cartridges," he answered. "I make my own bullets in a shed down behind my shop."

I couldn't believe what I was hearing. "You make your own bullets?"

"In my shed."

I stood up. "That little scrap of information might just save your life."

"Is it important?"

"You bet it is."

I went to the cobbler's shop that very afternoon. The front door was not locked. I stood in the shop at the foot of the stairs and called out, "Hello! Hello!" No one answered, and I deduced that no one was at home, so I took advantage of the situation to look around the shop. There were, of course, all the instruments of shoemaking, awls, leather punches, hammers, and boxes of nails, all within public view. At the back of the shop, there was a door leading to a shed in the backyard, and in that shed, I found a blacksmith's forge. There was also a box of gunpowder, some cartridges spread out on a workbench, and some raw lead. The prize I was seeking was a casting mould for slugs. I did not have to look far; the mould was sitting in plain view on the ledge of a window.

I had read about a case in England, some years before, where a Bow Street Runner had managed to find the casting mould of a servant accused of killing his master. On the basis of that evidence, the police were able to convict the servant of the murder, a criminal charge he had denied for some months. I snatched up Haggardy's mould and some raw lead, and then I headed for Joe Scriver's livery stable down the street.

When I arrived at the stable, Scriver was in his usual surly mood. Abel Dickson was sitting on a bale of hay, admiring his own fingers. "So, have you come to arrest me, too?" Scriver asked.

"Not to arrest you," I said, "but to ask for your help."

He looked mockingly over my shoulder. "I don't see no horse behind you, waiting to be shod."

"I need you to fire up your forge."

"My forge?" The old man scrubbed his bristly chin with one

hand and peered at me slyly. "My forge doesn't git fired up fer less than four bits."

"I can pay you that much."

"Fer what purpose do you want to use my forge?"

I showed him the mould. "I want to cast a slug."

"A slug?" He grinned at me. "Is the Mounted Police so skint that they're castin' their own bullets now?"

"It's an experiment," I said. "Can you help me?"

He held out one manure-stained palm. "Fer four bits I kin help."

I dropped four bits into his hand, and he led me down a narrow corridor and into his blacksmithing shop. Abel Dickson followed dutifully, as if he had been told never to leave Scriver's sight. The old man threw some shreds of paper into the firepot. He asked me to turn the blower slowly, then he lit the paper shreds with a match and covered them with coke. Soon the coals were glowing, and soon after that, the raw lead was in a molten state, resting in a large ingot spoon above the coals. Scriver poured the molten lead into the mould. We waited for the lead to harden and for the mould to cool. Steam rose out of a small half-barrel as we dipped the mould in cold water. An hour later, I was on my way back to the McLaughlin house with the mould and the slug I had asked the old man to cast. It had begun to snow, crystals wafting down from the heavens as I made my way to Belvedere with my prize.

Belvedere was upstairs in his room when I stepped into the house. Mrs. McLaughlin was either out or resting in her own room. I heard the dog's sly cry of a bark from behind Belvedere's door, as I climbed the stairs. The slug I had excised from the laundryman's body had been kept in a camphor tin in my medicine bag. After retrieving the slug from my bag, I knocked on Belvedere's bedroom door. He looked as though he'd just been sleeping for forty-eight hours. "Montgomery," he said, "what is it?"

I was barely able to contain my excitement. "I've found some new evidence."

"What's that you say?"

"I want you to look at something." Holding out the two slugs, one in each hand, I continued. "The cobbler is in the habit of making his own ammunition. He can't afford to do otherwise."

Belvedere rubbed his eyes impatiently. "Some do cast their own bullets, certainly."

Thrusting my left hand at him, I said, "This is the slug I dug from the laundryman's body." Then I showed him the slug in my right hand at closer detail. "This one is from the shoemaker's mould."

"So what?"

"The mould has a crease in it, and you can see that crease in the casting of the slug."

"Yes?"

"There's no such crease in the slug I found in the laundryman's body."

I handed him both slugs, and he looked them over with a wary eye. "Hmm," he said, "you might have something there, Montgomery. But if you do, it means we're no closer to finding the killer than we were a month ago."

A WEEK LATER, the magistrate rode into town in a frosty caboose, a weary driver by his side. The magistrate was a corpulent fellow with huge red splotches on his round, white face. His name was McCabe. When we met with him at the town hall, he informed us that the caboose had upset somewhere near Hoodoo Station, and the coals from the firepit had been scattered around the interior of the conveyance, scalding his face in the process.

He was not in a happy mood when he asked us about the evidence in the case. Belvedere told him about the argument between the two men and the fact that the cobbler's upper floor provided a direct trajectory into the laundryman's yard. "Purely circumstantial," the magistrate intoned. "But there is a possible motive. Have you confiscated the weapon?"

Belvedere looked at me and shrugged. Then he turned and faced the magistrate. "We've been trying to get a message to you for the past week."

The magistrate scrutinized Belvedere critically for a moment. "I've been on and off the road for most of the past week."

"My colleague here," said Belvedere, pointing at me, "has recently discovered evidence that has some bearing on the case."

"Oh, and what's that?"

"The cobbler makes his own slugs in a mould," I interjected, somewhat sheepishly, because I could see that the burly fellow was rapidly losing his patience. "The slug we found in the post-mortem does not match the slug created in the mould."

The magistrate's jaw dropped. He leaned back in his chair and contemplated the ceiling for a good long time. Returning to a more upright position, he looked at us as one looks at a pair of sickly curs. His face glowed red. "Gentlemen," he said at last, "you have led me on a merry chase through hill and dale and ice and fire. There is no case here. I recommend that you release your prisoner at once. And that you do not, under any circumstances, meddle with me or the law in so cavalier a fashion going forward."

Belvedere was in a surly mood all the way up the hill to the McLaughlin house after our meeting with the judge. I could feel the anger building in him. Finally, he kicked at a frozen road apple on the roadway, sending it flying toward one of the houses that lined the street. "Fekking hell!" he exclaimed. "We're no closer to solving these murders than we were two months ago."

I felt that I had to say something to defuse his anger. "At least we know two people who didn't do it." That was all I could come up with.

Belvedere stopped and looked at me as though I was wearing a hollow pumpkin on my head. "If this keeps up, no judge in the territory will take us seriously. If this keeps up, Herchmer's boot-marks will be up and down my back." He turned and marched away toward the house.

Haggardy was released from his drafty prison the next day. He returned to his wife and family without fanfare. A day after that, we could see Joe Scriver and his dray cart in front of the cobbler's shop on River Street. We watched from the front window of the McLaughlin house as the entire family, ragged and morose, was driven out of town.

"I still don't like it," Belvedere said to me. "We might be watching our prime suspect making an escape in the broad light of day."

IN THE DAYS leading up to Christmas, Belvedere was in a brooding mood. He spent hours alone in his room, no doubt pondering his next steps in the investigation. On Christmas Eve, we walked the considerable length of River Street. Belvedere asked every shop owner and passerby if they were acquainted with somebody named Scribang, but no one had a recollection of the man.

I had purchased a fat turkey for Christmas Day, and I awoke that morning with visions of drumsticks dancing in my head. The turkey had been salted in a vat of brine the day before, and I went downstairs that morning with a plan to create a stuffing of some sort, with bread and apples and an onion. To my delight, the wood stove had already been stoked. I could feel its heat on my forearms as I was coming down the stairs. I saw the turkey in a roasting pan on the kitchen table and Mrs. McLaughlin scurrying around it, a colourful apron over her customary black dress. She ceased her labours when she saw me. "I hope you don't mind," she said. "I thought I'd make myself useful."

I rubbed the sleep from my eyes. "I don't mind at all. But I think you should let me do the cooking."

She shook her head, and wisps of auburn hair curled like

tinsel around her dainty neck. "You were promised room and board," she said. "It's time for me to live up to my promise."

"Well, let me help at least."

"Certainly, you may help."

We spent the rest of the morning preparing our feast together. I sliced the few apples that were not rotten, and Mrs. McLaughlin cubed the bread with great fervour. We talked incessantly. It was good to see the poor lady beginning to recover from what must have been a great shock.

Belvedere strolled downstairs at ten o'clock and watched the preparations. His laudanum use must have abated; his eyes were clear and his demeanour was crisp. Perhaps the pain in his leg had subsided. The little dog, who had become as much a companion of Mrs. McLaughlin's as it was of Belvedere's, jumped into his lap as he sat at the kitchen table.

Mrs. McLaughlin became more jubilant as the day went on. By mid-afternoon, she was rolling dough for pies. The flour in her hair made her look like a barrister in the high courts, back in Toronto or Montreal, and I told her so. Her laughter had the soft trill of a babbling brook. When she shook her head, the flour cascaded off her like snow from the heavens. Her sleeves were rolled up, and her long arms were graceful with the rolling pin. She was humming "Silent Night" almost imperceptibly as she worked.

At suppertime, we feasted. Even Mrs. McLaughlin's questionable culinary skills were incapable of ruining the magnificent turkey. We ate with delight. The conversation around the dinner table was more animated than usual. Belvedere and Mrs. McLaughlin took turns slipping the whining dog precious morsels of the bird.

I had purchased a bottle of wine for the occasion and, between the three of us, we finished off the bottle. Mrs. McLaughlin might have been accused of slight inebriation, unused to alcoholic beverages as she was, but the drink brought out her natural glow, and if her conversation was more liberated than it had been, that was a healthy improvement. She reached across the table and placed her hand on my sleeve during the main course. "Surgeon Montgomery," she said, "you are a far better cook than I. But I do promise to get better."

Belvedere grinned at me.

We ate mince meat pies for dessert. The minced meat was a tad tallowy for my liking, and the outer crust had been charred in the hot end-of-the-day oven. We ate it, nonetheless, as though it had been prepared for us by a grandam in Montreal.

After supper, we repaired to the parlour for the gift opening. I retrieved a box, wrapped in newspaper, from under the Christmas tree and presented it to Mrs. McLaughlin. She opened it delicately, sliding the string off one end of the box and unfolding the newsprint without tearing it. A moment later, the box of chocolates I had procured for her stood open on her lap. She sampled one of the chocolates, her eyes closed as if savouring some long-forgotten delicacy, and then she thanked me and passed the box to Belvedere. He didn't bother taking a bonbon, passing the box along to me instead.

Then Mrs. McLaughlin scurried into her bedroom and returned with two soft packages, also neatly wrapped in the pages of *The Saskatchewanian*. She handed the packages to Belvedere and me, and we opened them. Two identical pairs of woollen stockings were her kind gift to us. They were not the most artfully designed stockings I had ever seen, but they were obviously knitted by her own hand. I was touched by her thoughtfulness and by the labour she had committed herself to in a difficult time.

Not to be outdone, Belvedere reached deep into his trouser pocket and produced a small box. He handed it to Mrs. McLaughlin. "Didn't know what to buy for a lady," he muttered. "The man in the store told me this would do."

Mrs. McLaughlin opened the box and closed it again. "I can't accept this."

"Well, I can't take it back," Belvedere replied.

She opened the box again, and I saw, curled around her

fingers, a silver necklace with a heart-shaped pendant. It did not look terribly expensive, but still, I wondered how Belvedere could have afforded it. Tears stood in Mrs. McLaughlin's eyes. "This is beautiful," she said.

"Then you must keep it." It was an awkward gift, the kind of present a beau might give his sweetheart, but I think that nuance was lost on Belvedere. He had simply gone out looking for something a lady might like and had made that purchase.

"It's lovely," Mrs. McLaughlin said, "but we will just have to put it away for now."

Not wanting the celebration to end on that note, I suggested that each of us might cap off the evening by delivering a party piece. The suggestion was met with moans and groans but also with a measure of good humour, so I led by example. I braced myself on the mantelpiece and warbled something like the tune of "Hard Times Come Again No More." There was special poignancy in the first lines of the song: "Let us pause in life's pleasures and count its many tears, while we all sup sorrow with the poor; There's a song that will linger forever in our ears; Oh! Hard times come again no more."

Tears were streaming down Mrs. McLaughlin's face as the song came to an end, but Belvedere, in his typical fashion, undercut the moment with a jeer. "Never knew you could sing, Montgomery," he said, "and I'm still not sure you can!"

Sufficiently buoyed by this attempt at humour, Mrs. McLaughlin stood up and commenced an oration. "I sometimes recite poetry to myself when I can't sleep at night," she said, "and usually it's a Keats poem, 'Ode to a Nightingale.'" Still slightly under the effect of the wine she had drunk, she began to recite: "My heart aches, and a drowsy numbness pains my sense . . ." She did quite well, too. Clearly, her overbearing husband had forced her to hide the light of her talents under a bushel. She possessed an agile mind and an appreciation of all things beautiful. The words came forth with poise and eloquence until she arrived at the sixth stanza. "Darkling I listen," she recited; "and, for many a time, I have been half in love . . ." Mrs. McLaughlin paused, searching for the words or afraid to say them, and then she spoke again. "For many a time I have been half in love with—in love with easeful Death." She paused again and looked up at the ceiling. "Easeful Death," she repeated, and then: "This is where I usually fall asleep." With that brief explanation, she resumed her seat and waited for the third act to begin.

I was wondering what talent Belvedere might bring to bear on the occasion. It seemed unlike him to sing or dance or recite a poem. He remained in his chair for a long time, one leg over the other and a bemused look on his weathered face. Finally, he said to Mrs. McLaughlin, "Have you got a deck of cards in the house?"

Mrs. McLaughlin looked troubled. "The reverend did not countenance playing cards," she said, "but I do have a deck in my bureau. I used to play solitaire late at night." She went into her bedroom once again and returned with a dog-eared set of playing cards, gilded with a pattern of gold. Belvedere took the playing cards out of their box and shuffled them with a degree of expertise that might have characterized a card shark or a casino dealer. He fanned the cards with a flourish. Handing the deck to Mrs. McLaughlin, he asked her to pick a card but not to show it to him. She picked the three of hearts, couching it in her palm and revealing it to me.

"Memorize that card," Belvedere said, "and return it to the deck."Mrs. McLaughlin did so and passed the deck back to Belvedere. He shuffled the cards three or four times and then placed the deck face down on the mantelpiece. "Now I want you to concentrate very hard," Belvedere said to Mrs. McLaughlin, "on the card you have memorized. See it and visualize it." Mrs. McLaughlin squeezed her eyes shut and concentrated. "Is it the three of hearts?" asked Belvedere.

Mrs. McLaughlin opened her eyes and stared at Belvedere in amazement. "It is."

"Now, I want you to stand up," Belvedere said. Mrs. McLaughlin did so. "Turn around and look at the chair." Mrs.

McLaughlin and I both peered at the chair upon which she had been sitting. A card lay there, on the seat, face down. "Now, I'll ask you to pick that card up and show it to Surgeon Montgomery." She picked up the card and turned it over in her hand. "What card is the lady holding, Montgomery?"

I could hardly believe my own eyes. "The three of hearts."

Belvedere threw his arms in the air and intoned a self-mocking "Ta da!" Then he sat down in his chair and looked smugly about.

Mrs. McLaughlin's eyes never left him. "That's impossible. How did you do that?"

Belvedere grinned at her. "A magician never explains his trick."

The party did not go on much longer. Belvedere excused himself at about nine and trudged up the stairs to bed. Mrs. McLaughlin and I sat and talked for some time. She told me about her life back in Ontario. She was a minister's daughter, she said, so it only made sense that she would fall in love with and marry a minister. Her husband had got the call, in a dream one night, to come to Saskatchewan and spread the Word. They had been offered a manse, gratis, but when they arrived, they found the manse to be a drafty log cabin. Their decision to purchase a house of their own, with help from her father, turned out to be fortuitous; it meant that she did not have to vacate after her husband's passing.

When she began talking about her husband's suicide, Mrs. McLaughlin's eyes filled with tears. "Will you put out the lamps?" she asked me. "I think it's time for me to retire."

"Certainly."

She paused for a moment in front of her bedroom door. "And Mister Montgomery."

"Yes?"

"Merry Christmas."

I dutifully extinguished the coal-oil lamps in the parlour and kitchen. Logs were still burning in the fireplace and in the kitchen stove, and the house felt warm in the way that Christmases were always warm in my memory. It felt suddenly like a home instead of a place to stay.

I was able to make my way up the stairs in the dark, having by then memorized the steps. My mind wandered to thoughts of Mrs. McLaughlin as I sat up in my bed. I wanted to help the poor lady in any way I could. When I found that I could not sleep, I went to my writing desk and composed a letter to my darling Emily. In the letter, I guiltily reassured her that all was well with me. The North-West, which I had so abhorred in earlier letters, was, I said, beginning to grow on me. There was majesty, I wrote, in her panoramic sunsets, in her mighty rivers and forests, even in her perilous snowstorms.

I did not set out that evening to unburden myself of the shame I felt over the scandal in Quebec City, a scandal of which Emily was quite unaware. The words simply spilled out of me. Like blood from a jagged wound, the ink blotted and stained the paper. I wrote to her of the epidemic of meningitis that had occurred in Quebec City a year earlier, of the children who died, of the parents who blamed me for their deaths. "It was the most unhappy moment of my life," I wrote, "for which I will never be able to properly atone." I told her of my plan to give up on a medical practice and that I would seek to buy a farmstead in Vermont when my career with the Mounted Police had come to an end. And then I told her about the contract I had signed when I enlisted in the force, admitting that I would not be home the next summer and that I had signed on for five long years of service. I pleaded with her to understand my situation, my shame, and the reasons I had not been truthful. "Upon reading this, you may have decided that our love is but a sham," I wrote, "and I do not blame you for thinking so. But know in your deep heart's core that I love you now and that I always shall."

12

It did not take long for the joy of Christmas to dissipate. On the twenty-eighth of December, a Captain Rynders rode into town. He was an ostentatious old fellow with a handlebar moustache and medals clearly displayed on his military tunic. He had been sent from Ottawa, he said, for the purpose of establishing a standing militia in the settlement.

I first encountered Captain Rynders at a public meeting at Treston Hall. The newspaperman Sylvester O'Rourke introduced him, after an oration about how Prince Albert settlement was "the emerald of the West." That upstart town Regina, he said, was built on shifting sands and dried-up creek beds. It had made noises about becoming the centre of the universe, although it had none of the natural advantages of a thriving metropolis near a waterway and a forest where furs might be trapped and traded.

"Rest assured," O'Rourke continued, "that Ottawa has a watchful eye and is always looking out for us. And to that end, they have sent an emissary, Captain John Rynders, to keep the settlement secure against all threats."

The crowd, all men, was silent as Rynders stepped gingerly toward the lectern. His demeanour was gruff; his silvery moustache shook with passion as he spoke. "Gentlemen," he announced, "our fledgling nation is under threat from all sides. To the south, the Americans, who have on several occasions expressed a desire to annex these fair lands. To the north and all around us are the Chipewyan, the Cree, the Assiniboine, and the Sioux. They far outnumber the good white settlers who want nothing more than to bring civilization and security and agricultural wisdom and good business practices to a heathen land. The savages far outnumber us and, if they wished, could annihilate this settlement in the blink of an eye. And then there are possible threats from within, from folks who do not see the value of good government and stability." There was a sudden disquiet in the assembled multitude. Perhaps Rynders did not know that at least half of the people who occupied Treston Hall that evening were Métis. "And so," he continued, "to defend against these threats, the benevolent government of Sir John A. has asked me to come out here and set up a local militia."

At the back of the hall, a man wearing a Métis sash shouted, "Who would we be fighting?"

Rynders cleared his throat. "We wouldn't be fighting anyone," he said. "We'd only be here to keep the peace."

"You've already got one of our number in jail," another man shouted. "Until he's released, I won't be joinin' no militia."

There was general tumult on the floor of the hall. "Gentlemen, gentlemen," Rynders interjected, "I know nothing about a man in jail. I'm only here to protect your interests."

It was too late. The multitude erupted into a fury of yelling and name-calling, which only ceased when Dan McQuaid stepped to the front of the hall and raised a meaty hand. The Métis fellow who had spoken first made a show of exiting the hall, and others followed.

After the mass exodus, there were fewer than twenty-five men left in attendance. I looked around. Three or four elderly shopkeepers and some younger men, perhaps loggers by their appearance, still seemed interested. One of the younger men spoke up. "Is there any payment associated with this militia?"

"There is," Rynders announced, although he looked somewhat bedraggled. "Twenty-five cents per day when the militia is training. Through a generous grant from the federal government."

"I'd be interested in that," one of the older men said. He was perhaps sixty years old, wizened and unhealthy-looking. I couldn't imagine such a man marching into battle. "Where do I sign?"

WE PAID a visit to Mr. and Mrs. Morley the next evening. Their small house, covered with tar paper but not sided, was located on the western edge of the settlement. Mr. Morley came to the door when we knocked. He was a small man with a wiry head of hair, and he looked somewhat rattled at the first sight of us. "We're here to speak to Mrs. Morley," Belvedere told him.

Mr. Morley was not particularly confident, but he had enough gumption to make a further inquiry. "To speak to her about what?"

"About her time at the church."

There was a pause, and then Morley said, "My wife no longer attends that church."

"Nevertheless, we'd like to talk to her."

Morley's eyes darted back and forth between us. "Come in and sit."

We sat at the plain wooden table in the dining room. Morley seemed hesitant. "Would you like a cup of coffee?"

Belvedere was getting impatient. "No, thank you."

"I'll see if my wife is able to come." With one last look at us, Morley exited into what must have been a bedroom. The walls in the house were thin; we heard Morley's conversation with his wife. "The mounted policemen are here," he said. "They want to talk to you."

Her voice was timid and afraid. "Talk to me about what?"

"About McLaughlin." He said the name as though it carried some baggage.

"Now?"

"Yes, now. You'd better come."

After a few fleeting minutes, Morley again appeared, this time with his wife in tow. She was a meek woman, as meek as her husband, and about thirty years old. Her face was pale, and her hair was blonde. She moved with the temerity of a mouse. She said hello, and then the two of them sat on chairs, opposite one another, at the table.

Belvedere started the conversation. "I understand you were the organist at the Anglican church in town?"

Mrs. Morley glanced at her husband and then spoke in a soft voice. "I was. Yes."

"We are investigating the murder of the laundryman, Chen," Belvedere said. "Do you think the minister might have had any knowledge of that?"

She looked confused for a moment. "I don't think so."

"How well did you know the reverend?"

Her eyes began to well up with tears. "I knew him quite well, I guess."

"Mr. Sandaker, at the church, said you knew him better than most."

Mrs. Morley inhaled some sharp breaths. Tears ran down her cheeks. Her husband stepped into the fray. "We might as well come clean," he said to his wife. She nodded her head. "My wife fell under McLaughlin's spell momentarily."

Belvedere's face darkened. "Meaning what?"

Mr. Morley's eyes were reddening. "She had an intimate affair with him."

"When did this happen?" Tact was not one of Belvedere's best characteristics.

"Last summer." Morley reached across the table and clasped his wife's hand. "I've forgiven her, as you can see."

"I can see."

Morley allowed himself to show some emotion, at last. "He was a wolf in sheep's clothing, was Minister McLaughlin. He used my wife's faith against her. It was child's play for him."

"I see." Belvedere stood up, and I followed suit. "Well, that's all the questions we have for this evening. If there's anything more, we will be in touch."

We left the Morleys staring at one another across the dining room table. When we were outside and walking home through the snow, I turned to Belvedere. "So the minister was involved in a romantic liaison."

"It seems so."

"And is that what he was so desperate to be forgiven for?"

"Quite possibly."

We walked the rest of the way to the McLaughlin house in silence. I couldn't help thinking of poor Mrs. McLaughlin and wondering what she might have known about her husband's relationship with another woman.

THERE WAS a New Year's Eve dance at the town hall, but neither Belvedere nor I attended. We stayed at the McLaughlin house, where the celebration that ushered in eighteen eighty-four had a muted tone. The Christmas meats did coldly furnish forth the New Year's table. There was no cheery rendition of "Auld Lang Syne," and Mrs. McLaughlin retired early to bed. Belvedere and I were in our rooms by nine-thirty. I went to work on a charcoal portrait of Mrs. McLaughlin, based on some sketches I had drawn earlier, which I thought to present to her sometime in the new year.

Asleep well before midnight, I was awakened by a clatter of rifle fire at precisely that hour. I wondered, momentarily, whether an insurrection was taking place or perhaps the militia was in the midst of target practice. Neither of those far-fetched scenarios was substantiated in fact. It was a Métis custom, as I found out later, to ring in the new year by firing rifles into the air. It was also a means of letting one's distant neighbour know that all is well with you and yours.

On New Year's Day, Belvedere and I trekked down to the livery stable once more for another meeting with Joe Scriver. Although the old man could be ruled out as a suspect, Belvedere thought, he might also be a valuable source of information about comings and goings in the settlement. We waited inside the stable doors as Scriver accepted cash from a gentleman I did not know. When the transaction was complete, the gentleman mounted his horse and rode south out of town.

Scriver turned his attention to us. "The Mounties is back."

"We have more questions," Belvedere said.

The old man chuckled, more to himself than to us. "Come into my office and have a seat." He escorted us into the tack room, and we sat on straw bales. The room was musty and dark. There were curry combs and brushes hanging from nails, salves and ointments on a ledge above the door, and sets of harness organized on pegs that protruded from the wall. A Winchester rifle was perched on two spikes that had been pounded into one of the walls. Scriver's nephew Abel Dickson was busy, in one corner of the tack room, making shapes with his mouth and laboriously repairing a harness with a long, sharp needle and some thick thread. "How can I help you?" Scriver asked.

Belvedere toed a frozen road apple with his boot. "You're aware that this is a police investigation."

Scriver spat chewing tobacco on the straw-covered floor. "I'm aware of that."

"A liveryman sees some things that others don't see." Belvedere was examining the sole of his boot as if this line of questioning were mere small talk.

"I s'pose that's a true fact."

"We figure you might have some insight into the comings and goings in this town."

"That I do," the old man replied.

"Any strangers come through here just before Christmas?"

The old man guffawed at Belvedere's question, almost swallowing a mouthful of tobacco in the process. "Plenty of strangers come through here," he said. "We got fur traders coming out of the north, we got guv'ment people travelling from the south, we got plain folks just tryin' to get from Winnipeg to Edmonton."

Belvedere stared a hole through the man. "Anybody with a name like yours? Screever or Scrivener or maybe Scribang?"

Scriver thought for a moment, then shook his head. "No one that I kin recall."

"Fair enough." Belvedere stood up. "We figure you see things that other people don't."

The old man's smile turned into a death mask. "I see plenty a things."

"Like what?" Belvedere edged toward him.

"I don't like to say too much," the old man replied, "because I don't know too much. Alls I kin tell you is this. If ya wanna know who's behind the skulduggery, ya gotta see where the dollars is spent."

Belvedere was two feet away from him, and he bent down to look directly into the old man's eyes. "What's that mean?"

Scriver didn't flinch. "Means just what I said. Look where the dollars is spent. And that's as much as I'm gonna tell ya."

We asked him other questions about money and motive in the town and about personal animosities. Scriver did not have many answers. He clearly thought he'd said enough and, whether out of fear or distrust, he wasn't willing to divulge much more information or opinion.

Belvedere was in a sullen mood as we walked back toward the McLaughlin house that morning. He was clearly befuddled by the old man's pronouncements. I thought to bring him out of his shell by reiterating the liveryman's words. "Look where the dollars are spent," I said. "That could lead us down a lot of blind alleys."

Belvedere exhaled warm air onto his fingers as we trudged

through the snowbound street. "Who's got money in this town? The logging company? The flour mill?"

"And who's got motive?"

"That's what we're about to find out." Belvedere tucked his jaw into the folds of his buffalo coat and trudged up the hill like an ancient buffalo bracing against the storm.

ON THE SECOND day of January, Colonel Herchmer arrived at the settlement, accompanied by four junior officers. His jaunt by horseback to the settlement had been cold and lengthy, and his visit was brief, as he had just moved his headquarters from Battleford to Regina and was in a hurry to return. Belvedere and I were summoned to the detachment office at the Hobart and Eden store at four o'clock that afternoon. The shadows of early evening had already begun to fall as we walked up the hill to receive what I could only imagine was our comeuppance.

As we entered the building, Sergeant Slade was just leaving. He said nothing but looked at us with a jaundiced eye as he hurried out the door. Belvedere raised an eyebrow at me. "Looks like somebody shat in his coffee cup."

In the office at the rear of the store, Herchmer sat at Slade's desk like he was the sole owner of the Hobart and Eden chain of stores. Belvedere knocked on the doorjamb. "Yes, come in," the grizzled colonel said. He took a long look at us. He did not ask us to sit down. "You two have been making quite a splash in the town by all accounts."

"All in aid of the investigation," Belvedere replied.

The colonel stroked his beard for another long moment. "It appears that Sergeant Slade has not been impressed by your carryings-on."

"Yes, well," Belvedere said, "the only thing that impresses Sergeant Slade is a well-written report."

I was expecting a severe dressing down after such a remark,

but the colonel seemed to know something of the relationship between my investigative partner and Slade. He leaned back in his chair and appraised Belvedere. "And how is the investigation coming along, sir?"

"There have been three murders now."

"Three of them?" Herchmer looked shocked. "And who might be the perpetrator?"

Belvedere remained at attention, but his stature was a little sloppy. "We had a suspect, and we thought he was our man."

"Yes?"

"But we were proven wrong." Belvedere looked sidelong at me. "We're currently following another lead."

"Another lead?" Herchmer leaned forward, a puzzled look on his face.

"We have a name."

Herchmer rubbed his whiskery chin again. "And what name is that?"

"Scribang, sir."

"And do you have a face to associate with the name?"

Belvedere sagged a little. "We have a description, but we have not located the man." I thought it a bit of a stretch to call what little we had heard of Scribang a description, but I did not say anything.

Herchmer stood up and peered out of the frost-laden windowpane at the village below. "You've been here for two months."

"Not every murder investigation is the same, sir." Belvedere was as close to pleading as I had ever heard him.

The colonel turned abruptly toward us. "Goddamit, Belvedere, you are a drunk and a drug addict and a royal pain in the ass. But you are also the right man for this job."

"I know that, sir."

"And yet the sergeant wants you gone."

"With respect, sir," I interrupted, "Sergeant Slade has been intolerant of Corporal Belvedere since the moment of our arrival here." It was no more than the truth, but I instantly regretted speaking up.

Herchmer looked at me as though I were a muskrat that had just crawled into the room and died. "I think I made it clear to you, Montgomery, when we were back in Battleford, that your two jobs were to keep this asshole in line and to regulate his habits. You have failed dismally on both counts." Then he turned back to Belvedere. "I'll give you until the thaw." He stepped toward Belvedere and stood three feet away, looking him in the eye. "But no more shenanigans before then. No more nights in the public house. Am I clear?"

"Yes, sir."

The colonel glared at him a moment longer. "That will be all, Corporal."

"Thank you, sir." Belvedere executed a military turn and marched out of the store. I glanced back at the colonel, who gestured at me to follow my partner, and so I did.

As we were walking down the hill toward the McLaughlin house after the meeting, I asked Belvedere why he thought Herchmer had let us stay on in the settlement and continue the investigation. He snorted with laughter. "Because the colonel knows that Slade couldn't find a stinking corpse in a bed of roses." His countenance turned dark again as we ambled into the wind. "So you've been told to keep an eye on me?"

I thought for a moment before admitting my guilt. "It wasn't my idea."

"Well, you'd better keep a close eye," he growled. "There's no telling what I might do next."

IT WAS NOT unusual for Belvedere to spend his evenings away from the house, whether on investigation or simply having a beer in the public house. He departed after supper that evening, leaving me and Mrs. McLaughlin to wash and dry the dishes. Mrs.

McLaughlin seemed distracted as we did so, and our conversation was as scattered as leaves in autumn. When I asked her what kind of day she'd had, she replied, "Oh, you know, just this and that."

Having finished the dishes, we repaired to the parlour, where I enjoyed a glass of wine while Mrs. McLaughlin sat down at the piano. She was an accomplished piano player, and she negotiated her way through Mozart and Bach with no sheets of musical notation in front of her. The emotion of the music was expressed in her back and in her long neck as she played, sitting very upright at the piano. Her fingers seemed to dance across the keys.

When she finished playing, Mrs. McLaughlin turned around on the piano bench and smiled at me. I told her that I had been working on her portrait in charcoal and that I was quite happy with the result. She said, "I'd like to see that."

Perhaps it was not wise to be telling Mrs. McLaughlin about her portrait or even to have been working on it in the first place. I went upstairs, took the charcoal drawing off its easel, and brought it downstairs for Mrs. McLaughlin to see. She asked me to place it on the piano's music rest, and we both stood some distance away to get a full view of the drawing. Mrs. McLaughlin examined the portrait for a good long time, and I began to wonder if she was perhaps displeased. She turned to look at me. "Do you find me attractive, Mr. Montgomery?"At a loss for words, the best I could manage was to stare back at her. She stepped forward and grasped my right hand, and then she kissed me on the lips.

Her kiss was addictive, and I found myself enjoying the taste of her because I had not experienced the taste of a woman in so long, but I pushed her gently away and blurted, stupidly, "I have a fiancée. At least, I think I do."

Mrs. McLaughlin looked befuddled. "You think you have a fiancée?"

"I'm sorry," I said. "I should have told you before."

The discomfort in the room was palpable. "But you're not certain that you have a fiancée?"

I felt the blood surge into my face. "I'm not certain that she loves me anymore."

"And why's that?"

"I have not been entirely truthful with her about my circumstances here."

Mrs. McLaughlin looked at me as one looks at a small child who has fallen off a playground swing. "About what circumstances in particular?"

I took a deep breath. "She thinks I'll be coming home next summer."

"And you won't?"

"I've signed a contract with the Mounted Police for a five-year term."

"Then you must be truthful with her," Mrs. McLaughlin urged. "You must write her immediately. You must tell her how you feel and why you feel that way."

"I already have."

Mrs. McLaughlin was not entirely ready to believe me. "What is your fiancée's name?"

"Her name is Emily."

She smiled at me in a motherly way. "I'm sorry I was so forward just now."

"I'm the one who should be sorry."

"You couldn't have known how I felt," Mrs. McLaughlin said. "There's nothing for you to be sorry for." She looked at me thoughtfully for a moment. "We'll pretend this never happened. I never kissed you, and you certainly did not kiss me back. And there will be no need to write your fiancée about it. Do we have a deal?"

Not being an expert in affairs of the heart, I was relieved that the two of us could arrive at so amicable an agreement. "Yes," I said, "we have a deal."

We interviewed the logging boss the next day. On our way to the mill by the river at the edge of town, Belvedere reminded me that he had interviewed the man early in the investigation and that the fellow had been rather obtuse. His name was Everett Markham. We were going to get answers today, Belvedere said, so be forewarned.

The logging boss was a burly fellow with a bright-red face and cheeks that looked like he was carrying two large apples in his mouth. He was out in the yard, on one end of a long swede saw, grinding away at a log laid across two sturdy sawhorses. The fellow on the other end of the saw was a skinny kid who looked like he could barely keep up. Whether because of the sawing or the sawing partner, the boss did not seem to be happy. His face was red with exertion, and there was fire in his eyes.

Belvedere approached him from the side. "Mr. Markham."

"Fuck off to hell," Markham replied, barely looking at us. Whether he was exasperated by his work or whether he simply did not like policemen, I was not able to confirm.

Pivoting on his good leg, Belvedere delivered a haymaker to the side of the man's head that sent him sprawling to the ground. The swede saw twanged and vibrated when the boss let go of it. The skinny kid was still holding on to the other end of the saw, his face ashen. Belvedere stepped over to where Markham lay in the snow and delivered a size-eleven police boot to the side of the man's head. Then he picked the man up by the collar of his winter coat and propped him in a sitting position against one of the sawhorses. "Perhaps you'll keep a civil tongue in your head now."

"Belvedere!" I exclaimed. "Enough!"

Belvedere glanced at me out of the corner of his eye. "None of your concern, Montgomery."

The skinny kid didn't move. I approached his boss, thinking to administer first aid, but Belvedere shoved me away. Markham's ear was bleeding, and he was a little groggy, but he still managed a "fuck you."

Belvedere kicked him again, this time in the groin. "I didn't hear that. What did you say?" The man was slouched forward, with his hands covering his genitals and gasping for air. Belvedere knelt beside him. "I'm going to ask you a question. I'd appreciate a straight answer. Have you had any dealings with Alexander McKay or with Herman Cantrell?"

"Never heard of either of them." Markham spoke slowly, through moans and groans; he had difficulty getting the words out.

"Are you certain of that?" Belvedere pressed a finger into the man's bloody ear. "Because I have it on good authority that you log right near their farms."

The logging boss looked up at Belvedere through swollen eyes. He had lost his spunk. "I don't personally know every homesteader north of the river."

"But you'd like to own their trees."

"There's four hundred miles of trees north of the river," the man said. "All the way to Stanley Mission and beyond. What would I care for two farmers with three hundred acres between them?"

Belvedere looked up at me and then back at Markham. "Those are all the questions I have for now," he said. "Thank you for your cooperation."

As we were walking away, the logging boss muttered something about common assault. Belvedere froze and then turned to look at the man. He was still sprawled against the sawhorse, and the skinny kid was still attached to the saw. "You were obstructing a police officer, sir. Maybe next time, you'll be more forthcoming."

BELVEDERE SAT at supper that evening as if it had been all in a day's work. He was even jovial, teasing his little terrier with a shard of venison and then laughing uproariously when the mutt jumped, knocking the morsel from his hand and scooping it off the hardwood floor.

Mrs. McLaughlin was jovial, as well. She seemed to have forgotten our tryst of the night before, or to have distanced herself from it, and her dark eyes gleamed in the light of the lamp as she told us about a fundraiser for the Prince Albert Arts and Letters Club. "I'll be reading a poem," she said, "and there will be room for paintings on the walls." She was caught up in the endless possibilities of such an evening, and I began to see how important the world of the beaux arts was to her. "Perhaps you'll allow us to show some of your landscape work, Mr. Montgomery? I know you also draw portraits, but we'll leave those for another evening."

I was noncommittal, especially since Belvedere had been quite derisive about my time spent with the charcoals and paint. "When will this variety night be held?"

"On the sixteenth of January," she replied. "Just the right antidote to the deep cold that has set in, wouldn't you say, doctor?"

"I'm sure it will be."

She went on effusively. "And there will be music. We have a string quartet in town now. And you can sing, if you wish."

"Good God, no," Belvedere shouted in my stead. "Please don't encourage him with another rendition of Stephen Foster."

Mrs. McLaughlin turned her attention to Belvedere. "And what could be better than a thrilling magic act to end the evening?"

Belvedere shook his head. "I'm content to be neither seen nor heard at such an event."

Mrs. McLaughlin reached across the table and touched his sleeve. "But you are so good. Please tell me that you will share your talents with us. It would be a crime to do otherwise."

Belvedere pulled his arm away self-consciously. "I do better in small gatherings."

"This gathering won't be large." Mrs. McLaughlin smiled at Belvedere coquettishly. "No more than a hundred people. I promise. And all of them eager to see the handsome corporal perform his magic act."

It was the first time I'd heard her, or anyone, refer to Belvedere's weathered face as handsome. Perhaps it was also the first time Belvedere had heard that epithet, as well. His face reddened. "I'll give that some thought."

More expansive than I had ever seen her, Mrs. McLaughlin went on. "I can see the advertisement in *The Herald* now." With a dainty wave of her hand, she created an imaginary headline in the air in front of her. "CORPORAL BELVEDERE AND HIS AMAZING FEATS OF LEGERDEMAIN!"

Belvedere sat back in his chair and appraised her for a moment, as one might examine a horse before purchase. "Well, I'll let you know." He snatched some grizzle off his plate and held it at shoulder height. His little dog leaped at the morsel of meat, and Belvedere chuckled deep down in his belly.

THE NEXT MORNING was colder than I had ever experienced. The thermometer outside Mrs. McLaughlin's kitchen window read minus forty-two degrees. Belvedere and I bundled up in as much clothing as we could find and marched down to the flour mill. The frozen air assaulted our lungs with every intake of breath. It crystallized in Belvedere's beard with every exhalation. I felt as though my bones were hollow sticks of bamboo as I walked. Inside my police-issue boots, my toes were blocks of ice by the time we arrived at the mill.

It was an oddly shaped wood frame building, as these mills are, with a variety of machines in the taller part of the building for stoning the wheat and separating the chaff, and a long, squat engine room from which protruded a chimney that poured black smoke into the sky. The smoke seemed not to dissipate but to cascade down over the nearby river. The steam engine that powered the operation was at full throttle already, and the din was mind-rattling as we entered the building. Flour floated in the air like dry dust, and I found myself with an incurable case of the sneezes.

"Get ahold of yourself!" Belvedere admonished after the umpteenth sneeze. I could see that his eyes were also inflamed from the onslaught of flour that was everywhere around us.

A man approached through the haze. He was small and wiry, maybe forty years old. Wheat chaff had settled on his shoulders and in his hair. "Can I help you, gentlemen?" Although he had to be loud, the man was decidedly more cordial than the lumber mill boss had been the day before. Perhaps word of Belvedere's nasty temper had got out.

"We're here on police business," Belvedere yelled over the din. "Are you foreman here?"

The man grinned at us. "Foreman. Owner. Operator. Cedric Wilson's the name." He extended a floury hand to both Belvedere and me. We shook it.

"Here to learn about your operation," Belvedere shouted. "Do you buy wheat from the farmers hereabout?"

"I do," the man said, "and I pay them top dollar."

Belvedere peered at Wilson through a small blizzard of dust. "What if they won't sell?"

Wilson bellowed out a laugh. "Everybody wants to sell," he replied. "I got no competition until the railroad gets here. Costs too much to ship a load of grain by boat, and boats only run in the summertime."

"Ever had any dealings with Alexander McKay?"

"I heard about the guy. Sounds like the Indians got him."

"Ever had any dealings with him?"

"He was just getting started out here," Wilson replied. "Hadn't produced more than enough crop to feed his own cattle."

"How about Herman Cantrell?"

Wilson grinned again. "Old Herman was an erratic sort."

"That he was."

"Used to bring in a gunny sack full of wheat every now and then. Enough to make about a dozen loaves of bread."

Belvedere thought for a moment. "Ever hear of anyone wanting to buy his land?"

Wilson shook his head, and a flurry of flour cascaded around him. "Can't say as I did," he replied, "but there's a lot of speculation going on right now."

"What are people speculating about?"

"All sorts of things," Wilson said. "Where the telegraph will go. Where the railroad might get built. Whether all that Métis farmland will come up for sale sometime soon."

Belvedere peered at the man through the floury haze. "Hmm. That's a lot of avenues to investigate."

"I reckon it is."

When his line of questioning was finished, Belvedere looked at me. "Anything you want to ask, Montgomery?"

"No." I was still choked up and trying not to sneeze.

"Then we're done here," Belvedere said. He turned to Wilson. "Thank you for your time."

My ears, nose, and throat were happy to exit the mill. I sneezed all the way back to the McLaughlin house, certain that I could bake an angel food cake with all the flour that had settled on my thick coat. Belvedere wondered aloud as we walked about what Wilson had said. "Christ," he muttered, "will we be able to untangle all these knots in three months' time?"

13

It was only a few days later when we received a visit from Sergeant Slade at the McLaughlin house. He was at our door at eight o'clock in the evening, smiling like a Cheshire cat. Belvedere and I had been smoking in the dining room. Slade did not bother to come farther inside than the front hall portico. His face was red with the cold but perhaps also flushed with pride. "I've come to advise you that your murder case has been solved," he announced. "You may begin preparations for your immediate return to Battleford."

Belvedere puffed on his cigar. "Solved?" he said. "How so?"

With a wave of his hand, Slade whisked the cigar smoke away. He did not bother getting angry, choosing instead to take solace in the possibility of our early departure. "I've personally apprehended the suspect," he said. His voice was dripping with delight. "He's admitted to all three murders. When the two of you proved yourselves to be unequal to the task, I decided to take a further interest in the case."

"You've found a suspect?" Belvedere inhaled another breath of the cigar and released a pungent exhalation into the air. "And who might that be?"

"A fellow by the name of Dickson," Slade replied. "Abel Dickson. He's been boasting around town for some time about having committed these murders, all the while the two of you were traipsing about the countryside."

Belvedere was incredulous. "Abel Dickson? The stable boy? The half-wit?"

"Witty enough, apparently, to have eluded you," Slade said. "We have him in custody now, up at the jail."

THERE WAS a four-way hullabaloo going on in the Mounted Police jail when we arrived the next morning. Abel Dickson was singing at the top of his voice, perhaps to help him forget his present circumstances. In another cell, Evert Sinclair was hollering at him to shut up. Abel had apparently been singing all night long, some song I didn't recognize about a lady who'd misplaced her bonnet. Standing in the corridor outside the jail cells, Joe Scriver was shouting at Evert Sinclair to mind his own damnable business. Assigned to guard duty for the day, Sub-Constable Parry made a feeble effort to quell the noise, but he was hardly able to squeeze a word out in the excitement. It was a sorry commotion.

The moment Belvedere and I walked in out of the January cold, Joe Scriver turned his attention on us. "Was this yer doin'?"

Belvedere looked at him squarely. "It was not."

Scriver continued speaking, knowing that his advanced age provided him with a degree of immunity. "You Mounties think yer God's gift to these territories," he shouted over the din, "when in truth, yer nothin but a cancer."

Belvedere shook his head and chuckled. "Have a care," he said, "or we'll have to put you outside in the snowbank."

Beside himself with anger, Scriver was vibrating like a rattlesnake's tail. Abel Dickson was still singing wildly, having changed his tune to "Camp Town Races." "Will you kindly shut the fuck up?" Scriver hollered at his nephew. "I'm trying to have an argument here."

Belvedere intervened, calling Sub-Constable Parry to action. "Escort Mister Scriver to the Hobart and Eden, Parry, or else I'll have to charge him with disturbing the peace."

Parry grasped the old man by the elbow and led him to the door, but not without a protestation. "Get yer greasy hands offa me, you sumbitch tongue-tied rabbit-slapper!" he said to Parry. Then he shouted back at Belvedere, "And I'm not done with you yet, either!"

When Parry and the old man had gone, Abel Dickson quieted down, and Evert Sinclair sat back on his bed. We approached Dickson's cell. He sat down and looked away from us, studying the wall beside him. "Abel Dickson," Belvedere said, "I have some doubts about you. Did you murder Chaoxing Chen?"

"Yeah." Dickson's voice sounded disconnected somehow, like it was coming from some place other than his mouth.

"Did you shoot Alexander McKay?"

"Yeah."

"How about Herman Cantrell? Did you shoot him, too?"

"I did. At least I think I did." Dickson was still staring at the bare wall beside him. "My uncle tells me different, but I'm pretty sure I done it."

Belvedere edged closer to the iron lattice of the cell. "What makes you sure you've done it?"

Dickson spoke to the wall, almost as though he was trying to deny our presence. "I'm pretty sure I wasn't dreamin'," he said. "I think I'd know if I was dreamin'."

Evert Sinclair spoke up from his own cell. "He didn't do a goddamn thing," Sinclair offered. "He's got but one testicle and half a brain."

"You shut up yourself," said Abel to Evert Sinclair. "I got me two testicles."

Belvedere turned to Sinclair. "Has he talked to you about it? Since he's been in here."

"I wish he would talk to me about it," Sinclair replied. "It'd be a nice change from his singin'."

Turning his attention back to Abel Dickson, Belvedere asked, "What did you shoot them with?"

"With my uncle's old Winchester. The one he keeps in the tack room."

"I'd advise you to keep quiet about all that," Belvedere said, "and to keep the peace in here. In the meantime, Surgeon Montgomery and I will look for a way to exonerate you." He headed for the jailhouse door. As we were stepping outside into the wintry blast, Belvedere looked sidelong at me. "I'm sure even Slade had sense enough to confiscate the firearm by now."

Old Joe Scriver was standing on the roadway about fifty feet from the jailhouse when Belvedere and I exited the building. His coat was open to the elements; it seemed that he didn't care a pin for his own health and well-being. He laboured through the snow toward us, his dung-encrusted boots kicking up a minor flurry as he made his way. "That boy is no more a murderer than I'm the Prime Minister of Siam," he said. "He wouldn't know which end of a gun to shoot with."

Belvedere stared him down. "Where is that gun now?"

"What gun?"

"The Winchester that was hanging on the wall of your tack room."

"That's another thing," Scriver shouted. "That gun ain't bin fired in two years."

Belvedere spat a wad of phlegm into the snow. "Where is it now?"

Scriver spat too. "Your sergeant already took it."

Belvedere took a deep breath of cold prairie air. "I don't think your nephew is guilty of anything," he said. "I'd like to prove him innocent."

This last statement caused Scriver to calm down a bit. He looked up and down at Belvedere. "How do you plan to do that?"

"Don't know," Belvedere said, "but I'm willing to give it the old college try. In the meantime, the best you can do is go back to your stable and keep your ear to the ground."

"Ear to the ground fer what?"

"For any information you can find about these murders." Belvedere turned and strode away toward the McLaughlin house.

I wanted to reassure the old man myself. "We'll keep our ears to the ground too," I said. "Hopefully, we can get your nephew out of jail before long." Having offered that little bit of reassurance, I thought it best to follow Belvedere down the hill, leaving Scriver to contemplate his nephew's fate and what he could do to ensure it was a happy one.

On Monday morning, Belvedere and I walked to the Land Titles Office on River Street. Colonel Rynders was busy, marching his ragtag recruits up and down the street, each of them shouldering a rifle. He shouted orders at them in a gruff voice, but they could not seem to march in step or to halt simultaneously. I would estimate the average age of the brigade at fifty-five. The militiamen were visibly shivering in their patent leather boots and light tunics. I understood that Rynders had set up a firing range at the edge of town. Although his troops would have been unlikely to hit anything, and they were three miles away from the encampment, I was sure that the incessant pounding of their rifles was reminder enough to the Sioux that another Little Bighorn would not be acceptable here.

The land office agent, bald and bespectacled, was sitting behind his immaculate desk near the stove when we entered. The nameplate on his desk read "Whitney." Other than the nameplate, the desk bore only an inkwell, a fountain pen, and exactly one sheet of paper. Seeing us, the man got up and approached the front counter. His face was pasty and his language was precise, delivered through colourless lips that always seemed puckered. "Can I help?" His articulation was as dry as hard tack in summer.

Belvedere spoke up. "We're interested in knowing where the telegraph office will be located."

Whitney looked over his spectacles at Belvedere. "That, as you probably know, is a matter of some concern."

"Oh?"

"People are already conjecturing that a new telegraph office will become a centre of business in this community," Whitney replied, "and the wealth will be shared with any of the businesses that happen to be located nearby."

I could tell that Belvedere did not like the man's precious attitude. "Where is the office likely to be built, in your esteemed opinion?"

"Three constituencies are vying for the office," Whitney said. "Pochaville, at the east end of town, wants it. There's a business group right here in the centre of town that has put in an application. And, of course, Lawrence Clark would like to have it near the Hudson Bay store."

"And the line will be coming right down River Street?"

"Likely. It's a matter of conjecture." Whitney pulled a white handkerchief from his pocket and meticulously scrubbed the lenses of his spectacles. "If the railroad comes through here, as planned, they will want the telegraph office to be located in the station."

Belvedere scratched at his beard. "And will the telegraph line be heading north across the river afterwards? Toward Whitehorse?"

"That would be far off in the future," Whitney explained. "For now, at least, Prince Albert is the end of the line."

On our way back to the McLaughlin house, huffing and puffing in the cold morning air, I turned to Belvedere. "Do you think the telegraph is involved in any of this?"

He spat a wad of phlegm into the snow. "Doesn't appear so, does it? If they're not going across the river with the line, why would two homesteaders north of the river be murdered?"

WE HEARD, the next day, of Evert Sinclair's escape from jail. According to Sub-Constable Parry, who stood in our porch that morning, the event had taken place on the night previous. Under the cover of darkness, one of Sinclair's friends—apparently, a young man named MacIvor—had strolled into the guardhouse, assaulted the guard who was on duty, and demanded the key to the cells. When the guard refused to hand them over, he was knocked to the ground with a rifle butt and the keys were taken forcibly from him.

In that manner, Sinclair's friend had extricated him from his cell, and the two of them had fled the town on horses that were waiting for them outside the jail. The escapees had taken the extra measure of unlocking Abel Dickson's cell, but Abel was sensible enough not to move. He was still sitting on his bed in the cell, staring at the wall beside him, when Sergeant Slade arrived to inspect the scene of the crime. After the alarm went up, Slade quickly organized a search party. He was out combing the area by the time Belvedere and I had heard about the escape.

Belvedere listened patiently as Parry finished his long speech. "Might've headed south to Duck Lake," Belvedere thought aloud.

Parry struggled through the next sentence. "The s-s-s-sergeant l-l-left me here to l- look after the d-d-d-detachment."

"A brilliant move," Belvedere said.

"I th-th-thought you m-m-m-m-might like to know in c-c-case you s-see Sin-Sin- Sinclair out and about."

"Yes, thank you, Parry," Belvedere said. "You've been most succinct. We'll keep an eye out for him."

After Parry had gone to oversee the detachment office, Belvedere turned to me, grinning widely. "Good luck with that," he said. "By now, those fugitives could be in any barn or log cabin between here and Willow Bunch."

THERE WERE two days of celebration in the middle of January, at the height of winter. A dog sled race commenced early on the morning of the first day. Its starting line was on the river ice. About a dozen drivers, their dogs sleek and barking, stood in the snow, waiting for the starter's pistol. They were mostly Métis fellows, dressed in two layers of fur and with leather moccasins tied around their feet. Their sleds were rough and wooden, with long runners. Those same sleds had probably been used on the trapline the day before.

The men were hard and brazen as their dogs. When the gun went off, the canines raced away, and the men pushed the sleds in front of them until enough momentum was created for them to jump on the skids and shout encouragement at their running hounds. Soon, dogs, sleds, and drivers disappeared around a bend in the river, only to reappear again, five hours later, the muzzles of the dogs and the men decorated with ice and snow. To have taken so long, the entire course of the race must have been at least twenty miles.

A young Métis trapper sped across the finish line first, his hounds sleek with sweat. A small group of locals were there to cheer the racers on. Others had already adjourned to the local public house and were deep in spirits.

That evening, there was a minstrel show at Treston Hall on River Street. The actors were all local men, blackened up with charcoal in the tradition of southern minstrelsy. Their performances were mostly cringeworthy. The interlocutor made lame jokes about chitlins and black-eyed peas. Dressed in their finery, the minstrels sang songs about life on the plantation. They performed "Old Log Cabin in the Dell" and "Miss Lucy Long." Between songs, the interlocutor asked Tambo some hard questions. "Tell me, Tambo, how do you make a lean baby fat?"

"How?"

"You drop him out of a third-story window, and he'll come down plump!" I found it difficult to laugh at the interlocuter's question and his response, as did Mrs. McLaughlin. We had witnessed, only months earlier, her husband's fatal fall from his church's peak to the frozen ground below.

On the next day, which was a Saturday, there was a marksmanship contest, again on the river ice. I stood on the ice in the afternoon and watched as the marksmen competed for a coveted turkey that had been donated by the local butcher's shop. There were paper targets pinned to haybales near the far bank of the river. Some excellent marksmen were in attendance. Several of the local Métis, hunters by trade, were superb shots. Belvedere took part in the contest and acquitted himself well, although he did not win. The victor, who recorded bull's eye after bull's eye, was the local sheriff, Dan McQuaid.

In the evening, we adjourned to Treston Hall for the much-vaunted variety night. Mrs. McLaughlin had prevailed upon me to decorate the interior walls of the hall with my charcoal drawings. I overheard several of the local denizens commenting upon my work. "Not bad for a Mountie doctor," one of them said.

Another exclaimed, in reaction to one of my landscapes, "Why would anyone want to draw that?"

The local poetry league was in full force, as well. The newspaperman O'Rourke recited a poem he had written about the coming railroad and its hoped-for effect upon the people of Prince Albert. "And we will ride to glory," the poem ended, "on that bright beast's iron wheels!"

Then Mrs. McLaughlin came to the podium and read one of her poems, about how, at the end of winter, our griefs and unhappiness will melt with the snow. I thought she had undeniable literary skill, and she read with such quiet passion that it was impossible to take one's eyes off her. There were several other poets who later shared their work, but none of it was as memorable as Mrs. McLaughlin's piece had been.

After the poetry reading, Belvedere mounted the stage and performed a brief magician's act. I was surprised to see him there, as he had been non-committal even three days before the event. He performed a card trick, to the amazement of all those assembled, and then he asked for a volunteer to come up on stage. When no one else stepped forward, Mrs. McLaughlin volunteered, probably out of a sense of obligation after having coerced him to perform.

She was instructed to aim Belvedere's service revolver at his heart and to fire. Belvedere demonstrated how to hold the revolver, coaching Mrs. McLaughlin to aim with an outstretched arm and eyes over the barrel. Then he cocked the weapon and moved to the other side of the stage. Mrs. McLaughlin was still reticent to fire the gun, or even to aim it at a living human being, but Belvedere exhorted her. "Pull the trigger!" he shouted. "Now!" She did so. There was a deafening report as the gun went off, and the smell of gunpowder was everywhere. Belvedere reached forward with his right hand and plucked the speeding bullet out of mid-air, without injury to himself. He showed the slug, in the palm of his hand, to all assembled. Amazement once again ensued.

There was a dance to end the evening. Before it was over, Belvedere escorted Mrs. McLaughlin home because she was tired. I stayed for an hour and watched the festivities. The Métis jigs were particularly remarkable. One fellow, in moccasins and dancing all alone, executed a jig based on the gait of a horse that was so convincing you might have sworn an actual horse had been led into the hall.

When I arrived home that evening, Mrs. McLaughlin was sitting on the chaise longue in the parlour, and Belvedere was leaning on the mantlepiece across the room from her. I immediately felt that I had interrupted something. Mrs. McLaughlin's curls looked slightly awry, and she sat smoothing the folds in her dress as I entered. Stroking his moustache furtively, Belvedere looked like he was in possession of a deep, dark secret.

There was no conversation. The three of us looked at one another for a long few seconds, and then I said the first thing that came to mind. "Frosty out there."

There was a barrage of responses. "Yes," Belvedere replied, "quite warm in here, though."

"Quite warm," Mrs. McLaughlin added.

I had little more to say. "Well then." I kicked off my boots. "Guess I'll be heading up to bed."

BELVEDERE and I rode north again early the next morning. It was another cold day, but the wind had died down mercifully. I tried to strike up a conversation as we rode. "Seems like you and the missus are getting along quite well," I said, as our horses laboured through the wagon-rutted snow.

"What's that supposed to mean?" Belvedere looked at me sidelong.

"Just that you seem suddenly quite close."

"And is that any business of yours?" He kicked his horse in the flank, spurring the animal through a heavy patch of snow.

"She's in a fragile state," I warned. "Her husband died only two months ago."

Belvedere peered at me peevishly. "She's a grown woman," he said, "capable of conducting her own affairs."

We arrived at the Glendenning farm at two o'clock in the afternoon. The house was wood-frame and unpainted, two stories tall. We didn't go inside. Oliver Glendenning was out in the yard, carrying a sheaf of hay on the tines of a pitchfork from the stack to the barn. He was tall, rangy, and plain-spoken. Neither of us had met Mr. Glendenning before. We asked him the usual questions. Had anybody offered to buy his land recently? Did he have any idea who might have wanted to kill his neighbours? When the answers to these questions were all negative, Belvedere asked him if he'd seen anything untoward out there in recent days.

"Nothing out of the ordinary," Glendenning replied. "There's loggers out on the road, but that's about it."

"Seen anyone by the name of Scribang? Little bespectacled fellow?"

"No, sir, I haven't."

"We want you to be vigilant," said Belvedere. "Especially with people you don't know."

"Oh, I am," Glendenning said. "You can bet on that."

One mile further up the logging road was another homestead. Belvedere had been told that a young man named Colbishaw lived there, but we could find little sign of Colbishaw, when we arrived in the yard. There was no livestock in the small corral behind the barn. We knocked at the door of his squat log cabin, but there was no response.

Belvedere pulled the door open, and we entered. The cabin was bare, with no sign of any food in the cupboard and no bedding on the makeshift wooden bed. The stove was cold, and there was an absence of wood in the box beside it. We could see our breath in the air, even inside the building. It was so cold that even the rats had vacated in hopes of better quarters.

When we went outside again, Belvedere called the man's name five or six times. There was no answer.

"Gone," I said.

"Maybe gone back to Ontario for the winter," Belvedere replied. "One can only hope." Before leaving, we performed a cursory inspection of the barn and the pasture and could not find any sign of the man.

We visited two other homesteads before heading back to town. Neither Jack Parsons nor Emil Landis had been coerced into selling their land, and neither had any idea who might have shot McKay or Cantrell.

We were travelling south along the logging road as darkness fell. I didn't think it was the right time to bring up Mrs. McLaughlin again, although I was worried about her, so we rode in silence through the quiet forest. I was comforted by the warmth of Emily's scarf around my neck.

Shots rang out. I felt a rush of cold air as a slug whizzed by my face.

"Get down for gawd's sake, Montgomery!" Belvedere was already on the ground beside his horse. Rifle in hand, he hobbled toward a tree at the edge of the clearing and took cover behind it. Not as practiced as Belvedere in these matters, I was late and awkward. Sliding off my horse, I hit the ground with a thud as another slug displaced the air behind my head. Then I, too, rushed for cover behind a fallen log, some twenty feet away from Belvedere. It was amazing that the horses had not been hit. They stood their ground along the logging road as if gunfire was routine and expected in their brief lives.

Belvedere yelled at me. "Are you hit?"

"Don't think so."

"Have you got your revolver?"

"I do." I had only ever fired the gun in target practice at some tin cans on the upper rung of a fence.

"Stay here!" Belvedere exhorted. "And shoot anything that moves." He paused for a moment and grinned, as if to put me at ease. "Except me."

It was difficult to tell where exactly the shots had been coming from, as they echoed through the forest in an unspecified way. I unholstered my revolver and glanced about frantically. Belvedere stood at a crouch, his rifle in one hand, and charged farther into the forest.

All was silence. He arrived at the cover of one tree and then another. Soon, he was out of sight. There were more gunshots, none of them fired at me as far as I could tell. Then there was silence again.

I kept vigil. Minutes passed, and the grey shades of early evening descended into a deep abyss of blackness. There was no sound. The snow began to fall in soft flakes. My feet and hands were numb with cold. There was a rustling in the bush not more than fifty feet in front of me. I called Belvedere's name. When he did not answer, I opened fire, aiming the Enfield as I had been taught, one eye directly over the barrel. After a moment, a deer leaped out of the thicket and bounded off, deeper into the forest and away from the commotion of my poorly aimed handgun.

I heard a voice behind me. "You called?" Wheeling around, I aimed my revolver again. "It's me, Belvedere."

"My gawd, you frightened me!" I lowered my weapon.

Belvedere sauntered toward me, his rifle at his side. "Thank you for not shooting at me. Not that you were likely to hit anything."

"Did you find the man?"

"I saw the back of him," Belvedere said. "He high-tailed it toward town."

"Are you sure he's gone?"

"He's gone." Belvedere sat on a tree stump near me. "He was riding a fast horse, maybe fifteen hands high."

I holstered my gun and took a deep breath. I must have looked ashen. Belvedere asked if I was all right.

"Never been shot at before, that's all."

"We must be getting close to something." He spat into the snow.

Relief washed over me, and I found myself grinning at Belvedere. "He wasn't a very good shot."

"Either that," Belvedere said, "or he was only hoping to scare us off."

14

We arrived back at the McLaughlin house well after midnight. As soon as we walked in the door, Mrs. McLaughlin came out of the parlour in her dressing gown. Her ringlets were hanging down around her face, and her eyes were dark with exhaustion. “You’re here,” she said, more to the room than to anyone in particular. “I was worried about you.” She was holding Belvedere’s mutt in her arms, and I could see that she was wearing the heart-shaped pendant he’d bought for her at Christmas.

Suddenly more polite than he had hitherto been, Belvedere kicked off his boots and stood sock-footed in the foyer. “Busy night,” he said.

“I’ve left some supper for you on the table.”

She escorted us into the kitchen. On the table was a feast of roast chicken and boiled potatoes. China plates and cutlery had been placed meticulously on either side of the table in front of two chairs. A candle, once tall and new, sputtered at the centre, rivulets of wax cascading down toward the brass holder. “It’s cold now,” Mrs. McLaughlin said, “but perhaps still edible.” Belvedere dived right in, prying a leg off the chicken with his bare hands, spooning a mess of potatoes onto his plate. I followed suit, and we ate gluttonously. Mrs. McLaughlin perched on a chair at the head of the table. "Was it an eventful evening?"

"Not to speak of," Belvedere replied.

Mrs. McLaughlin's gaze fell upon me. "No excitement?"

"Nothing really." It didn't seem right to worry the lady over a police affair.

We ate the rest of the meal in silence. When Belvedere dished up a second helping and appeared to be going nowhere for some time, I excused myself and went upstairs to bed. Sleep came early and hard after such a strenuous and anxiety-provoking day, but I did awaken briefly at about two o'clock when I heard Belvedere climbing up to bed.

BELVEDERE WAS SITTING at breakfast the next morning when I clumped down the stairs, tired and bedraggled. He was gnawing at a piece of stale toast while his mutt sat expectantly at his feet. Mrs. McLaughlin poured a cup of coffee and placed it before me on the table. There was something different about her. Perhaps it was merely that she had abandoned her usually severe hairstyle and that her ringlets hung down around her shoulders. But it was more than that. A light gleamed in her eyes that I had not seen before; it seemed that she had regained her appetite for living. She remarked on my unkempt appearance. "You look like you've been dragged through a knothole backwards, Surgeon Montgomery."

I took a sip of the bitter coffee. "Haven't been sleeping well."

"Is your bedroom too cold?" she asked. "Is there something wrong with the bed?"

"No, it's nothing like that," I said. "Can't really put my finger on it."

She made herself busy, frying an egg at the stove. Belvedere slipped a morsel of salted pork to his dog. "We're riding out after breakfast," he said to me. "You'll need to pack your handgun and some ammunition."

I warmed my hands around the coffee cup and thought about how cold it was outside. "Where are we off to today?"

Belvedere looked at Mrs. McLaughlin surreptitiously. He dandled his dog, and the hound bristled with the joy of being attended to. "Can't really talk about it here."

After eating my meal of fried eggs and salted pork, I went upstairs to retrieve my revolver and some ammunition. Having lived through the previous evening, I was worried about the events of the coming day. It seemed that violence followed Belvedere wherever he went, and it was the first time he'd ever requested that I pack my firearm. I knew that I would be of little use in a gunfight.

As we walked to the Mounted Police stable on that crisp, wintry morning, I questioned Belvedere again. "Where is it that we're going?"

"You'll see." He was favouring his hurt leg again. The cold must have penetrated through to the bone. I could smell the strong scent of the salesman's lineament as we walked.

We saddled our horses and ventured south and east of the town, over vast windswept meadows that were almost bereft of snow and past stands of poplar. In a small valley shielded on all sides by trees, we reined our horses to a standstill, and Belvedere jumped down from the saddle. "Why are we stopping here?" I asked.

"Because you need to learn how to shoot," he said. "Otherwise, you're a liability to me and a danger to yourself."

I climbed down from my horse. "That's why you brought me here?"

"I'm paying you the honour," he said, "of teaching you how to save your life. Since no one else seems to have done that for you."

I did not bother to tell him that my own father had been killed in action at Antietam when I was barely two years old. After he died, there was no one in my family who might have taught me how to use a firearm. I'd had a brisk training in the use and care of a handgun when I joined the Mounted Police some months earlier, but had only fired at a target on one occasion. "I was hired as a surgeon," I told Belvedere. "I'm paid to save people's lives, not take them."

Belvedere's eyes narrowed. "You wouldn't shoot somebody? Not even to save your own life?"

I saw my breath form white crystals in the air as I exhaled. "Well, I suppose if it was to save my own life—"

"You'd better be willing to do as much as that," Belvedere said, "or you have no business being a mounted policeman." He grabbed his saddle bag and limped to the edge of the clearing. Fishing three empty whisky bottles out of the saddlebag, he placed them in the snow, some fifty feet away from me. Then he strolled back to where I was standing. "Let me see your weapon."

I handed him my revolver, and he examined it for some time. "These goddamn Enfields," he said, "they loosen up at the barrel break after a while, and then you can't hit the broad side of a barn with them. But yours is still in pristine condition." He handed the gun back to me and stepped to one side. "I want you to take aim at one of those whisky bottles and squeeze off a shot."

I had sense enough to spread my feet and look down the barrel of the revolver before I fired. The gun recoiled, and I could see a small puff of powdery snow a good five feet from where the whisky bottles were placed. Belvedere looked on, and I did not read in his appearance anything like optimism. "We'll try that again," he said. "This time, I want you to stand sideways to your target and look down your shoulder like the gun is just an extension of your arm."

I took aim again.

"Relax your eyes," Belvedere said. "Blink a few times and make sure you're seeing correctly." My eyes were watering from the cold, but I did manage to blink a few times before pulling the trigger. There was another puff of snow, this time closer to the empty bottles."Better," Belvedere said, "but you still would have missed your man. Try it again, but this time, concentrate on your breathing."

"What do you mean?" I asked.

"Take a deep breath and hold it, just before you shoot." I did so, and the puff of snow was closer to the whisky bottles than before. Belvedere thought for a moment. "You're pulling the trigger like it's a mechanical thing," he said. "You've got to caress it like a beautiful woman's earlobe."

I couldn't help but smirk. "Caress it like a woman's earlobe?"

"And squeeze it like a lady's hand at a church service."

I tried to put this advice to good use, but I was nearly shaking with mirth. I fired the gun three more times and still did not smash any of the bottles. We spent the better part of the morning taking target practice, and I think I got to be a marginally better shot, but Belvedere did not see fit to shower me with praise. "You're never going to be a marksman," he said at last, "but at least you're using the firearm correctly. I'll give you that."

We rode quietly back into town in the early afternoon. I prayed, all the way there, that I might never be forced to use my handgun in anger. At the stables, Belvedere was quicker unsaddling his horse than I, and he was already eating a late lunch by the time I returned to the McLaughlin house.

Sergeant Slade and his men rode back into town three days later. I met them at the police stables, where I was checking up on Belle after our sojourn to the country. Slade looked like a man who had just walked the entire length of the Northwest Passage barefoot. His nose was almost black with frostbite, and his fingers, as he blew on them, looked like the uncured meat one might see hanging in a butcher's shop window. He walked with the gait of a fellow who had been frozen into his own saddle.

His men did not look like they had fared much better than their commanding officer during their days and nights on the farmer's trail. The search for Sinclair had been fruitless, Slade told me. "The blighter evaporated into the night air!" he said. "But don't worry. I'll have every Mountie between here and Maple Creek out looking for him by this time tomorrow!"

At breakfast the next morning, Belvedere announced that we would once again be visiting the site of the first murder. "Why?" I wondered aloud. I thought we had pretty much gone through the place with a fine-toothed comb.

Belvedere shoved a slice of burnt toast into his mouth. "Something's not quite right."

Again holding the dog, with which she had become quite inseparable, Mrs. McLaughlin saw us off at the doorstep. We strode downtown, and Belvedere's step seemed full of resolve, but we did not go directly to the laundry. Instead, Belvedere led me again to Sam Gee's hole-in-the-wall café on River Street.

Some men sat in one corner of the café, playing a dominoes game. Still in his traditional cap and tunic, Gee approached us as soon as we walked in the door. "Gentlemen," he said, "are you here to see Ruby Chen again?" Belvedere said no. "Maybe you like a cup of coffee? Maybe green tea?"

Belvedere didn't mince words. "We need you to come with us."

Sam Gee looked suddenly deflated, as though he were about to be deported back to China. "My papers are in order."

"Put your coat on," Belvedere said, "and come with us."

The man was hesitant, but he did eventually find a coat in the back room. When he returned to the dining area, Gee exhorted the men at the corner table to leave their payment for the tea on the counter. We went outside into the cold and walked toward the laundry. "Were you friends with the laundryman Chen?" Belvedere asked him as we huffed down the street.

"Of course."

"Any idea who killed him?"

"It wasn't me."

We arrived at the back door of the laundry. Nothing much

had changed except that four feet of snow now covered the ground where the laundryman had died. Belvedere kicked snow away from the sill and pried the door open. "Dogs!" he shouted before entering. "Get the hell out!" There were no dogs on the premises. Nevertheless, we ventured inside tentatively, edging through the darkened back room and through to the front desk. Sam Gee looked stunned. He was likely wondering if he was about to be charged with the murder of his countryman.

We were standing in front of the blackboard on the wall. "Do you read Chinese?" Belvedere asked.

"I read Mandarin."

Belvedere pointed his mittened hand at the Chinese lettering on the blackboard. "Is that Mandarin?"

"It is."

"What's it say?"

Gee pondered the lettering for a moment. "It is a name, I think."

"A name?"

"Not sure how to translate." Gee pointed to the four Chinese letters in order. "*Si kei bei ang*. Not sure how you translate."

"C.K. Bang?" I offered.

Gee looked at me with what could only be described as a soupçon of derision. "Is a proper name. *Si kei bei ang*. Maybe an English name?"

Belvedere took his mitten off and raked his beard with his fingers. "Can you write it down for us? In English letters?"

"I can." Gee found a piece of chalk on the ledge and wrote the English lettering at the bottom of the blackboard. Belvedere stood, for some time, memorizing the four words that Gee had spelled out. Gee looked at him expectantly.

"Thank you, Mister Gee," Belvedere muttered. "You may go now."

The creases in Sam Gee's face softened. "I may go?"

"And thank you for your help."

Gee smiled at Belvedere and then at me, and then he hurried

out the door. His step was sprightly again, as it had been when we first saw him in the café.

Belvedere was still gazing at the blackboard. "*Si kei bei ang*. *Si kei bei ang*. Who might that be, Montgomery?"

"I haven't the foggiest."

"Is it possible that Mr. Scribang paid a visit here, as well, in the days before the laundryman was murdered?"

I looked back at the blackboard and then at Belvedere as the logic dawned on me. "Yes, yes, yes. Yes, of course."

As we exited the abandoned laundry, Belvedere noticed a surveyor setting up his sextant on a tripod on the riverbank across the street. The surveyor was a young man, ruddy-faced and blond-haired. He was working without mittens, attempting to sight the sextant at the bright morning sun. There was a semi-circle of dogs around him, and he swore and kicked at them occasionally.

We approached the man. The dogs scattered when they saw Belvedere. "Are you with the telegraph?" Belvedere asked the surveyor.

"No, sir," the young man said, "I work for the Canadian Pacific Railway."

"Is the railroad coming through here soon?"

"That remains to be seen," the surveyor said, shuffling from foot to foot in the knee-deep snow. "Sir John A. can't make up his mind."

Belvedere pulled a handkerchief out of his pocket and wiped his nose. "How so?"

The surveyor shook his head, grinning. "Some say it's comin' north along the river, all the way to Whitehorse. But they're also talkin' about a line across the southern plains."

Belvedere thought for a moment. "Must be serious about coming through here if they sent you."

"They got surveyors down south, as well," said the young man. "Tryin to suss out the best route, I guess. This route has been surveyed once before. They sent me out here again to make sure of the coordinates."

Belvedere squinted into the distance. "If the railroad comes through the northern route, is there a plan to bridge it across the river?"

"There'd be a bridge right here," the young man replied. "Runnin' due north."

I looked to the north and to the south. The proposed bridge seemed to line up directly with Chen's laundry. A coincidence, maybe? I couldn't be sure.

"And does the Canadian Pacific Railway own the land on which this line will run?" Belvedere asked.

"Not yet." The surveyor was blowing on his fingers to keep them warm. "But the company'll pay top dollar if it comes this way."

Belvedere looked at me and then back at the young man. "We'll let you get back to your work."

The surveyor had his eyes on the dogs that were huddled in a pack about fifty feet away. "Wisht I could keep these mutts at bay for the next half hour."

Belvedere unholstered his revolver and fired a shot in the air. The dogs scattered across River Street. "That ought to hold the bastards for a minute or two."

WE PAID another visit to Mr. Whitney at the Land Office the next day. He was attired in the same suit, immaculately, I might add, collar starched high around his skinny neck. His desk was also as tidy as it had been: one pen, one ink well, one sheet of crisp white paper. It seemed as if nothing had moved. Whitney donned his spectacles when he saw us enter, got up from his desk, and approached the counter. "Yes?' he said. "Can I help you?"

"We're interested in the railroad," Belvedere replied. "Do you have a surveyor's map?"

Whitney peered at us over his glasses. "And what business do you have with the railroad?"

Belvedere straightened up and glared at the man. "Never mind what fekking business," he growled. "We're officers of the gawd-damn law."

Whitney's eyes widened behind his thick glasses. "I was merely making pleasantries," he said. "No need to get excited." When Belvedere didn't respond verbally, the land agent scurried back to a filing cabinet and located the map. "Ah, yes," he said, "here is what you are looking for." He returned to the counter and unfolded the map carefully in front of us. Perhaps two feet by two feet, the map was a conundrum of squares, straight and curved lines, and numbers.

Belvedere studied it for some time. "I can't make this out." He pointed at a set of numbers. "What's this mean?"

Whitney grew officious again. "Those, my good man, are a set of coordinates. One hundred and five degrees and forty-five minutes west of the second meridian."

"Christ," Belvedere said, "it's all Greek to me." With his forefinger, he traced a line up the centre of the map. "Is this the coming railway?"

"It is."

Belvedere pointed at a half-section north of the river. "Whose property is that?"

"I'd have to look it up," said Whitney.

"Please do."

Mumbling to himself, Whitney went to another filing cabinet, slid the door open, and combed through it with a trained hand. He pulled out a file and brought it to the counter. "That appears to be the homestead of Alexander McKay."

Belvedere's eyes were like blazing meteors. "McKay owned that land?"

"Correct."

He pointed again with his finger at the map. "Then this to the north would be Herman Cantrell's?"

"If Cantrell homesteaded directly north of McKay, yes."

Belvedere pressed his forefinger into the map again, at a point near the south bank of the river. "And this is where the railway comes through town?"

"Yes."

"Who owns that property?"

"I'll check."

I don't think the land agent was certain what the excitement was about, but he was somehow caught up in it. He trotted off to the second cabinet and came back with another file. He placed it on the counter in front of us, and Belvedere flipped open the cover. In bold letters was the name of the laundryman, Chaoxing Chen.

"As I expected." Belvedere shot a stern glance at Whitney. "All these people are now deceased. What will happen to their property?"

"They have been put up for public tender, of course."

"Meaning what?"

Whitney took off his spectacles and began polishing them with a spotless handkerchief. "Meaning that we are even now in the process of accepting sealed bids on each of them."

"Any idea who is bidding?"

"We won't know who the bidders are," Whitney replied, "until the bids are unsealed on the fifteenth of February."

Belvedere was almost beside himself. "The fifteenth of February?"

Whitney smiled at him inscrutably. "That is the law," he said. "Unless you're of a mind to break it."

As we walked back to the McLaughlin house afterwards, I broached the idea of opening the seals before the due date. "Couldn't we get a judge to issue a warrant or some such?"

Belvedere spat furiously into the snow. "How?" he asked. "The nearest judge is in Regina. It'd take a week for our letter to get there and another week for the judge to get his fat ass up here."

We trudged past gloomy houses up the hill. The winter seemed suddenly long. "Looks like we're doomed to wait, then."

"Looks like it."

THE FIFTEENTH of February was two weeks away. In the meantime, Belvedere and I busied ourselves canvassing landowners south of the river on whose property the railroad might eventually be situated. We extended our reach as far as Egil Johnson's homestead, where I had poached a Christmas tree some time earlier. Mr. Johnson was an elderly man. When we met him at the door of his wood-frame house, he was wearing a tweed waistcoat that looked about as old as he. His white hair was neatly parted. He looked to be a country gentleman. Smiling genially, he said, "The Queen's cowboys have finally arrived."

Belvedere stepped forward. "May we come in?"

"Don't see why not." The old man escorted us into the kitchen of his warm house. "Take a seat, if you please." Still dressed in our buffalo coats, we dutifully sat on his wooden chairs. "Would you care for a cup of tea and apple cider vinegar?"

"Tea and apple cider vinegar?" I'd never heard of such a concoction before.

Johnson winked at me. "Good for the circulation."

"We'll pass on the tea," Belvedere said. "We want to ask about your homestead. Has anyone offered to purchase it?"

The old man was pouring himself a tin cupful of his circulation medicine. "As a matter of fact, yes. Some months ago. Fella named Scribante offered me two hundred dollars for the place."

"That's not a bad price," I said. Belvedere looked at me like I was an idiot.

"I didn't accept his offer," Johnson said.

"This fellow Scribante," Belvedeere said. "What did he look like?"

Johnson placed his cup on the table and looked up at the ceiling. "Can't rightly remember much about him. He was an eastern-looking fella. Little man with a leather satchel. His hair and beard were trimmed. Kinda looked like a muskrat."

"Ever seen him around here since?"

"Nope," the old man said. "I expect he went back to wherever he calls home."

WE WERE ENTERTAINED, a few evenings later, with a production of *My Old Blue Bell*, produced and enacted at Treston Hall by members of Sergeant Slade's regiment. Belvedere and I attended in uniform because we had no other formal clothes. We escorted Mrs. McLaughlin to the hall. She clung to both of us for support as we traversed the snowbound streets. Then, inside the hall, she sat between us, a beautiful portrait of Venus between two likenesses of Mars.

She had positively bloomed over the past month. Gone were the drab, dark weeds of mourning. She was attired in a bright-blue dress on that evening, and it set off her eyes in the most dazzling way. Witty, too, and enlivened by the evening, she charmed us with her conversation. When she saw the backdrop for the play, an interior with doors, windows, tables, and chairs crudely painted, she nudged me and said, "I see they've spared no expense, hiring the best artists money could buy."

The remainder of the evening was equally worthy of laughter. First Sub-Constable Parry mounted the stage. He was got up as the heroine of the play, wearing a blue gown, but not nearly so well as Mrs. McLaughlin. Somebody had plastered his face with about two inches of makeup. He ambled and lisped and stammered his way through the early lines to great comedic effect, although I am not sure that was the only effect for which the production was striving.

There was much hijinks and pandemonium when Sergeant Slade himself entered as Parry's first suitor. Either he had recovered from his frostbite, or he had used ten pounds of stage makeup to disguise its ill effects. It was clear from his overwrought performance that Slade fancied himself the poor man's Henry Irving. He strutted about the stage and delivered his lines in a pseudo-British accent that produced guffaws both intended and unintended. While Slade attempted to woo Sub-Constable Parry on bended knee, Belvedere turned to me and whispered, a little too loudly, "That ponce belongs on the stage."

For his part, Parry was reticent to accept the hand of an esteemed soldier, the like of which Slade was playing. Retreating to one side of the stage, and with the back of his hand to his forehead, he exclaimed, "N-n-n-never sh-sh-shall I w-w-w-wed!" At last, a more suitable and younger constable came into view as the object of Parry's real affections, and Parry was induced to marry the young man. The burletta ended with a triumphal wedding march and many curtain calls. Sergeant Slade seemed particularly chuffed by the attention he was receiving.

Our walk home after the play was full of frivolity and fun. There was a southern wind, and with it came the warm promise of springtime. When we arrived at the house, Mrs. McLaughlin poured a glass of sherry for each of us, and we sat around the dining room table, critiquing the play and its actors.

I excused myself early and went upstairs, where I penned a letter to Emily, finally taking Mrs. McLaughlin's advice and writing further about my feelings regarding my medical practice and the possibility that I might not return to it. Belvedere and Mrs. McLaughlin conversed in hushed tones for some time, and then all went silent. I was in bed by the time I heard Belvedere's footfalls on the stairs.

I must admit that I was more than a little rankled by Belvedere's seduction of the poor widow and by her acceptance of him. She had, just over a month before, displayed a passing interest in me. I felt that Belvedere was the wrong man for Mrs. McLaughlin. Sometimes, women who have been subjected to abuse blame themselves, and they willingly seek out other abusers. Belvedere was not a man who would have much to offer a woman outside of his mere presence from time to time. I worried and believed that he would hurt Mrs. McLaughlin in the end.

A WEEKEND WAS ONCE AGAIN upon us, and I decided to revisit the Sioux encampment where I had twice administered medical aid to the young boy. It was the second day of February, and it was still quite cold, but the journey to the encampment was only a distance of about three miles. I wore almost every article of clothing in my possession, and my heavy coat on top of all of that. Even so, my feet were petrified by the time I'd saddled Belle and led her out of the stable. I could have wished for a nice caboose with a coal stove blazing in front of me as I rode.

The encampment was quiet when I arrived, but the dogs ran up to greet me. They were much more well-behaved than the town dogs; they barked, but they did not offer to bite me or to nip at the haunches of my horse. I dismounted without incident and tethered Belle to a tree. Moments later, a tipi flap opened and Good Voice emerged, a blanket around his shoulders.

"I've come to look at your grandson," I said. "Is he—" I was suddenly apprehensive, fearing that the boy might have died.

Good Voice studied me cooly. His face was difficult to read. "The boy is well."

"May I see him?"

He gestured toward another tipi with his hand. "Follow me."

Entering the grandson's abode, I was greeted with a domestic scene. A small fire was burning in the middle of the tipi, smoke rising through a buffalo hide flue twenty feet above us. The space was surprisingly warm, with hides of various animals spread on the ground. The boy was sitting off to one side with his father. They each had a toy in their hands that looked like a piece of bone attached with sinews to a short stick. The father was showing his son how to whirl the bone until the sinew was taut and twisted. As the sinew then unwound in the opposite direction, the toy made a buzzing noise like mosquitoes in summer. With his own toy, the son perfected the motion, and his father uttered words that sounded encouraging.

The boy was clearly in good health. He looked up but did not recognize me. His father said something to the boy and gestured with his eyes toward me. His mother sat on the other side of the fire, beading a swatch of leather. She smiled shyly at me but did not attempt to say anything. Approaching the boy cautiously, I asked, "Do you remember me?" The boy shook his head, perhaps more out of fear than understanding. I tried to reassure him with a smile, and then I laid my fingers gently across his wrist. His pulse was normal and strong. I retrieved my stethoscope from the medical bag and showed it to him. "May I listen to you with this instrument?"

The boy nodded. He at least knew that I was asking a question. I rubbed the scope's chest-piece in my hands to warm it up, and then I held it against the boy's chest, just below the neck. He winced at the foreignness of it all. I could hear no rasp in his breathing. I slipped the stethoscope down the back of his shirt and listened. Then I turned to Good Voice. "He has recovered." It felt like a wave had washed over me, a wave that washed clean all my despair and guilt. I had made my recompense to the universe.

The old man nodded. "My daughter has made you a gift." He said some words in Lakota to his daughter, and she retrieved a pair of moccasins from the inside perimeter of the tipi. She gave the moccasins to her father, and he handed them to me. "In gratitude."

The moccasins were beautiful, painstakingly beaded. "Thank you," I said. Because my feet were still blocks of ice, I resisted the urge to take off my boots and try on the moccasins.

Good Voice led me out of the tipi, and we walked back toward my horse. The old man put his hand on my shoulder. "If there is anything else I can do—"

"There is one thing," I said quickly. "I would like to sketch you."

He seemed taken aback. "To sketch me?"

"To make a picture," I said, motioning vaguely with my hands to demonstrate what that might look like.

Good Voice's brow was furrowed. "Why?"

"So that I can remember you when I am away."

He seemed suddenly a little frightened. "A picture from a box?"

"No," I said, "a drawing. With charcoal."

It was clear that the chief did not think much of the idea, but he did agree to let me make his portrait, probably out of a sense of indebtedness. We went into his tipi, where an old woman was tending the fire, and I remained there for the better part of two hours, rendering the man's likeness onto a skein of parchment. I drew him in profile, making sure to capture the furrows around the old man's eyes, his majestic nose, and the long grey hair that hung in braids over his shoulder.

15

On Valentine's Day, Belvedere and I trudged down to our morning breakfast while Mrs. McLaughlin stirred a pot of porridge that was congealing on the hot stove. Mrs. McLaughlin's culinary skills had not improved over the intervening months, but she was beginning to approach the task with more zeal. On the table beside our respective bowls were two small paper hearts. Mrs. McLaughlin had written, on the back of mine: "To Surgeon Montgomery. Always in my heart. Olivia." Signing her first name seemed odd to me; I had only ever addressed her before as Mrs. McLaughlin. Belvedere had read his own paper heart by the time I looked up at him. He smiled to himself and deposited the heart in his breast pocket, wearing it like a knight wears a talisman from his lady. Mrs. McLaughlin dolloped the porridge into our bowls.

That afternoon, I had some business downtown. When I returned to the house at three o'clock or so, Belvedere and Mrs. McLaughlin were in her bedroom. The little dog was barking at the bedroom door, left out of the festivities. I tiptoed up the stairs so as not to embarrass them and wrote my Emily another long and passionate letter. I asked again for her forgiveness. Then I told her that I loved her and hoped to be with her in whatever future the good Lord had planned for us.

WE WERE STANDING at the Land Office door at quarter to nine on the morning of February 15. There was a dampness in the air, coming off the nearby river, which was somehow more chilling to the bone than forty below zero had been. The land agent came trundling down the boardwalk at 8:55 precisely. He smiled as though he had won some precious victory over us, and then he slid his key into the lock. We followed him inside. Meticulously, he unfurled the woollen scarf that was wrapped tightly around his neck. He placed his hat on the top hook of the coat rack and slowly unbuttoned his tweed overcoat. After blowing his nose into a handkerchief, he went to his desk and traded his winter boots for a pair of oxfords. The clock on the wall struck nine, and the land agent proceeded to the other side of the counter. "May I help you, gentlemen?"

Belvedere's face was a death mask. "We're here for the opening of the tenders."

Whitney took his spectacles off and began cleaning them frantically. "We usually wait until noon to open the tenders."

"Is there another mail wagon coming in before noon?" Belvedere's hands were twitching.

Whitney paused in his pursuit of clearer vision. "I don't believe so."

"Then we'll open them now."

His resolve crumbling, Whitney put his glasses back on his face. "Very well. If we must." He went to the black metal safe near the rear of the building and blew on his fingers like a safe cracker at the beginning of a robbery. Shielding the lock with his body so that we could not see the combination, he worked at opening the safe. When at last the door was ajar, Whitney produced a manila envelope and brought it back to the counter. With a letter opener, he meticulously unsealed the manila envelope and dumped a stack of smaller envelopes onto the counter in front of him. Using the letter opener again with dexterity, he proceeded to open each smaller envelope in order.

There were several tenders for McKay's property and for Cantrell's, one of them coming from McKay's neighbour, Jack Parsons, who had offered the tidy sum of two hundred dollars for each quarter-section. We were most interested when Whitney opened a legalistic-looking envelope from the law firm of Walters and Scribante. The return address on the envelope clarified that Walters and Scribante had their offices in Winnipeg. Acting in proxy for an unnamed individual, they offered three hundred and fifty dollars for each of the two properties. Whitney was jubilant. "Looks like we have a clear winner," he said.

Belvedere thought for a moment, then peered at the land agent. "Do you know anything about this law firm?"

"I do not, sir," Whitney said, "but I believe them to be reputable."

On our way home that morning, Belvedere asked me to pen a letter to police headquarters in Winnipeg on his behalf. "I see you posting letters all the time," he said. "You're a better writer than I." He wanted me to ask the commanding officer for an investigation into the law firm of Walters and Scribante and to find out whom they represented.

I wrote the letter that afternoon, read it to Belvedere upstairs in his room, and had him sign it. The letter was posted promptly, but I knew that we were in for a wait. The mail wagon crawls slowly across the prairies, especially in the waning days of winter, and it would most certainly be weeks before an investigation could be conducted and a reply obtained.

As luck would have it, Judge McCabe careened into town five days later, with a view to trying Abel Dickson for the murders to which he'd confessed. He was the same judge who had appeared for the Haggardy case. We hoped he'd had a happier journey to Prince Albert settlement this time around, with no upsot cabooses and no coal burns on his face. Belvedere heard, from Sub-Constable Parry, that the preliminary hearing would take place in Treston Hall in two days' time.

I had an interest in the case, believing Abel Dickson to be innocent of the murders, and so I walked down to Treston Hall on the day of the hearing. There were not many people present in the hall as the hearing was preliminary, only Judge McCabe, a fellow from Regina who served as prosecuting attorney, Hayter Reid, Prince Albert settlement's only lawyer, Sergeant Slade, and Old Joe Scriver. Shackled at his wrists and ankles, Abel Dickson sat at a desk with Reid, who was his defence attorney. Dickson looked like he didn't know where he was. He glanced around the cavernous hall furtively, his gaze settling on no one in particular. The voices of the judge and lawyers echoed in the empty space, making it difficult to hear some of the proceedings.

Judge McCabe read the charges against Abel Dickson and asked him if he understood what those charges meant. Dickson looked at his uncle for confirmation, and then he said to the judge, "I think so. Yes. I think so."

Then the prosecuting attorney began his spiel, acting as if it were an open-and-shut case. The defendant had already confessed to the crimes, he said, and while motive was yet to be discussed, the defendant certainly had the opportunity to commit the murders. He called Sergeant Slade to the stand. Slade was puffed up by all the attention he was receiving. "Sergeant Slade," the prosecutor began, after Slade had recited the oath, "you were the arresting officer, were you not?"

Slade's voice boomed through the hall. "I was indeed."

The prosecuting attorney meandered back and forth in front of his witness. "And why did you see fit to arrest this individual?"

"The search for the murderer had been ongoing for some time," Slade replied, with a glance at me. "The defendant was well-known in the town, and he had been boasting about killing all three men for some time."

This assertion stopped the prosecuting attorney in his tracks. "Boasting? To whom?"

"To the local sheriff, for one." The sergeant was in his element now. He enumerated all the people he had interviewed. "But also to the butcher. And to the local dentist."

"He told all three of them?"

"Yes."

The prosecutor edged closer to Slade. "And have you ascribed a motive for these killings?"

Slade shook his head. "Some people simply enjoy the suffering of others," he said. "Human life is not meaningful to them."

At that moment, Joe Scriver fairly leapt out of his seat. "That's malarkey, plain and simple!" he shouted. "You know he don't have the wherewithal to kill no one!"

The judge was quick to intervene. "Order in this court," he said, "or I will have you forcefully ejected." Suitably chastened, Joe Scriver sat down again.

The prosecuting attorney continued with his interrogation. "And you've confiscated the murder weapon?" he asked the sergeant.

"I have."

"Where is it now?"

Slade pointed at a Winchester rifle that lay upon an evidence table to his left, the same Winchester rifle I had seen in the livery tack room. "That's the gun, right there."

The prosecutor returned to his desk. "I have no further questions, Your Honour." He sat down with a flourish.

Judge McCabe turned to Slade. "You may step down." Having enjoyed his time in the sun, Sergeant Slade seemed reticent to step down from the stand, but eventually, he did.

It was Hayter Reid's turn to speak up in defence of Abel Dickson. More homespun than the prosecutor, Reid spoke in quiet tones about Dickson's infirmity, about his lack of a criminal record, and about his generally pleasant bearing. "The people of this town love him," Reid said. "He's like a good-luck charm to everyone he encounters. I mean to prove that these confessions are nothing more than the result of a dream. Of a bad dream."

He called Joe Scriver to the stand. Scriver gave the judge a cussed look as he hobbled across the room. The oath was read and recited, and Reid began his examination. "Where were you on the afternoons of October 3, November 16, and December 12, Mr. Scriver?"

"I was at the livery, shovelling shit and currying horsehair," Scriver replied. "Where else would I be?"

"And was the defendant with you on those dates?"

"He most certainly was."

"You're sure of that?" Reid asked.

"Sure as God created Heaven and Earth."

Reid approached the bench. "I submit, Your Honour, that those were the dates upon which the murders were committed."

The prosecuting attorney rose with an objection. "Your Honour," he intoned, "this man is the defendant's uncle, and he's liable to say anything that might exonerate his nephew. He's an unreliable witness, Your Honour."

"Duly noted," said the judge. "Have you got any other witnesses, Mr. Reid?"

Reid called Abel Dickson to the stand. When Dickson did not seem to understand what had been asked of him, Reid took him by the hand and led him to the witness box beside the judge. Reid's gambit seemed risky to me; Abel Dickson was liable to say anything under the duress of a cross-examination. Before Reid could speak, Joe Scriver shouted an encouragement at his nephew. "You tell 'em the truth now, and none of that baloney you were spoutin' around town."

"Order!" the judge exhorted. He read the oath to Dickson and asked him if he agreed to tell the truth.

"I surely will."

Reid began his examination, speaking to Dickson in terms he could understand. "Did you kill those men, Abel?"

"Yup. I think I did. My uncle says I didn't, but I think I did."

The judge's jaw nearly dropped to the floor. He decided to intervene. "Do you realize, young man, that the penalty for murder is hanging?"

Dickson looked uncomprehendingly at the judge. "My mama used to say that God hates a liar worst of all."

Reid stepped back into the fray. "You might have dreamed it one night when you were asleep. Don't you think that might be a possibility, Abel?"

"No, sirree, I don't think so."

It seemed for a moment that all was lost and that Abel Dickson might go to the gallows after all. Then Joe Scriver spoke up again. "Ask him about the gun."

The judge had lost his patience. He pointed a finger at Scriver. "Will you kindly shut up?"

Scriver didn't. "Ask him to load the gun, if he's so sure he killed someone!"

"Sir," said the magistrate, "you've left me little choice but to have you removed from my courtroom." He nodded at Sergeant Slade, who immediately got up and took Scriver by the arm. As he was being led out of the courtroom, Scriver continued to natter on about the rifle that was lying on the evidence table. He reached into a pocket with his free hand and produced a handful of bullets, flinging them across the room toward Hayter Reid.

When Scriver was safely out of the building, the proceedings continued. Reid went to the evidence table and picked up the Winchester, holding it with the barrel pointed indiscriminately about, like a man unused to firearms. "May I conduct a little experiment, Your Honour?"

Judge McCabe was immediately apprehensive, crouching forward as if to make himself a smaller target. "If you can do so without getting anybody shot."

Reid found a bullet on the floor in the gallery. He handed the bullet and rifle to Abel Dickson. "I want you to load this rifle," Reid told him. "Load it the way you loaded it when you shot Mr. Chen."

I must admit that I was not entirely comfortable with this turn of events. A rifle and a bullet had been placed in the hands of a mentally incompetent man. I watched closely. Abel Dickson scrutinized the weapon from all angles. He pulled the trigger several times, and the entire room gasped with relief every time a click was heard instead of a bang. He looked down the barrel of the rifle like an astronomer looking through a telescope. Then he tried forcefully to shove the bullet down the end of the barrel, slug first and then cartridge first. When he was unsuccessful in that attempt, he gave the gun back to Hayter Reid. "I can't rightly remember how I did it."

On his feet again, the prosecuting attorney protested loudly against this piece of grandstanding, as he called it. "Any killer might pretend that he did not know how to load a gun," he said, "if it means escaping the noose."

"But the defendant has already admitted to the murders," the judge replied. "He's been complicit in proving his own guilt."

The prosecutor approached the bench. "Perhaps he's had a change of heart, Your Honour. Perhaps he's now complicit in proving his own innocence."

Judge McCabe turned to Abel Dickson. "I'll ask you again, Mr. Dickson: did you murder the laundryman?"

"I think I did," Abel responded, but he was suddenly unsure of himself. "Unless it was a dream like my uncle said."

"And have you ever killed anyone else?"

Abel thought for a moment. He seemed to be deciding which of his exploits were safe to discuss and which were not. "I killed six Mounties one time in a shoot-out down by the forks. Three years ago, I killed a whole band of Indians acrost the river. And once I shot a moose that was twenty feet high."

The judge looked incredulously at the prosecuting attorney

and at Sergeant Slade, who had returned to the room while the attempt to load the gun was being made. "How can the fellow murder if he can't load a gun?" he asked.

When there was no response, he tapped on the desk with his gavel. "This fellow is a nincompoop," he pronounced, "no more capable of murder than a child." He looked squarely at Sergeant Slade. "This is the second time I have been brought to this community for the purpose of trying an ill-conceived case. I must ask that, in future, the North-West Mounted Police ensure their charges are substantial and provable before calling upon the judicial system." He tapped with his gavel again. "This case is dismissed."

The next morning, at breakfast, Belvedere announced that we would be vacating the house for an indeterminate period. "Pack your belongings, Montgomery," he said. "We could be away for some time."

Mrs. McLaughlin, pouring cups of strong coffee, was immediately concerned. "You're going away?"

"Yes."

"Where?"

"That's police business," Belvedere replied. "I'd appreciate it if you would take care of my dog while I'm away."

"I will," she said. "Of course, I will." Her lips trembling, Mrs. McLaughlin placed the coffee pot on the stove and left the room.

I spoke to Belvedere in hushed tones. "Where are we off to?"

"We're going to spend a few nights at Egil Johnson's farm," he whispered back. "He's the only living man we know of who's had an offer from this Scribante character."

After breakfast, I packed my gear in a saddlebag and carried it down to the foyer. Belvedere was waiting for me, coat draped over his broad shoulders, looking impatiently in the direction of Mrs. McLaughlin's bedroom. When she did not come out to see us off, he harumphed once and picked up his saddlebag. "Come on," he growled. "Time's a-wasting."

We arrived at Johnson's homestead before noon. The old man

was surprised to see us. He strolled out of the house with his overcoat absentmindedly unbuttoned as our horses trotted into the yard. "The Mounties have returned!" he exclaimed.

Belvedere dismounted and handed his reins to me. He approached the old man. "We believe you are in some danger."

Johnson looked puzzled. "Why?"

"Because of this fellow, Scribante."

"Because of that muskrat-lookin' city-slicker?"

"Everywhere Scribante has appeared, people have died."

The old man chuckled, more to himself than to us. "Guess it's time to bust out my old fowling piece."

Belvedere did not share in the mirth. "We'd like to keep our animals in your barn," he said. "Have you got a spare room for us in the house? Just for a day or two?"

"There's a bedroom up the stairs," the old man said. "Doesn't get much heat but enough to keep the frost off the pumpkin."

After stabling our horses, we went into the house. Johnson was cleaning his fowling piece in the kitchen, rubbing oil on the two barrels with a dirty rag. "I ain't really got nothin' to be afraid of," the old man said.

Belvedere looked at him squarely. "Three men have already been murdered. They were all able-bodied."

The old man grinned and shook his head. He polished the gun with more vigour. "I figger I can look after my own self."

"We'll be here as back-up," Belvedere said, "in case something should go awry."

After he had finished cleaning his weapon, Johnson escorted us upstairs to our temporary quarters. "Hope this'll do," he said. There were two beds, side by side, in the room. "I raised my sons in this house. This is where they slept."

"This'll do quite nicely," I offered.

The old man grew suddenly wistful. "It'll be kinda like havin' them home, with you here."

After we'd gotten settled in, Belvedere and I went back downstairs. Johnson was standing over a cast-iron stove, stirring a pot of broth with a wooden spoon. "Hope you don't mind dried-pea soup," he said. "Fresh peas are in short supply this time of year."

"Dried-pea soup'll be fine," I replied. Looking around the room, I could see the old man's fowling piece propped against a wall near the door. It was an ancient weapon, a muzzle loader from a bygone era, but Johnson had kept it in reasonable shape. Still, I did not understand how such an antiquated weapon might be used for hunting, let alone for self-defence.

"And would you have some tea and apple cider vinegar?" Johnson asked. "It's good for the circulation."

"We'll pass on the tea," Belvedere said. "I'd like to take a walk around the place before dark."

Having eaten our repast—and the pea soup was mighty good after much of what we had suffered at the McLaughlin house—we donned our coats and proceeded on a stroll around the old man's homestead. Johnson did not bother to accompany us. Belvedere and I walked the fence line and then entered the woodlot at the edge of his quarter-section. The snow was crusty, as it tends to be in the middle of February on the plains, sometimes bearing our weight and sometimes not. It made for tough slogging, but we did manage to find another set of footprints that approached the fence with a clear view of the house and then retreated. "Hard to say what those footprints are," Belvedere muttered. "Could be hunters again."

We stayed with the old man for three nights, checking the fence line daily, perpetually on the lookout for intruders. A policeman's work, I had found, was ninety-nine per cent boredom and one per cent utter terror. Johnson kept us entertained by telling us stories from his past—sometimes the same stories two or three times over—and by feeding us a seemingly endless quantity of pea soup. When it became apparent that there was no immediate danger, Belvedere broached the subject of our leaving. "You must keep an eye out," he warned the old man. "Have your fowling piece loaded and shoot anything that comes through that door."

On the third night, as we were lying in our beds, we heard the nicker of a horse somewhere in the vicinity. The night was moonlit, and moonbeams reflected off the snow, illuminating even the inside of the house. Belvedere sat up in his bed. "Did you hear that?"

"I did."

He pulled his service britches on and then his boots. "I'll go and take a look." He threw his coat over his shoulders and grabbed his handgun in its holster.

"Wait," I said. "I'm coming with you."

When we'd opened the front door of the house and stepped outside, I could see no sign of a horse or rider. Belvedere stopped in his tracks and peered at the trees on the other side of the pasture. "Do you see that?" he murmured.

"See what?" I was still strapping a holster around my waist.

He nodded toward the trees. "That glint of light over there. Somebody's looking at us through a pair of binoculars."

I followed the direction of his eyeline until I could see a faint glint of moonlight, reflected from a pair of lenses. Belvedere drew his service revolver out of its holster and strode toward the place from whence the glimmer of light had emanated. I drew my Enfield as well, hoping against hope that I would not be required to kill a human being that evening. When we were halfway across the pasture, trudging through snow that resembled ice at times, I could no longer see the reflection of light off binocular lenses. Clearly, our watcher no longer had need of an ocular aid. It occurred to me, as we continued walking, how easy a target both Belvedere and I had made of ourselves. With a rifle of any sort, the man in the trees might easily have disposed of the two of us. I held my breath as I walked and waited for the report of a gun.

As we neared the forest's edge, I saw a bit of red cloth moving among the trees. The cloth disappeared momentarily in the darkness of the forest, only to reappear some twenty feet away. Judging by the pace at which it moved, I surmised that the wearer of that red cloth was in a hurry to escape our attentions. A horse nickered again. Belvedere knelt in the snow near a tuft of dead grass and aimed his handgun at the red cloth as it scurried along. "Come out!" he shouted. "Whoever you are, come out, or I'll be forced to fire my weapon."

There was a pause, and then Sergeant Slade stepped into the clearing with his hands above his head. "Put down your weapon, Corporal," he said. "I outrank you."

16

Belvedere stood up slowly, trying to process what had just materialized before his eyes. I was surprised, as well, having never seen the sergeant at work in the field before. He seemed much more at home in his office at the Stobart and Eden store. My heart was still pounding from the tension of the moment. We had been on the verge of firing shots. Belvedere lowered his gun. "Slade," he said, "what the hell are you doing here?"

"Investigating a case," Slade replied, "same as you."

I holstered my Enfield, but Belvedere did not do the same. "Why here? Why now?" Belvedere said. "Have you been following us?"

Slade lowered his hands. "Please, please," he said, "give me a little bit of credit. I have at least as much jurisdiction over this case as you have. And it is possible I might have some leads of my own."

Belvedere was having none of it. "And so you've left the warm confines of your bed to ride out here on a night such as this?" he said. "Doesn't seem like you, Slade."

Slade chuckled quietly to himself. "It doesn't take a genius to understand that three murders have occurred in a straight line, north and south, on the exact route of the proposed railroad," he said. "But I'm sure you knew that."

From long experience, I understood that there was no love lost between the sergeant and Belvedere. It would have been easy for Belvedere to squeeze off a shot at that moment and put an end to a longstanding antagonism. But for me as a witness, Belvedere might have claimed that Slade had been mistaken for an intruder and shot dead.

Belvedere slid his weapon into its holster. Slade approached us. "Now that I see the two of you are on the job," he said, "I believe I'll head back to town before anyone gets shot."

"I think that's a good idea," Belvedere replied cooly. "You never can tell when an accident might happen."

We watched as Slade led his horse out of the trees. It was a tall sorrel, perhaps fifteen hands high, shoed as if ready for a parade along cobblestone streets. Slade climbed into the saddle and nodded at us. Then he spurred his horse toward town. We were left standing in the crisp snow, with the moon shining down upon us. Belvedere was lost in thought for a moment. "So Sergeant Slade enters the picture," he said. "That silly fek is up to something. I know it."

RIDING my horse back to town early on the fourth day, I saw a red-throated woodpecker banging his head on a pine tree, and I knew that there would be spring after all. Belvedere was grumpy all the way home. "That was a waste of our fekking time," he said, spurring his mount through the wet snow.

We arrived home to a frosty reception. Mrs. McLaughlin met us at the door. She was wearing her black mourning dress again, and her hair was swept back severely. Her eyes were blackened with lack of sleep. "Hullo," she said to me, almost in a monotone. "Did you have a good time?"

"Not particularly," I told her.

Belvedere was standing behind me, looking like a dog that had been kicked. Mrs. McLaughlin glanced up at him. "There's soup in a pot on the stove." She turned on her heels and exited through the parlour. I could hear the bedroom door close quietly behind her.

The look in Belvedere's eye was steely. "Well, there's soup on the stove," he said. "That's a start."

THERE WAS a terrible blizzard in March. It left three feet of snow in its wake, just as I was expecting a massive thaw. I had been out in the fields drawing that morning, taking advantage of a mild day when temperatures were at last above freezing. Hardly recognizing the storm clouds that rose in a bank to the north of the river and remained there for some time, I continued sketching landscapes until early afternoon. It was a relief to have my fingers outside my mitts and exposed to the elements after such a hard, long winter.

I did not notice the wind beginning to blow or the first crystals of snow swirling around me. The wind had begun to surge by the time I packed up my supplies and mounted my horse. I galloped back to the settlement at breakneck speed and made it to the stables before visibility became a problem. Happy to be inside the McLaughlin house as the blizzard worsened, I sat in front of the fireplace in the parlour and warmed my hands around a cup of hot tea.

Others did not fare so well in the storm. We heard, some days later, that our comrades Stevenson and Chartrand, two stalwart mounted policemen still stationed in Battleford, had been lost in the storm near Cut Knife and had frozen to death in their canvas tent. Belvedere had been particularly fond of Stevenson, and the news of his death threw my housemate into a blue funk that lasted for some time. I began to see evidence of laudanum use in his eyes once again, usually in the mornings as we took our breakfasts.

Mrs. McLaughlin's attitude toward us had softened in the intervening weeks, but I did not have the sense that she and Belvedere were as thick as they once had been. A quiet civility characterized their conversations, or, at least, the conversations that I heard. They did not touch one another when I was present in the room with them, and I neither saw nor heard more evidence of Belvedere in her bedroom.

After the storm, the weather began to soften, as well. The streets of Prince Albert settlement turned to slush and mud. It was difficult to keep one's attire to the immaculate standard of the police code. I spent hours in my room, cleaning and polishing my boots.

Belvedere and I trudged through the slush down to River Street early one morning, with thoughts of interviewing the sheriff about Cantrell and McKay. The sheriff seemed relaxed in his small office, with his muddy boots up on his desk as though he didn't give a hoot for authority figures or police business. We knew that McQuaid's jurisdiction did not extend outside town limits, but we questioned him anyway. He had no answers for us, no suspicions as to who might have murdered the men. There had been another dispute on the east end of the settlement, involving a Métis farmer and the telegraph men, and the sheriff told us that he planned to spend the rest of his day attending to that incident.

"There's something shady about that fellow," Belvedere said to me as we were walking back home. "I can't quite put my finger on it."

That's when I remembered meeting McQuaid on Egil Johnson's land, three months earlier, while I had been searching for a Christmas tree. I told Belvedere about the incident, about how the sheriff had been poised with his gun to take a shot at me. "He said he was out hunting."

"At Johnson's farm?" Belvedere's interest was piqued.

"Yes," I said, "just before Christmas."

"And he pointed his rifle at you?"

"Yes."

Belvedere was silent for a moment as we laboured up the hill. "We'll have to keep an eye on the silly fek," he said at last.

THE GOINGS-ON in the McLaughlin house had gotten slowly back to normal during the month of March. Mrs. McLaughlin dispensed with her black weeds as springtime approached, and she danced around the house in sprightly colours, crafting largely inedible meals, playing the piano, and sometimes retiring to her bedroom, probably to compose poetry whenever inspiration struck. Her relationship with Belvedere also seemed to recover, though perhaps in a more restrained manner than had hitherto been the case. I did see them sitting on the chaise longue in the parlour one evening, she with her dainty fingers touching the side of his knee.

Belvedere was his old crusty self. Occasionally, I would see the gleam of intoxication in his eyes. I think the dampness of early spring had gotten into his bones somehow. Once, when I was sorting through my medicine bag, I noticed that my own bottle of laudanum had gone missing. When I confronted Belvedere with that fact, he blamed my own carelessness. "Probably happened when you were falling off your horse," he muttered. Our wages were far from astronomical, and I often wondered how Belvedere could afford to keep up with his laudanum habit. Nevertheless, at the end of each month when our pay packets would arrive, I would see Belvedere limping down to the Hudson Bay store to purchase a bottle of the precious liquid.

I continued sketching landscapes and people until the deteriorating ice on the river became impassable. A frequent visitor at Good Voice's camp, I made charcoal sketches of the men and women at work, of the encampment and the nearby river, and of the boy I had treated for pneumonia. He was a spirited lad and could hardly sit still long enough for me to draw his likeness. When I was finished, he stood up and asked to see my drawing. I turned it toward him. "Is that me?" he asked, as though he had no idea what he looked like.

"Yes." I was always a little wary of showing my portraits to their subjects, lest they might disapprove.

"Pretty handsome, me."

"You are." I admired the drawing with him. The boy was handsome in his buckskin suit, with his hair pulled back in a braid.

I wrote again to Emily that evening, not having heard from her in some time, but I did not tell her about my sketches or my work as a mounted policeman. I told her again how much I loved her, how much I longed to be at her side. My fear was that she had hardened herself against me. Had she found solace in the arms of another man? Living far from her and in a limbo of unknowing, I was like a man tangled in barbed wire, where any movement was guaranteed to rip the flesh from his bones and his heart out of his chest.

WHILE WE WAITED for a letter to arrive from Winnipeg, Belvedere began a surveillance of Dan McQuaid. In the first weeks, Belvedere discovered little that was out of the ordinary. McQuaid did his daily round of the community in the mornings. He was usually in the public house by three in the afternoon, and he was seen beating up a drunken sot at nine o'clock one evening. The one thing Belvedere noticed was an inordinate amount of time spent in the company of the newspaperman O'Rourke. "Stops in there every day," Belvedere told me. "I wonder what's going on between them."

One evening after supper at the end of March, Belvedere strolled into my bedroom at the McLaughlin house. He was wearing tweed trousers, a white collarless shirt, and a cloth coat, the only casual clothes he had brought with him from Battleford. "Get your civies on," he said. "I need you to come with me."

I was in the middle of writing another letter to Emily. "Come with you where?"

"To the public house," he said. "We're going to loosen the sheriff's tongue."

Placing my pen in the ink well, I asked, "And how are we going to do that?"

He leaned on my doorframe and folded his arms. "How do you think we're going to do that?"

While I was not one for spending a great deal of time with inebriated people in public houses, I thought it might be interesting to see more of Belvedere's strategies for interrogation. I hastily donned a shirt and trousers and followed Belvedere down the stairs. Mrs. McLaughlin was still in the kitchen, putting away pots and pans, and she inquired about our plans for the evening. Belvedere was his usual indecipherable self. "Don't wait up for us," he said. "We might be rather late."

There was a cool breeze blowing across the mighty North Saskatchewan as we strode down River Street. "Why do you need me to accompany you on this fact-finding mission?" I asked.

"My good fellow," Belvedere replied, "because I may be in no shape, by the end of the evening, to remember so much as one word of what will be said."

The public house was located on the ground floor of the local hotel, a wood-frame three-story building that stood like a beacon overlooking the river. As we entered the building, a rush of moist hot air, perfumed with an odour of rancid beer, assaulted my nostrils. Inside the public house, working men of all generations were quaffing alcohol and speaking at high volume. A group of the telegraph workers partied it up around one table. Some other burly men looked to me like loggers. I recognized three of the Métis dogsledders sitting quietly around another beer-spattered table. McQuaid was standing at the bar, blowing hard about his exploits to another local who looked only slightly interested.

Belvedere and I found a table in the corner and spoke quietly about the sheriff until a waiter appeared. Belvedere sat with his back to the wall. When the waiter approached, a pale black-haired man who looked like a cadaver at an anatomy lesson, Belvedere ordered whisky. The waiter turned to me. "And what's your pleasure?"

Before I could speak up, Belvedere butted in. "My friend will have a small glass of beer, thank you."

We drank quietly for a quarter of an hour before McQuaid noticed us and stumbled over to our table. "If it ain't the Queen's cowboys," he bellowed, "come to purge this fair land of its demons."

Belvedere surprised me by not being quick to anger at that moment. He grinned at the sheriff, but I could see behind Belvedere's eyes a host of other thoughts. "Sit down, Dan," he said. "Join us for a drink." McQuaid's mountainous frame dwarfed the chair he sat on. "What are you drinking?"

"Whisky, always whisky."

Belvedere called the waiter again. "Bottle of whisky and two glasses."

The waiter grinned like a skeleton's skull. "We only have Usher's."

"That will do."

While the waiter was getting us a bottle, Dan McQuaid began asking questions. "So, how's the investigation going?"

"Peachy," Belvedere replied.

McQuaid waited for more, a silly smile on his face, and when more did not come, he prodded further. "Any leads?"

"A few."

When the bottle arrived, Belvedere poured the sheriff a drink of whisky. As McQuaid grasped the shot glass in his thick fingers, I noticed that he was wearing a silver ring embossed with symbols of carpentry, a compass and a square. Belvedere noticed the ring too. "You a freemason, McQuaid?"

The sheriff smiled drunkenly. "I am a member of that hallowed fraternity."

"And so am I." Belvedere held out his hand, and McQuaid shook it with the same grip he had used on me, out at Johnson's farm.

McQuaid's eyes never left Belvedere. "I wouldn't have guessed."

"I spent some years in the military before I took this posting." Belvedere was grinning back at the man. "In fact, I've found something you may have lost. I've been carrying it around for weeks." Belvedere reached into his coat pocket and produced the pewter flask he had found at McKay's homestead, the one with the letter "G" engraved on it. "Do you recognize this?"

The sheriff gazed at the flask for a long moment. "Where did you find that?"

"Just a block down River Street. Does it belong to you?"

McQuaid looked bewildered for a moment. At last, he said, "I believe it does."

"Well then, the lost article has found its rightful owner." Belvedere handed the silver flask to the sheriff, who stowed it in an outside pocket of his coat. "I'm afraid I couldn't resist imbibing its contents."

"That's quite all right," McQuaid said. "Just happy I got my sweet little flask back."

Belvedere and McQuaid drank, glass for glass, the rest of the evening. Sipping on my small beer in the meantime, I was amazed at how much alcohol each of them could put away. The conversation was far-ranging, from hunting south of the river to the abscondment of the Métis farmer Sinclair and his whereabouts. McQuaid boasted that he was the best shot in the country next to a man from Duck Lake named Gabriel Dumont, and that he was also the toughest with fist or boot. Belvedere sat back in his chair and smiled. "Good to know," he said. Around midnight, the conversation turned back to the murder investigation. "What do you know of a lawyer named Scribante?"

I saw a flicker of recognition in McQuaid's eyes, but then he said, "Never heard of him."

"Are you sure?"

The sheriff just smiled.

"Because I have it on good authority that he's buying up land in these parts."

The sheriff chuckled to himself like this was better than Grimaldi in a pantomime. "One thing for certain," he said. "This traipsing around the countryside, asking all sorts of questions, ain't gonna git you nowhere. Or at the very least will git you shot at agin."

Belvedere sat up straight in his chair. "Shot at again? What do you mean?"

"Just what I said."

"How do you know we've been shot at? We've told no one." Belvedere peered at me for confirmation, and I nodded.

For a moment, McQuaid looked like a skunk that's been caught in a chicken coop. Then he grinned again. "I have my sources."

"And who might they be?"

"Well, that would be none of yer business, cowboy." McQuaid's demeanour suddenly grew steely. "You got yer sources, and I got mine."

Belvedere got steely, too. "You'd impede a North-West Mounted Police inquiry?"

"I might."

"Then you're a donkey's arsehole."

McQuaid placed a gnarly hand on the table in front of him. The knuckles were ragged, and I could see the sausage fingers twitching slightly. "Have a care."

Belvedere did not flinch. "You might have a care, as well."

The big man stared at Belvedere for a long moment. Slowly, he got to his feet and adopted a boxer's pose. "Care to go a round or two with me for bragging rights?"

I stood up, too, but Belvedere remained seated. "We'd have to discuss the rules."

McQuaid grinned drunkenly. "There are no rules in a bar fight."

"In that case, here." Quick as a wolverine, Belvedere gripped the neck of the whisky bottle in his hand. Quicker than that, he smashed the bottle over McQuaid's bullish head. While the sheriff stood there, wondering what had just happened, Belvedere threw the table aside and kicked him square in the genitals. The sheriff dropped to his knees like a gut-shot buffalo, and Belvedere delivered a round-house blow with his clasped hands that sent the big man sprawling backwards across the whisky-soaked floor.

17

There was little opportunity to speak with the sheriff for several days after the incident in the public house, but Belvedere's set-to with the man was soon the subject of public discourse. While it went thankfully unreported in both local newspapers, the scandal of one policeman assaulting another was on the lips of every citizen. Even Mrs. McLaughlin commented on it at the breakfast table. "I hear that the big oaf has finally got his just rewards," she said, casting an appreciative eye on Belvedere's swollen knuckles.

Among the first to hear was Sergeant Slade. He arrived at our door in person, three mornings after the fight, with two sub-constables. Mrs. McLaughlin gasped audibly when she opened the front door and witnessed the sea of red serge before her. Slade spoke to her sharply. "Is Corporal Belvedere here?"

Before Mrs. McLaughlin had time to compose herself and offer a reply, Belvedere spoke up from the dining room. "Who wants to know?"

Belvedere's response must have enraged the sergeant, for he swept past Mrs. McLaughlin and found his way into the dining room, where Belvedere and I were seated. He addressed Belvedere directly. "I'm arresting you in the name of Queen Victoria."

"Arresting me?" Belvedere stared incredulously at the sergeant. "On what charge?"

Slade continued, crimson-faced. "On a charge of common assault, sir."

"And who is pressing this charge?"

"I am," Slade hissed. "Until further reports are received."

I felt it was my obligation to intervene and plead Belvedere's case at this unexpected visit. "But, Sergeant—"

Slade turned toward me and spoke with severity. "I understand you were present during the altercation, Montgomery. You may count yourself lucky that you are not also being charged as an accessory."

Belvedere grinned at me. "It appears the sergeant has a bee in his bonnet."

Slade's body shook with rage. He produced a pair of handcuffs. "Arise, if you please, Belvedere, and come with me."

Belvedere chuckled. "May I get my coat first?"

"No, you may not." Slade marched Belvedere to the front porch, where he offered the further indignity of manacling Belvedere's wrists behind his back. At that moment, Belvedere's little terrier emerged from under the dining room table and pounced at the sergeant. The mutt had Slade's pant leg in his teeth and was tearing at it in all directions, ripping a nice triangle out of the well-cared-for material. I could tell that the sergeant viewed the dog's attack as a final indignity. "Get out of it, you mangy cur!" he shouted, kicking at the animal with his unencumbered foot and sending the dog sprawling across the hardwood floor.

Manacled as he was, Belvedere approached the sergeant and confronted him face-to-face. "Kick my dog again," he said, "and it'll be the last thing you kick."

Fortunately, the terrier did not mount a second offensive. Slade turned, red-faced, to his sub-constables and issued an order. "Take this miscreant to the lock-up now!"

Mrs. McLaughlin, who had receded into the parlour, looked

pale and stricken. "Please feed my hound while I'm away," Belvedere said to her. "And not too much fat. It's bad for his kidneys." Then he turned to me and winked. "Keep up the good work, Montgomery."

Mrs. McLaughlin and I watched from the front porch as Belvedere was marched in his shirt sleeves up the hill toward the jail. She turned to me, her eyes swimming in tears. "He needs his coat on such a cold morning as this."

I visited Belvedere in his jail cell early that afternoon. His cell was no better or worse than the cages they keep lions in at the zoo. If the purpose was to make a man feel like an animal, then that purpose was quite evident in the design. When I arrived, Belvedere was pacing back and forth in the eight or nine feet that the cell afforded. He was somehow too large for the space, too large for captivity of any kind. I began to suspect that he might erupt at any moment, with an otherworldly snarl, and rip the crisscross iron to shreds. When he saw me, in the gloom of the jailhouse, his eyes did not seem to belong to a human being. "Anything further on McQuaid?" he snapped.

"Nothing."

"Keep an eye on him, Montgomery. He's up to no good."

I had brought along Belvedere's buffalo coat, which would prove useful in that barely heated shack. Placing it on the wooden bench opposite the cell, I said, "The guard has promised to give you the coat next time he's here." Through the metal grate, I slipped Belvedere a small jar of canned blueberries that Mrs. McLaughlin had sent along for him. "And the missus wanted you to have these."

Belvedere received the jar, and his demeanour softened appreciably. The animal had gone out of him. "Thank you, Montgomery. And give my thanks to the missus, as well."

Six days later, an emissary from Battleford rode into town. He was a fresh-faced mounted police constable, hair the colour of sunlight, no more than nineteen years old. I had never met him before; he must have been a new recruit. I happened to be visiting Belvedere in his cell that afternoon. Slade strode into the jailhouse, a gaggle of keys in his hand, with the young man at his side. He shoved one of the keys awkwardly into the lock and threw open the cell door. "As I cannot persuade the sheriff to lay charges, it seems you are free to go." His words were spat like molten lead in Belvedere's direction.

After Slade had exited the building, the young Mountie offered some further explanation. "Colonel Herchmer himself ordered your release, sir. I came into town this morning with the news. The sergeant did not take it well."

"I didn't expect he would," Belvedere said, standing fully upright outside the cell for the first time in several days. I could almost hear his spine crack as he straightened up. "Slade is a shit of the first water."

It was a happy reunion in the McLaughlin house that afternoon. Mrs. McLaughlin flitted about the house like a red robin on the first day of spring. Belvedere sat at the dining room table, sipping a warm cup of tea she had made for him. I returned to my room after some time and engaged in a charcoal drawing of the scene outside my window, leaving Belvedere and the missus to reacquaint themselves.

Belvedere's relationship with McQuaid did not return to normal after the incident in the public house. When the sheriff saw us coming down the boardwalk on one side of River Street, he would either cross to the other side of the street or dip into a shop to avoid us. For his part, Belvedere made no attempt to apologize or to cajole McQuaid out of his bad humour.

Because McQuaid was wary of us, surveilling him became problematic. We were reduced to watching his activities from curtained windows or behind buildings. We did finally converse with the man on River Street, one afternoon and seemingly by chance, while he was performing his daily rounds. The sheriff was walking gingerly, and the bruises around his eyes had begun to change in colour from a midnight turquoise to a rainbow of blues and greens.

He seemed overjoyed to see us. The grin on his face, coupled with his cuts and bruises, was reminiscent of a sad clown at the circus. "Gentlemen," he said, "we got off on the wrong foot there a few weeks ago. I put it down to the evils of drink, and I hope you harbour no hard feelings."

Belvedere was not one to apologize, but he was not one to hold grudges either. "No hard feelings on this side."

"Aw, there you are, and I'm glad of it." The sheriff offered his meaty paw, grasped Belvedere's hand, and squeezed it a little too long. Seeing the steely look on Belvedere's face, I began to think that another fight might materialize, right there on the street. "I was a trifle inebriated at the time," McQuaid added, "and you got the drop on me. I wouldn't count on such luck in the future."

Belvedere looked him in the eye. "You still haven't told me about your sources."

"And I will not, either." There was another uncomfortable silence, and then the sheriff let go of Belvedere's hand. "Well," he said, "be seein' ya." He strolled on down the street, looking in shop windows and greeting passersby as merrily as if he were part of an Easter parade.

Belvedere watched as the man lumbered away. "We'll keep an eye on that gentle giant," he said. "He might soon need another lesson in manners."

IT WAS early April when the news came out that the Canadian Pacific Railway was on the verge of building a line through Prince Albert to Edmonton and on to Whitehorse. The headline in O'Rourke's paper was larger and inkier than any I had seen before: "NEW RAILROAD A BOON TO PRINCE ALBERT

SETTLEMENT!" The article below it, written by O'Rourke himself, explained that the coming of the railroad was inevitable now. It would make Prince Albert a transportation hub, as goods manufactured in the east would be hauled by rail across the country and eventually to Vancouver. Local shopkeepers would flourish, O'Rourke argued, and property values would soar sky-high. There was no downside to the news. All that remained was for the spokesmen of Canadian Pacific to arrive in Prince Albert and make the announcement, and that announcement would be made sometime in the month of May. Prince Albert settlement was about to become a flourishing metropolis. "Hold on to your hats, folks!" the newspaperman veritably shouted. "The train is on its way!"

In the meantime, we had moved our surveillance of Dan McQuaid to another level. The business of one police officer surveilling another is a precarious one, like peering through a keyhole at someone who is also peering through a keyhole. On the other hand, an experienced police officer is sometimes so used to watching that he is perhaps oblivious to the fact of being watched. Our hope was that McQuaid did not suddenly turn away from his own keyhole to spot us studying him.

It was easy to underestimate a man like McQuaid. His demeanour was affable and bumbling, an oversized man with an apparently undersized brain. Sometimes, though, the book and its cover do not coincide. Perhaps the bumbling exterior was a mask for the calculating individual underneath.

We made a point of watching McQuaid as he walked his daily rounds. Belvedere positioned me in Sam Gee's café on some of those days and in the Hudson Bay store on others, while he crouched under evergreen branches down by the river with a pair of binoculars trained on the sheriff. My job was to listen for snippets of conversation that might incriminate or exonerate McQuaid, but the sheriff was quite tight-lipped whenever I was near.

On one of those days, he remarked on the amount of time I

was spending downtown. "I've never seen a doctor drink so much coffee," he said. "Is this a cure for hemorrhoids or constipation?" He giggled at his own joke, and I began to wonder if our little game of hide-and-seek had been found out.

After a few days of surveilling the sheriff from the bushes on the riverbank and risking frostbite in early spring, Belvedere was suddenly waxing philosophical. He had caught a springtime cold. His voice was even lower than usual, and he punctuated his bursts of speech with a wet, mucous-laden cough. I heard him across the corridor, in his bedroom at night, hacking and swearing.

One morning at the breakfast table, he dandled his dog and spoke with bleary-eyed tenderness about the loyalty of animals. "Dogs are better than people," he said. "They're loyal, they're forgiving, their love is beyond reproach. There's no greater joy in life than a well-trained, happy dog." He scratched the mutt on the top of its head, and the dog stretched its neck longingly toward Belvedere. "I'm not talking about these mangy ferals that roam the streets here at night, searching out rats and mice. Dogs can be ruined, the same as people can."

Gently, he placed the dog on the floor, and it clattered across the hardwood to where Mrs. McLaughlin was sitting. She was holding a teacup, two dainty fingers on the cracked china. "Sometimes, people can be loyal and forgiving, too."

Belvedere coughed and smiled at her. Somehow, he always looked wicked when he smiled and especially when he was sick. "Sometimes." Then he turned in his chair and looked at me. "Are you ready for a ramble, Montgomery?"

"Always ready," I said, and I *was* always ready, in full uniform by nine in the morning, boots shone to military standards.

"Good," Belvedere said. "I'll get my tunic on, and we'll go for a walk."

It was difficult to keep one's feet dry in the Great North-West during the month of April. Springtime came late out there and began with a continuous cycle of thawing and freezing. The roads turned to slush by midday, and wagon traffic made it a muddy business. When the sun went down again, at seven-thirty or thereabouts, those same roads turned into stalagmites of sharp ice, hazardous to the walker.

Belvedere and I picked our way down the street more carefully than usual that morning, eager to avoid the puddles and slush that might cause us to spend extra hours, later, polishing our boots. The wind was brisk—a chilling springtime wind that carried the moisture of the melt and pierced the body like an assortment of dull scalpels. We were still wearing our buffalo coats, and we fully expected to do so until May was at hand.

Belvedere coughed and spat a wad of green phlegm into a puddle. He pulled his collar up around his ears and sidled close to me. "I'm going to need a brace and bit," he said. "Any idea where I might find one?"

I remembered that the shed behind the Presbyterian Church had various tools of carpentry hanging on its walls. We stopped there and found the brace and bit that Belvedere was looking for. He hid the instrument under his coat, and we proceeded down River Street. Through the window of Gee's Café, we could see Sheriff McQuaid engaged in an animated conversation with several townsmen. "Good," Belvedere muttered as we passed the café. "We'll have a bit of time while the sheriff blows hard about his exploits."

More briskly then, we walked to the town hall, where the sheriff's tiny office was situated. The building was mostly empty. There was a skeleton lock on the alley door. I was surprised when Belvedere pulled two lock-picking tools from his pocket. "I confiscated these some time ago," he whispered, "from a thief who wasn't a very good thief." He inserted one of the picks into the lock and then the other, and I heard the bolt snap open.

We entered and proceeded to the sheriff's office. At the other end of the building, we both knew, was the town office, reigned over imperiously by a frumpy, middle-aged woman named Mrs. Halvorsen. I followed Belvedere down a narrow corridor to another door, this one labelled "JANITOR."

Belvedere smirked at me. "Judging from the looks of it, there hasn't been a janitor in this building since it was built." He opened the door and peered into the darkness of the tiny closet. "I'll need you to stand here," he said, "just for a minute or two." Producing the brace and bit from the folds of his coat, he entered the small room and closed the door behind him. After a moment, I could hear the bit's sharp edges biting into the wooden wall of the closet.

"Can I help you?" Mrs. Halvorsen, primly dressed, was standing at the far end of the corridor. In the closet, Belvedere must have heard her voice too; he ceased turning the bit.

I tried to be nonchalant. "I'm looking for the mayor's office." I had no idea what I might say to the mayor when I met him.

Mrs. Halvorsen took a step or two toward me and then, thankfully, stopped. "The mayor isn't in today. May I be of service?"

"It's quite personal," I said. "I'll come back another day."

"How did you get in here?"

"The alley door was open." Hearing a muffled cough from inside the janitor's room, I tried to cover for it by coughing loudly myself.

"That's odd," said Mrs. Halvorsen. "It's supposed to be locked at all times."

"It wasn't."

"Perhaps Sheriff McQuaid forgot to lock it." She appraised me for a moment. "You're one of the mounted policemen."

"And I take it you are the mayor's secretary."

"I'm the town administrator," she said imperiously.

"Well, I'll come back another day."

"Please do."

Having no other recourse, I followed Mrs. Halvorsen to the front entrance of the building, leaving Belvedere to fend for himself. She closed the door behind me as I stepped out into the street, and she stood watching me through the window for some time. I sauntered down the boardwalk and saw the sheriff exiting

Gee's Café and walking toward me. "Hullo, Montgomery," he said. "On your way for a little of Gee's black mud?"

"I'm quite addicted," I said. McQuaid marched past me in the direction of his office. Concerned about Belvedere's well-being, I watched as the sheriff entered the front door of the town hall, and then I hurried to the alley.

Belvedere was already outside the building. He coughed up a wad of phlegm, spat it into a puddle of mud in the alley, and we strode away in the direction of the church again. Belvedere grinned at me. "That little aperture in the sheriff's wall will make surveillance easier."

I was not convinced that Belvedere's new plan would work. "You're not worried that he'll see it?"

He chuckled. "I drilled the hole behind his gun rack, where he'll be unlikely to notice it." He punched me playfully on the shoulder. "Didn't you observe the layout of his office? We've been in there together on three separate occasions." He laughed again, loosening some of the infection in his lungs, and the laughter turned into coughs and snorts and wheezes.

THE NEXT SUNDAY, I rode south of town with my satchel again full of charcoals. My initial impulse was to draw the ghostly shapes of poplars just as they were leaving their winter hibernation, but I came upon the telegraph line, quite by accident. Some of the tall wooden posts stood like beacons on the open prairie. Others were situated on trails carved through the forest, only distinguishable from the trees by their barkless appearance. The line itself was stretched taut from one pole to the next, with a straightness that led to a vanishing point in the distance.

Something about those telegraph poles intrigued me. Perhaps it was their lifelessness amid such a panorama of living nature. Perhaps it was their abiding loneliness. Perhaps it was the fact that they stretched in a line all the way back east, all the way to Montreal, all the way to my sweet Emily. I sketched that telegraph line for most of the morning and from several different angles, but no angle seemed right in the end. The wind came up, and my fingers began to freeze. I headed back to town just after lunch.

I arrived at the McLaughlin house that afternoon to a cacophony of lovemaking. Neither of the two lovers heard me as I entered. Belvedere's little dog sat on the chaise longue in the parlour outside Mrs. McLaughlin's bedroom, where he was never supposed to sit, and stared at me balefully. I stared back for a moment, then trudged up the stairs to my room.

At supper that evening, the two lovers pretended that none of this had ever happened, though they shared meaningful glances across the table when they thought I wasn't looking. Belvedere was still dealing with the remnants of his cold; his face was haggard, and his breathing laboured. Mrs. McLaughlin was decidedly more cheery and talkative than usual. As I spooned the barley soup to my lips, I tried to appear oblivious to it all. I knew they were wondering when I had returned home and what exactly I might have witnessed, but I gave them no inkling.

WITH THE HELP of his confiscated lock-picks, Belvedere spent the next week crouched in the dark confines of the janitor's closet behind McQuaid's office, listening for the sheriff to utter a tidbit of information that might shed light on one or two or three murders. No such tidbit was forthcoming in the first few days, and Belvedere was mightily discouraged, but then, on a late afternoon, he heard Sylvester O'Rourke and the sheriff talking. It was a muffled conversation, conducted mostly in whispers, but Belvedere strained his ears to hear the bulk of it. He reported this conversation to me the next morning, outside my bedroom.

Belvedere had witnessed O'Rourke giving the sheriff his orders. "It has to happen soon," O'Rourke had whispered. "I think these Mounties might have picked up the scent, so be careful. He's an old man. You'll need to make it look like an accident or some such."

"I'll make it look like the others looked," the sheriff had replied. "No one will be the wiser."

Standing at the top of the stairs in the McLaughlin house, I was shaken by this news. I looked into Belvedere's eyes, which were burning like the light of home after a far-flung journey. "Shouldn't we be making an arrest post-haste?"

Belvedere shook his head. "You saw what happened with the last arrest I made."

"But now a life is in danger."

"We're likely to see that same judge somewhere down the line." I could tell that Belvedere was weighing the danger of another murder against the possibility of justice. "A conversation overheard from a janitor's closet is not likely to stand as admissible."

"Yes, but—"

"I have an inkling it was Egil Johnson they were talking about. We'll set up camp in Johnson's woodlot and keep our eyes peeled."

"The old man won't be able to defend himself."

Belvedere placed a reassuring hand on my shoulder. "Sometimes old men are wilier than we give them credit for."

I looked down at the cracked birchwood floor. "This doesn't feel right."

"You're not paid to feel anything," Belvedere said, his voice steely again. "And I'm not going to let this investigation slip through my fingers because of your squeamishness."

18

We spent the next three nights in the woodlot near Egil Johnson's fence line. Belvedere felt that our presence in the house might be too obvious, especially as we had occupied the upstairs bedroom on an earlier occasion. We fashioned a tent out of a bolt of canvas and a length of rope, and we slept, whenever we slept, as best we could on the damp ground of spring. A fire would have disclosed our location, so we subsisted those three nights on jerky and hardtack and water. Belvedere had brought his terrier along with us. I was worried that the dog might bark and reveal our hiding place, but the mutt proved to be a stealthy soldier, never straying and never making a sound. On the promise that he would feed and water them twice a day, we'd left our horses in Mr. Johnson's barn.

It was about three o'clock in the morning when I was awakened by the terrier's quiet growl. There was an uncanny stillness in the air. Belvedere was awakened by it too, and we both sprang to our feet to take a look. There in the darkness across the pasture, we could see the sheriff's sorrel, standing patiently in the yard outside Egil Johnson's house.

I couldn't see McQuaid from where I was standing, but perhaps Belvedere could. "He's here!" Belvedere whispered, and then he climbed through the fence and broke into a run toward the yard. I followed him, running for all I was worth across the uneven pasture. The dog bounded along behind us.

We were halfway to the house when I caught a glimpse of McQuaid. With his Winchester over his shoulder, he was approaching the door of the house. I saw McQuaid throw open the door. I saw him go inside. I heard a loud crack, like distant thunder. It echoed through the forest and reverberated in my ears. The sound of the gunshot stopped us cold in our tracks for a moment, but then we were running again.

Once in the yard, Belvedere and I drew our sidearms. We approached the house with trepidation. Belvedere peered around the doorjamb while I stood behind him. The dog remained at Belvedere's feet. It took a while for my eyes to adjust as there was no light, by candle or kerosene, inside the house. In the darkness, I could see McQuaid lying on the floor, face up, and Egil Johnson standing over him, ancient fowling piece in his hands.

The old man turned and aimed the gun at Belvedere when he saw us in the doorway. "It's me, Belvedere!" my partner shouted. "Put down your weapon!"

The old man lowered his fowling piece. "It was self-defence!" he declared. "He come in here with a view to shootin' me, but I got him first."

Belvedere rushed into the room and pushed the old man aside. McQuaid was still breathing, but there was a gaping hole in his chest, made by a close-range concentration of pellets, and blood was spurting from it. Recognizing that an artery had been severed, I knelt beside the sheriff and applied pressure to the wound, but I knew it would be of little use. Belvedere knelt too and gazed into the sheriff's rapidly fading eyes. "Who put you up to this?" Belvedere asked.

McQuaid opened his mouth to speak and blood gurgled forth. His face was a mask of pain and anger. "Fucking O'Rourke," he murmured. "I knew he'd be the death of me one day." He chuckled morosely, as though it had been nothing more than a merry chase. Then he swallowed hard, a mouthful of blood, stiffened for a moment, and died.

We took the old man's gun away and sat him down on a chair in the kitchen. The mutt crawled up into Johnson's lap, seemingly aware of a man who needed comforting. Belvedere and I went outside to discuss the next steps in our investigation. "Goddammit!" Belvedere was seething. "We needed to take the sheriff alive!"

I peered into the kitchen. Johnson was still sitting there, lost in thought, silently petting Belvedere's terrier. "Why?" I asked. I tucked my woollen scarf into my coat collar to ward off the cold of early spring.

"He was our link to O'Rourke and our best evidence against him." Belvedere toed the dirt in front of him.

"Do you think McQuaid was responsible for all the killings in this town?"

"I'm pretty sure of it. We found his flask in the bushes where the homesteader McKay was murdered. The fact that he knew all about you and me being fired at near the Cantrell place suggests he was the man doing the shooting."

I looked again into the kitchen to see if we were overheard. The old man had buried his face in his hands. He was visibly shaken. Belvedere's dog had jumped down from the old man's lap and was on the floor looking up at him. "What are we going to do with Mr. Johnson?"

"There isn't much to do," Belvedere replied. "I'm not going to arrest the man. He did what he did out of self-defence."

The night had taken a ghoulish turn. In the darkness, shadows among the black spruce trees were like witnesses to the unhappy events of the evening. We went inside and had a conversation with Egil Johnson. Then we dragged the sheriff's lifeless body to where his horse was still standing. It was all we could do to lift the dead weight and drape the body over the saddle. We rode slowly back to town with our sad cargo. Nestled inside Belvedere's buffalo coat, the dog travelled with us.

The undertaker was asleep when we arrived, but we awakened him. He shook his head ruefully when he saw McQuaid's visage, grimacing in death. "How did this come about?" he asked Belvedere.

"I'm not at liberty to say."

The undertaker tutted and shook his head again. "What is this town coming to?" he said, as much to himself as to Belvedere and me. Then he led us into the mortuary.

THREE DAYS LATER, the town was abuzz with news of the sheriff's death. News travels fast in a community of that size, especially news about a citizen as prominent as the sheriff, and especially when the undertaker is a gossip. There were plenty of rumours about how McQuaid was killed and why. When it became known that Belvedere and I were at the scene, theories of wrongdoing on the part of Johnson or on the part of the sheriff, or even on the part of Belvedere and me, were rife. There was conjecture about where and when a trial would be held.

Belvedere and I were called into Slade's office for a dressing-down. What were we doing out there? Was the sheriff suspected of anything for which we might be surveilling him? Did Johnson really shoot the sheriff, or was it one of us?

His coat open, Belvedere slouched on a chair. "I can tell you that McQuaid was a suspicious character," he declared, "and you know that somebody's been murdering property owners in the nearby countryside."

Slade sat poker-straight behind the desk. "So, you didn't shoot the sheriff?"

"No, sir, I did not."

"Well, that's a relief," Slade responded. "I had visions of another incident like the one you were involved in down by Fort Walsh." Slade looked at me with a shit-eating grin on his face.

"Did he ever tell you about that? About how he shot six wolfers in cold blood?"

Belvedere shook his head. His lips curled into a remorseless sneer. "They'd done their share of killing, too."

Slade's face reddened with the joy of the telling. "He sneaked into their encampment and shot the first one in the back. Then he murdered the rest of them while they were reaching for their guns."

Belvedere stood up, pulling himself to his full height. "Well, that's my report. Will there be anything else?"

"No."

Standing at the door, Belvedere turned to Slade for one last shot. "You're quite the play-actor, Slade," he said. "A regular William Terris, that's what you are."

As we made our way back to the McLaughlin house, Belvedere was in a black mood. He was silent for most of the walk, only speaking up as we neared the house. "You've no doubt heard rumours about me and my time at Fort Walsh."

I did not feel it was any of my business, and part of me couldn't bear to hear ugly truths about the man. "No," I lied, but there had been plenty of rumours. Some of these implied that Belvedere had been a coward on that evening, although that characterization did not seem plausible to me. Another version of the story hinged on the notion that Belvedere had a brother and that this brother was also a Mountie who had accompanied Sergeant Walsh on his journey west in '74. According to that rumour, Belvedere's brother had been ambushed by wolfers and brutally murdered. Later, when Belvedere joined the Force, he was allegedly bent on avenging his brother's death. I did not know how much to believe of this, or any other, version of the story.

It was getting cold, and I wanted to change the subject. I found it odd that Belvedere hadn't mentioned the connection between McQuaid and the newspaperman O'Rourke in his discussion with Sergeant Slade, and I told him so.

"Everything in good time, Montgomery," he said to me.

"But surely," I said, "if you told him about the conversation you overheard—"

"There are good reasons for not doing so at this time." Belvedere spat a wad of phlegm into the snow. "Not the least of which is that I didn't obtain a search warrant before listening in at McQuaid's office."

I looked up at the big sky, clear and blue. "So, how do we implicate O'Rourke in all of this?"

"That remains to be seen," Belvedere replied. "We'll press him when the time is right."

THE ICE along the Saskatchewan River broke up with a terrible thud that woke people in their beds late at night. When we ventured out in the morning, sharp islands of white were floating downriver toward Hudson Bay. The opening of the river meant that boats would once again navigate freely along the watery route to the east. The ferry would run again as soon as it was safe to do so.

We got sad news in the middle of April that the farmer Sinclair had been located and shot to death on a property near Willow Bunch in a southern stretch of the territory. Mounties had surrounded the farmhouse in which he was sheltered, and when he would not give himself up, had lit the building on fire. Sinclair was shot in the back while he attempted to flee.

His body was transported to Prince Albert settlement by Red River cart for burial. His young wife was understandably distraught at the funeral, and anti-police sentiments were rife in the town. The Métis of Pochaville were less in evidence in the businesses along River Street. I suspected that revolution was in their hearts. When I tried to talk about this turn of events with Belvedere, he turned grey and shook his head and said nothing. I imagine Sergeant Slade was quite chuffed at the news.

On the twentieth of April, we learned that Egil Johnson had

been charged with the murder of Sheriff Dan McQuaid. Belvedere and I went to the trouble of marching up to Sergeant Slade's office to protest the arrest.

Complacent and happier now that spring had arrived, Slade sat at his desk with the serenity of Buddha and listened to our pleas. "McQuaid was the aggressor here," Belvedere said.

The sergeant sat back in his chair. "And how do you know that?"

"McQuaid showed up, with a rifle in his hands, in the middle of the night. He was there to kill Johnson."

"To kill him? For what purpose?"

Belvedere's fury did not make him more articulate. "So that the newsman O'Rourke could buy up his land."

Slade clasped his fingers and smiled at Belvedere. "Sounds like a crackpot theory to me."

"I've heard the two of them conspiring to commit murder."

"Heard them? Where?"

Belvedere stopped short, then fairly shouted, "If you will give me time, I'll prove it to you!"

Slade shook his head. "Justice must be done," he said, "and it must be seen to be done in a timely fashion."

On the twenty-first of April, Sylvester O'Rourke published this headline in *The Herald*: "EGIL JOHNSON TO BE TRIED IN COURT." A circuit court judge would have to be brought in from Regina, the article informed us, as well as a prosecuting attorney. Johnson had elected to be represented by the only lawyer in the settlement, Hayter Reid, and I worried that the homespun defence attorney would be no match for whomever was brought in to prosecute the case.

A letter from Emily arrived for me shortly thereafter. It must have been sent before she had received my last letter. Mrs. McLaughlin came upstairs that May morning with the envelope in hand. It was white and business-like. There was something about the crisp lettering that spelled my name that was both familiar and unfamiliar. Even without opening the envelope, I could sense that something was amiss, that the world was not spinning on its axis as freely as it had spun the day before.

I thanked Mrs. McLaughlin for the delivery and retreated to my bedroom to read the letter. Something hard and cylindrical fell out of the envelope when I opened it. I looked down at the floor, and there I saw the engagement ring that I had given Emily two years earlier. I picked up the ring and stared at it until I could stare at it no more, and then I read the letter.

The hand was severe, the calligraphy stark as leafless branches. I stood, like a man stunned by fire and flood, and read:

My dearest Virgil,

It is with the greatest sadness that I begin to write this letter, for I have waited—God only knows how patiently—while you have been away in service. When you departed, it was with the promise of a swift return, but now I see that you no longer harbour those thoughts and feelings. I am sure that there is much that draws you and your adventurous spirit to wild and unchartered territories, and I will not be an impediment in that great adventure. You know that I have loved you faithfully and true these many days, but I hear in your letters a reticence to return to my side.

I have decided to break off our engagement, and so you will be a free man. It would be foolish for me to do otherwise. I am of a marriageable age, and I do not lack suitors here in Montreal. Our schoolmaster, Mr. Kimble, has asked me to marry him on several occasions, and I am inclined to accept.

There have never been hard feelings between us, and I bear you no animosity now. I wish you well in all future endeavours. I will always think of you as a friend.

Sincerely,

Emily

Having seared my eyes with this epistle, I immediately sat down to write a letter of my own, but as I wrote, I became aware that everything she had said was true, that I did love this land, and that I did love these adventures, and that I would not be returning to her side as soon as I had planned. At last, I threw down my pen on the desk, buried my face in my arms, and wept piteously.

TWO DAYS LATER, a letter arrived from Winnipeg. Sub-Constable Parry brought the legal-looking envelope to our door. We were in the middle of supper. Mrs. McLaughlin and I watched from the table as Belvedere tore open the envelope and read the letter. Parry remained in the foyer as if he were waiting for a tip. Belvedere looked up at him. "Why are you still here, Parry?"

"Only w-w-waiting to s-s-s-see if there was any f-further business you w-w-wanted me to c-conduct."

Belvedere folded the letter again. "That will be all, Parry."

"Th-th-thank you, sir!" Parry executed a precise military turn and stepped out into the cold spring air. He closed the door softly behind him.

The letter was not mentioned again until after we'd finished our meal. When the dishes were done, Belvedere nodded at me to follow him upstairs. In the confines of his bedroom, and out of range of Mrs. McLaughlin's hearing, he turned to me and said, "I think we've found our man." He unfolded the letter once more and handed it to me. It bore the signature of a Corporal Haye of the Winnipeg detachment, and it told of an investigation. Its author had found that the law firm of Walters and Scribante had been acting as proxy for one Sylvester O'Rourke, journalist and editor of *The Herald*.

We visited Mr. O'Rourke in his office the next morning. He was not so busy as he had been during our first meeting. We found him seated comfortably behind his gnarled desk, reading the latest missives from Mr. Davin's newspaper in Regina. He folded *The Leader* and placed it on the desk before him as we entered the office. "Gentlemen," he said, "to what do I owe the pleasure?"

"We have questions," Belvedere replied, "about Sheriff Dan McQuaid."

O'Rourke looked serious. "I knew the poor man," he said. "Shot by a childish old homesteader—what a tragedy."

"Perhaps you had more than a passing acquaintance," replied Belvedere.

"Where are my manners?" O'Rourke motioned toward two chairs in front of his desk. "Would you care to sit down?"

"We'll stand," said Belvedere before either of us could take a seat. "You're a freemason, aren't you?"

The ring on O'Rourke's right hand was on full display. "I wear the compass and the square."

"McQuaid was a freemason, too."

The newspaperman sucked on his own teeth for a moment. "Oh, really? I hadn't realized."

Belvedere stared holes through the man. "Is it possible, in a town this size, that two freemasons wouldn't know one another?"

"Quite possible, I assure you."

Placing the Winnipeg letter on the desk in front of O'Rourke, Belvedere said, "Have a look at this."

O'Rourke unfolded the letter and perused it for some time. "Yes," he admitted, "I've successfully tendered for the properties of McKay and Cantrell."

"Land on which the proposed railway will run."

"There is no law against making a profit, is there, in this glorious new territory?"

Belvedere grasped the edge of O'Rourke's desk and leaned towards him. "There's a law against murdering innocent people," he growled, "or having them murdered when they refuse to accept your offer for their land."

O'Rourke's chair squeaked as he leaned back and looked at us with feigned disbelief. "That's a rather large accusation to make on the basis of so little proof."

"We know your man Scribante made the offers," Belvedere continued, "and that the laundryman and the two homesteaders both refused those offers."

"Is there a prohibition against offering to buy land?"

"And we know you and McQuaid were thick as thieves," said Belvedere. "He was in this office every day."

O'Rourke grinned like a cat. "He was providing me with a daily report on crime." He picked up the letter again and thrust it toward Belvedere. "Really, I wish you would take this to a court of law, if you think there's any merit in it, rather than troubling me with unfounded accusations at my place of work."

Belvedere erupted, as I knew he might, grabbing the newspaperman from across the desk and hoisting him to his feet by his lapels. "Listen to me, you simpering fek. We know you're behind all of this, and we won't rest until you're hung for it."

Choking and red in the face, O'Rourke managed to squeeze out a few words. "This is common assault, sir."

Belvedere threw O'Rourke back into his chair. "You'll pay for this, I promise." He snatched the letter out of O'Rourke's hand and marched out of the newspaperman's office.

I stood for a moment and gazed at O'Rourke, who was coughing and adjusting his coat. "What are you looking at?" he sputtered. "Get the fuck out." He looked like a guilty man to me. I couldn't help shaking my head before following Belvedere out the door. The corporal was already halfway down the street by the time I caught up with him.

THE PROSECUTING attorney arrived in Prince Albert a week before the trial. He was a tall, unctuous fellow with pomaded black hair. Because Sergeant Slade had been the arresting officer in the Egil Johnson case, the prosecutor's interview with Belvedere and me was brief and cursory. We met him in the mayor's chambers at the town hall on a bright day that felt suddenly like springtime. He looked up from his notebook only long enough to offer us a seat. "My understanding," he said, "is that you were surveilling the Johnson farm on the night of the murder?"

Belvedere shifted in his chair. "That is correct."

The prosecutor looked over his spectacles at Belvedere. "And did you have probable cause to do so?"

Belvedere had not gotten much sleep the night before. He rubbed his forehead with his hand. "We knew McQuaid was up to something."

"And how did you know that?" The attorney was toying with Belvedere like a parent toying with his child.

"We found his flask near the McKay murder site."

"The McKay murder site?"

"Yes."

The prosecutor left off writing and stared Belvedere in the eyes. "And that murder took place when?"

"Some months ago."

"Is it not possible, or even likely, that the sheriff was himself there to investigate McKay's murder?"

"Not likely, no." Belvedere was growing somewhat piqued at the prosecutor's tone. "The sheriff's jurisdiction was in town."

The prosecutor pushed his chair back and stood up. He looked out the window at the faint new green of the leaves on the trees. "We're not here to try a dead man for the murder of Mr. McKay," he said. "We're here to try the man who killed Dan McQuaid."

"I understand that," Belvedere replied, "but we have good reason to believe that McQuaid was in league with the newspaperman O'Rourke—"

"Sergeant Slade has another theory." The prosecutor sat on the edge of his desk and began to lecture Belvedere. "His theory is that Johnson and McQuaid had a longstanding antipathy."

It was Belvedere's turn to stand. "McQuaid was a hired killer!"

The prosecutor shook his head and returned to his chair. "Sergeant Slade tells me that you and McQuaid were also at loggerheads."

"Yes," Belvedere shouted, "because he was a murderer!"

The prosecutor took a deep breath. "I think this interview is over." He waited for Belvedere and me to take our leave. When we were almost out of the door, he said, "The murder of a lawman is a frightful thing, and we are here to protect the rule of law. You, of all people, should be able to understand that."

EGIL JOHNSON'S trial was held at Treston Hall. It lasted three days, and I watched with interest from the gallery. Brought into the courtroom each day in shackles, Johnson looked like a man in extremis. His lawyer maintained that he had hardly slept since his arrest three weeks earlier.

Johnson seemed not to understand the charges or why he had been brought to trial. The prosecution's case rested on the notion that an animosity had grown between Johnson and Sheriff McQuaid after the latter had been caught poaching game on Johnson's homestead. It was a slender assertion, but the defence attorney, Reid, had little evidence with which to make a counter-argument.

On the second day of the trial, Belvedere was called to the stand. He told the judge and jury that McQuaid had been a suspect in the murders of Cantrell and McKay.

When Hayter Reid was finished with his line of questioning, the prosecutor rose from his chair. Looking even more unctuous in his grey wig than he had during our preliminary interview, and speaking with an affected, stagey cadence, he scoffed at Belvedere's suspicions. "What possible motive could Sheriff McQuaid have had to murder two homesteaders in cold blood?"

"It was a land grab," Belvedere replied, "in advance of the coming railroad."

"And did Sheriff McQuaid offer to buy either of these properties when they became available?"

"No, but his associate did. They were members of a secret society together."

The prosecuting attorney's eyebrows ricocheted off the ceiling. "A secret society? Really? What's next? That they were transported here from the moon? Or perhaps they were summoned to this town by means of a séance?" The assemblage rocked with mirth at this assertion. The prosecutor turned to the judge. "Your Honour, I am not certain to whom the corporal might be referring, but I would ask that his assertion be stricken from the record. Whomever he thinks might possibly have had a hand in the deaths of Mr. McKay and Mr. Cantrell is not on trial here. Mr. Johnson, however, is." The judge agreed with the prosecuting attorney, and Belvedere's assertion was labelled inadmissible.

The attorney turned his attention again to Belvedere. "You were not on friendly terms with the sheriff?"

"I wasn't his best friend, no."

"Is it true, Corporal, that you had a rather public altercation with the sheriff only a month or two ago?"

Belvedere's eyes grew steely. "He was withholding evidence."

"And so you beat him senseless?"

"He threw some punches himself."

"But you beat him senseless. Is that not true?"

"I don't know about senseless," Belvedere said. "He fell down and hit his head."

"And so you don't mind damaging the poor man's reputation now that he is deceased?" The prosecutor strode away from the witness box and gave the jury a knowing look. "Are you in the habit of beating people, sir, when they withhold evidence?"

"No."

The attorney paused for theatrical effect. "But you also beat poor Mr. Markham, the owner of the sawmill, for much the same reason. Is that not correct?"

From where I was sitting, I could see the blood rising in Belvedere's face. It was all he could do to keep from leaping out of the witness stand and throttling the slippery fellow. "What's that got to do with anything?"

The attorney leaned, with both arms, on his desk near the front of the courtroom. He smiled at Belvedere, and in his smile was the gleam of intellectual superiority. "Do you have a drinking problem, sir?"

Belvedere harrumphed. "Sir, I do not."

"And yet you were seen, on numerous occasions, quaffing alcohol at the local public house. While in uniform, I might add."

"I was conducting an investigation."

"An investigation?" It was the prosecutor's turn to laugh, quietly and mirthlessly. "An investigation into the inebriating effects of the demon rum?" Before Belvedere could answer the rhetorical question, the attorney brought up another salient fact. "And is it true, sir, that you are also no stranger to the laudanum bottle?"

Belvedere was seething. "I've been dealing with a battlefield injury, sir. Something you would know little about."

The attorney sat at his desk with a flourish. "I have no further questions, Your Honour. The corporal is not a credible witness."

Hayter Reid declined to question the witness further, and Belvedere was asked to step down from the witness stand. He looked embarrassed and angry, and I was embarrassed and angry for him. I noticed Sylvester O'Rourke, at the back of the hall, scribbling frantically on a notepad when a brief adjournment was announced.

Others were called to give evidence. A neighbour of Mr. Johnson's testified that he had seen McQuaid hunting on the homesteader's property several times in the past year. Another neighbour had heard Johnson say that he didn't trust McQuaid "any farther than he could throw him" and that he thought McQuaid might be plotting against him. The local doctor was called in to provide an assessment of Johnson's mental acuity. He asserted that Johnson usually appeared to be of sound mind, but also that a preliminary state of dementia could not be ruled out.

The jury did not spend long deciding the fate of Egil Johnson. I had thought the jurors might be divided, given that there was some antipathy toward McQuaid in the town, but evidently, he had plenty of coffee-row friends. They were out for only an hour on the third day and, when they returned, the foreman was quick and clear-voiced in his pronouncement of a guilty verdict. In the prisoner's dock, Johnson looked like he hadn't heard the foreman's words.

On that same day, poor Mr. Johnson was sentenced to serve ten years at the Stony Mountain Penitentiary for the murder of Sheriff Dan McQuaid. I watched as Sergeant Slade led him out of the hall. The old man was still in shackles, and he looked at me, as he passed, with an expression of disbelief. His ancient face sagged; the light in his eyes seemed to have gone out.

19

Belvedere's drug habit worsened over the next few days. He was frequently late getting out of bed and coming downstairs to breakfast, and, when he did appear, his eyes were even more glazed than usual. Although he was largely non-communicative on those occasions, he did manage to politely scold Mrs. McLaughlin one morning for burning the gruel.

He spent most of the next two weeks in his bedroom, coming out only for meals and then eating hastily and returning to his room. His beard went untrimmed, and he did not bother to get properly dressed on any of those days, wandering around in his britches and bare feet. The laudanum was in his eyes, two feet deep, and their normally sharp blue seemed dimmer somehow. The whites had a yellow, filmy sheen. Mrs. McLaughlin looked at him worriedly as he ate, and then her eyes found mine as if to say, *What can you do about it?* The ice on the river had broken up. Time was running out.

Once, at the supper table, I asked Belvedere about a return to Battleford. "Where's that?" he replied, as if he had lost a sense of geography.

"The case has been tried," I told him. "A verdict has been reached."

"There's no justice in this fekking town," he said.

Even his dog regarded Belvedere as a stranger, refusing to sit on his lap anymore, even when offered a choice morsel of meat. The mutt whimpered when he looked at Belvedere and spent most of his time following Mrs. McLaughlin about the house. Perhaps I was delusional, but the dog seemed incurably sad.

During the nights, as I tried to sleep, I would hear Belvedere padding around in his room across the hall. He muttered profanities to himself and banged into the few pieces of furniture. Then there would be periods of unmelodic snoring, loud enough to wake me from even the deepest sleep. I heard a loud thump one night and surmised that he had fallen out of bed.

Finally, I decided to take matters into my own hands. I knocked on his bedroom door one fine morning and was told to go away. "I will not go away," I replied through the closed door, "until I have had a word with you."

"Go away, Montgomery."

I opened the door tentatively. Belvedere was sitting, shoeless, on the side of his bed, looking like he didn't know where he was. He didn't bother to look at me. "What do you want?"

I steeled myself against what I was about to say. "I want you to behave like a police officer," I told him. "I want you to do your job."

Belvedere harumphed weakly, and his harumph turned into a coughing spell. "As if you'd know how a police officer behaves."

I was still standing at the door, not wanting to venture farther into his room. It smelled of urine and vomit. Clothes were lying in haphazard piles on the floor. "You can laugh at me all you want," I said, "but I know you're a capable officer of the law, and I expect better of you."

He picked up a small brown bottle from his nightstand and examined its contents. "Is this you following Herchmer's orders again?" he asked. "Keeping an eye on me? Making me toe the line?"

"No," I said, "it's me telling you that you're better than this."

Belvedere uncorked the medicine bottle and downed its meagre contents. “You heard the lawyer. I’m a laudanum addict and a drunk and a violent bastard. Not fit to walk the Earth.”

“And you’re the only man who can bring this case to a conclusion,” I said. “But you’ve got to pull yourself up by the bootstraps. No one can do it for you.”

“That’s where you’re wrong, Montgomery,” he muttered. “I don’t have to do a goddamned thing.”

“But you should.”

Belvedere looked up at the ceiling, and his face drained of blood. I could see the drug was taking hold of him. “Why should I?” His voice had an otherworldly tone. It was almost as if he were talking to God. “There’s no justice here.”

“Not unless you make it so.”

He turned to look at me through tired yellow eyes. “Leave me in peace,” he said, and then he fell backward into his bed. His eyes fluttered shut, and he was snoring by the time I walked out of the room.

BELVEDERE LANGUISHED like that until the day his dog disappeared. It was a bright spring day. I had taken to spending my mornings in Sam Gee’s café in the hope of gleaning some tidbit of information about Sylvester O’Rourke’s involvement in the murders. When I returned to the McLaughlin house, just before noon, Mrs. McLaughlin was beside herself, combing through the newly green caragana hedge in the front yard. She was calling the mutt anxiously by the name she had given it. “Mufti!” she called. “Mufti! Come out now!”

The terrier was nowhere in sight, but a congregation of other dogs, big and small, had amassed on the other side of the road. “I’m worried about Mufti!” Mrs. McLaughlin said to me. “I must have left the door open when I was hanging bedsheets on the line. I haven’t seen him all morning.”

I looked around the back of the house and in the neighbour's yard. After chasing the band of dogs away as best I could, I searched through the scrub brush on the other side of the road. Belvedere's dog did not reveal himself.

Awakened from a deep slumber by Mrs. McLaughlin's frantic calling, Belvedere staggered down the stairs. He was wearing only trousers and boots, no shirt over his long johns. His hair and beard were an even greater mess than they had been the day before. I heard him ask Mrs. McLaughlin what the caterwauling was about, and I heard her confess that the dog had gone missing. "Jesus Christ, woman," he said, "can't I rely on you for anything?" Mrs. McLaughlin burst into tears at his response and ran back into the house.

I walked up the steps of the veranda. "You can't blame the missus for your own lack of get-up-and-go," I said. "It's your dog. Not hers."

Belvedere's eyes were suddenly full of steel. "Are you looking for a clout?"

"I'm looking for you to behave like a man."

There was a moment's standoff, and I was pretty sure that Belvedere would take a swing at me, but he didn't. He stood appraising me for some time. It was the first I knew that he had a modicum of respect for me. The sun was bright as a shiny penny that morning, and Belvedere's eyes were narrow. He shook his head as if to rattle the cobwebs out. "Well, let's go find him, Montgomery."

We searched the town for the better part of the afternoon, the cortege of feral mutts following behind us at some distance. Passersby asked us what we were looking for. Belvedere told them we were looking for lost treasure. With each passing hour, he stood more and more upright. His eyes lost their glaze, and his conversation became more coherent. I began to see that there was still hope.

I found the mutt at the foot of some wolf willows down by the river. The terrier was shaking when I lifted it out of its hiding place. I could not help but think that the dog had found its way to the river in an effort to escape the treachery of Prince Albert settlement.

Belvedere greeted the dog as one greets a beloved child who has fallen on a roadway in front of frantic horse traffic. He dandled the mutt's head. "There you are, my little sausage," he said, and then, growing more serious, "Don't you ever run away like that again." He cradled the shivering mutt in his arms all the way back to the McLaughlin house. "I want to thank you," Belvedere said, as we walked, "for standing by me through all of this. It's been a brutal time, but we're on the other side of it now."

"Are you ready to get back to work?" I asked.

"Yes," he said, and his voice was again direct and clear. "I think I'm ready."

On the first of June, we read in *The Saskatchewanian* that the Canadian Pacific Railroad had elected to build a southern route across the plains rather than to invest in a route through Prince Albert settlement to Fort Saskatchewan and beyond. Belvedere was sitting at the breakfast table when I read the article to him. He had been in a morose mood all the past week, but he guffawed loudly at the news. "Looks like our dear Mr. O'Rourke has laboured in vain, and now the railroad won't be coming through here at all."

"Looks like it," I replied. "The land along that proposed northern route won't be worth much now."

Belvedere placed his coffee cup on the table, and his face contorted into a grin. "Serves the bastard right."

We encountered O'Rourke on the street near his offices later that morning. He looked suitably chastened by recent events, his face a little washed out and haggard from lack of sleep. Belvedere stepped in front of him as O'Rourke was about to slide a key into the lock on his front door. "Looks like all your plotting was for naught, sir."

O'Rourke backed away and stared at Belvedere warily. "I don't know what you mean."

"I mean, sir, that you will not make a cent on your ill-gotten gains." Belvedere was frequently surly, but I do not believe I had ever seen him more so than at that time.

"Money is immaterial, sir," O'Rourke replied. "It can be lost and gained in a heartbeat."

"Was it worth killing three people over?"

O'Rourke smiled. "Again, I don't know what you mean."

"You know full well what I mean."

The newspaperman shook his head and looked with mock pity at Belvedere. "Baseless theories. Now, if you'll get out of my way, I have further business to attend to."

Belvedere stepped aside, and O'Rourke opened *The Herald's* front door. Before the door was shut behind him, I heard Belvedere hiss, "Was it worth sending an innocent man to prison?"

WE KNEW of O'Rourke's involvement in the murders, and we knew that Dan McQuaid was a paid assassin, but there was still one missing piece of the puzzle. Belvedere conjectured that Sergeant Slade was that missing piece. Hadn't he been at the scene of at least two of the murders? Couldn't he have shot the laundryman from a vantage point high on the hill above the settlement? Was he not frequently an obstruction to our investigation, and was he not in a hurry to see us out of town? And who told the lawyer of Belvedere's laudanum habit? Slade certainly had a motive to involve himself with McQuaid and O'Rourke, according to Belvedere, because his meagre salary, even as a sergeant and commanding officer, might have led him to try and profit from a land grab.

I was present at the Hobart and Eden store two days later when Belvedere confronted Slade about his possible involvement. It was a bright spring morning, and the pelts in the store reeked in the warmth of the day. Slade was sitting at his desk at the back of the store, spruced up in his spotless tunic, his hair parted neatly and pomaded, his face washed to a ruddy sheen. He glanced up at Belvedere and me as we entered. "Still in town," he said. "I thought the two of you would have absconded days ago."

Belvedere plunked himself down in the chair opposite the sergeant. "Some unfinished business keeps us here."

Slade went back to his paperwork. "Well, if you stay long enough, you can attend the groundbreaking of the new barracks sometime in July."

"The new barracks," Belvedere said. "So you'll be able to move your office out of this shite-hole."

Slade's face reddened. "Please refrain from the use of profanity in a public space, Corporal." He dipped his pen in a bottle of ink and continued writing.

Belvedere sucked on his own teeth for a moment. "I'm curious about your involvement in all of this."

"In all of what?"

"In these murders." Belvedere couldn't have said it more plainly.

Slade looked up, and his look was utterly serious. "Are you accusing me of something, Corporal?"

Belvedere grinned at him like a devil from the seventh ring of hell. "I'm tying up the loose ends," he said. "I can understand why you might have wanted me out of town from the start. We were never close. But why would you supply the prosecution with evidence against me?"

Slade looked over Belvedere's shoulder to see if a stray customer was eavesdropping upon their conversation, then chuckled mirthlessly. "I can assure you, Corporal, that your many foibles are the stuff of public knowledge. There was no need for me to supply the prosecution with anything."

Belvedere nodded slowly. "And do you not think it was more than a coincidence when you showed up on the Egil Johnson homestead even as we were investigating out there?"

False pity drenched Slade's next words. "You haven't a leg to stand on, Belvedere. I have as much right to conduct an investigation as you."

"What's in it for you?" Belvedere asked as if he had not really heard Slade's last response. "Were you hoping to have a share of the cash once the land had been sold?"

Slade stared at Belvedere long and hard. "I'm tired of this line of questioning, and I think you should take this matter up with whomever is not tired of listening to you," he said. "In the meantime, I must ask you to disappear at your earliest convenience."

Belvedere did not move. "If I find out you were involved in any of this, I'll put your sorry ass in jail, so help me God."

Slade was back at his paperwork. "Disappear, Corporal, and take your medical man with you. And don't let the door slap you on the backside on your way out."

PARRY ARRIVED EARLY the next day with a letter from Herchmer. Belvedere asked me to read the letter to him. The substance of the missive was that we were being summoned back to Battleford by the end of the week. Belvedere did not seem surprised by the news. "Herchmer says we are needed," I told him. "There are rumours of a Métis insurrection down by Carlton."

Belvedere's eyes were fixed on the coarse grounds in the coffee cup in front of him. "Not entirely unexpected." The dog jumped into his lap, and Belvedere petted the animal absentmindedly.

I was suddenly beset with the injustice of it all, the murders unpunished and the newspaperman allowed to go free. More than that, the futility of days and months spent on an investigation that had not convicted its kingpin burned like lye water at the back of my throat. We knew who that kingpin was, and we knew that he had murdered three men out of greed. "But we haven't brought O'Rourke to justice for his crimes."

"Justice isn't always served." Belvedere's face was hard.

"I suppose it isn't."

"There are different kinds of justice," he opined, "one for the rich, and one for the very poor." Absentmindedly dandling his mutt's forehead, Belvedere stared out the greasy window at the town. "Somebody's got to wash the dirty linens in this godforsaken place," he muttered. "Isn't that right?" I couldn't be sure if he was talking to me or to the dog, and I couldn't be sure if it was the laudanum talking and not the man.

Mrs. McLaughlin was in the dining room with us, washing pots and pans, and she had overheard our conversation. She looked squarely at Belvedere. "You're leaving?"

He looked at her foggily. "I have my orders."

After supper that evening, Belvedere dressed himself in civilian clothes and left the house. He told me he was off to the pub for one final hullabaloo before leaving the settlement, but he did not invite me to come along. The laudanum was in him, and he looked like a mangy coyote as he departed at eight o'clock that evening.

Unbeknownst to Belvedere, I penned a letter of my own to Colonel Herchmer after I had gone to my room that night. In the letter, I recounted the events of recent days and told the colonel of our suspicions about the sergeant. "We have reasonable grounds to believe that Sergeant Slade was involved somehow in these murders," I wrote. "It would be a great boon to our investigation if you would see fit to visit Prince Albert settlement one last time." Having marked the letter confidential, I stuffed it into an envelope and resolved to mail it the next morning.

I was awakened in the middle of the night by Belvedere's drunken return. I fumbled bleary-eyed for my pocket watch and discovered that it was four o'clock in the morning. He clumped up the stairs in his usual heavy-footed fashion, tripped, and fell on the landing with a loud thud. I heard him mutter a profanity before making his way to the bedroom.

He did not come down for breakfast the next morning, and he was still in bed at lunchtime. When he did awaken and stagger down the stairs at half past two, Belvedere looked like he'd seen a night of debauchery. His eyes were glazed again, as though under the influence of King Laud, and his manner was tired and unhappy. Most alarming of all was a gash on his forehead that was covered with coagulated blood. Over a cup of coffee, I asked him how he had received the wound.

"A little altercation," he muttered. "You know how these drunks are."

I also noticed a semi-circle of teeth marks on his left hand. "Must have been quite a fight."

"Short but sweet." Belvedere examined the contents of his coffee cup as though expecting a snake to slither out of it. Then he brought the cup to his lips and drank.

Mrs. McLaughlin, who had already begun to recede, became even more uncommunicative after that. She spent countless hours in her bedroom when she was not busy cooking for us. I sensed that the relationship between Mrs. McLaughlin and Belvedere had cooled completely. They were no longer chatty at the dinner table, and I do not think they spent much time together except at meals, where they studiously avoided looking at one another.

I MADE one last trip to the Sioux encampment before heading back to Battleford. The tipis were in the process of being dismantled; the band was moving south toward what was left of the buffalo herd. They were such remarkable people, alive to the very roots of their hair. One with the land in every way, they moved with the seasons. They lived in a world of trees and grass and water, as much a part of it as the deer and the otter and the black bear.

New leaves were budding on the stands of aspen, and the wind was soft as melted butter. Good Voice strode cheerily to where I was standing. "I was hoping to see you before we left," he said. "I wanted to thank you again for the help you gave my grandson."

"It was nothing," I replied, quite truthfully.

"He is with us today," Good Voice said. "That is as much as we can hope for." He pointed with his lips at the boy, who was loading supplies onto a travois. Then he turned his attention back to me. "There is a sadness about you. Too great for one so young."

I was startled by his pronouncement. "You see that in me?"

"I do." The old man seemed capable of looking into my soul. His hand was on my shoulder, and his gaze was unwavering. "You carry a heavy load. And you should not. Life belongs to no man. Only the Great Spirit can give life. And when death comes, it comes. We are the flash of the firefly in the night."

Unused to his philosophizing as I was, I found the old man strangely consoling. "Do you mind if I have another word with your grandson?"

"I'm sure he would like that."

I unstrapped a saddlebag and carried it with me as I approached the boy. He stopped in his labours and grinned at me. We exchanged hellos. "How are you feeling?" I asked.

"Good," he said. "I feel good."

We stood appraising each other for a moment. And then I said, "I've brought you something." I opened the saddlebag and produced the boy's portrait. "I wanted you to have this."

"For me?"

"Yes."

He showed the drawing to his mother, and she murmured something that sounded complimentary.

"I wish you well," I said.

The boy nodded his head.

I turned and walked back toward my horse.

"Mister!" the boy shouted at me. "I want to thank you,

mister." He ran toward me and clasped me around the waist. I'm not sure what he was thanking me for, but it was a moment of great joy for me. Whether or not I had effected a cure was questionable, but I had done no harm at least, and I took some comfort in that.

After I had said my goodbyes, I rode my horse a short distance and was then captivated by the impossible green of the new aspen leaves. I dismounted and breathed in deeply the scent of the forest, with its eternal rhythms of growth and decay.

Having climbed back into the saddle, I turned to see the last of Good Voice's tribe in the distance. People and horses plodded, in single file, toward the southwest, toward a hunt that would hopefully be happier than last year's had been. I spurred my horse toward the ferry crossing.

When I was back in the confines of my bedroom at the McLaughlin house that evening, I sat down at my desk and penned another letter to Emily. "I must apologize for my behaviour," I wrote. "I never meant to deceive you, but perhaps I have deceived myself more than you. I cannot leave this land just yet, but when I am able to depart, my fondest hope is that you might still carry me in your heart."

In truth, the culmination of our investigation had thrown a pail of freezing water on my enthusiasm for the North-West and for the notion of policing its peoples. It appeared that all my work —the training, the hard journey west—had been for naught. I began to wonder about the nature of humankind. I'd always thought that people, at their core, were generous and good, created in the image of God, but O'Rourke and his associate, McQuaid, had left me reeling. Worse yet, I began to wonder about my own purpose, if there was one, in coming west. Had I come for the right reasons? And were those same reasons strong enough to make me stay?

THREE DAYS LATER, we learned that Sylvester O'Rourke was dead. When he had not been seen or heard from in some time, a neighbour had kicked in the door and entered the newspaperman's stately brick house. He found O'Rourke hanging from a short rope that had been roughly tied to a newel post and flung over the railing at the top of his stairs.

There were rumours that the neighbour had heard some yelling four nights earlier, and bruises on the newspaperman's face were, according to Parry, inconsistent with the theory that he had committed suicide. The furniture in his elegant parlour had not been upturned or, if it was, chairs and tables had been placed in order again.

When I asked Belvedere, at the breakfast table, if we would be investigating the death, he sat in his chair and shrugged and looked out the window at the greening leaves. "We're off the case, remember?" He tried to smile, but he did not look happy. "We'll let Slade do the investigating. You know how he gets."

I did not know how to put my next question, so I asked it baldly. "Have you ever visited O'Rourke at his home?"

Belvedere's face darkened. "What are you getting at, Montgomery?"

"I just want to know—"

He locked his glazed eyes upon mine. His was the cold stare of a timber wolf. "Are you accusing me of something?"

"No, I—"

His lips curled into a vicious grin. "Give your head a shake, Montgomery. I would not be so stupid as to put my life and reputation at risk in such a way."

20

For reasons unknown to me at the time, Belvedere later relented in his insistence upon not getting involved in the investigation of the newspaperman's death. With O'Rourke out of the way, he decided that an inspection of his newspaper offices might be warranted.

Sergeant Slade had left a sign in the front window of the offices, prohibiting the public from entering the building. When Belvedere saw the sign, he snickered. "We're not the public," he said to me. "We're police officers." We walked to the rear of the building, where Belvedere unceremoniously kicked the door in.

The printing press stood at the back of the room like a big black bear that had gone into hibernation. The light was dim, but I was able to see that the offices had already been searched. Sheaves of paper were scattered haphazardly across the floor. The drawers of a desk had been opened and sifted through. I made my way to the compositor's table, where I could see that an article had been prepared for publication in the next edition of the newspaper, had that edition reached fruition. Although the headline was composed backward and upside down, I found I could read it after a moment's cogitation. "THE HERALD CLOSING DOORS," it said.

I took another moment to decipher the first paragraph of the unpublished article. *The Herald* would be shutting down by the end of the month, it read, and Sylvester O'Rourke would be moving on to new opportunities in Vancouver. These did not seem like the words of a man who had been contemplating suicide.

While I read through the article on the compositor's stick, Belvedere ransacked the office for further proof of O'Rourke's involvement in the murders. He searched through the open drawers on the newspaperman's desk, leaving their contents—mostly letters and receipts—in a pile on the floor. He looked for a safe but could not find one. Finally, he lifted a braided rug that covered the floor in front of the desk. The floor was constructed of hardwood of some sort, but there was an odd board of a blonder variety that seemed loose among its fellows. Belvedere clawed at the board with his fingernails, prying it out of its moorings. "What have we here?" he muttered, as he peered into the cavernous space below the floorboards. I came to his side for a better view. I could see brown earth two feet below the floorboards, but I could also see, in the gloom, a small metal box. Belvedere reached down and extracted the box from its murky confines.

The box was locked. Belvedere stomped on it with his boot several times, but to no avail. Then he found a screwdriver in a tool kit at the back of the shop and used it to pry open the metal container. Inside the box was a series of cancelled cheques and a letter. The cancelled cheques were addressed to Dan McQuaid and Eli Slade. The letter, which was signed by Sergeant Slade and dated 8 October 1883, notified the newspaperman that Herchmer was sending two Mounties to investigate Chen's murder and promising that Slade would do what little he could to impede the investigation. Why O'Rourke would have kept these cheques and letters was later a matter of some conjecture. Perhaps he had planned to use them if it became necessary to blackmail his confederates into silence.

Belvedere grinned at me churlishly as I perused the letter. “That’s convicting evidence,” he said. “It looks like our friend Sergeant Slade is on his way out.”

I was not present at Belvedere’s second confrontation with the sergeant. He reported it to me later. He found Slade again at his desk at the back of the Hobart and Eden store, beavering away at some paperwork. From the sound of it, Belvedere did not waste much time getting to the issue of the found letter. Slade did not believe that such a letter had been found until Belvedere showed it to him from a safe distance across the desk and told him of its contents. Slade scoffed at the notion that there was incriminating evidence in the letter.

“Incriminating or not,” Belvedere replied, “it contains evidence that you willfully betrayed the trust of your mounted police colleagues. And that you defied the orders of your commanding officer.”

There were several customers in the store at the time, and Slade was constantly looking over Belvedere’s shoulder to see if anyone was within hearing distance. “Kindly lower your voice,” Slade whispered. “You are making a grave mistake, sir, with these allegations. And you may be at risk of creating unrest in the community by calling a sergeant of the police force into question.”

“These are serious allegations,” Belvedere said, “and I want you to take them seriously.”

Slade leaned forward at his desk. “I didn’t murder anybody.”

“But you were willing to benefit from the murders.”

There was a long pause, and then Slade asked, quite confidentially, “What do you want from this?”

Belvedere was taken aback. “What do I want?”

“I can see to it that you have a share of whatever money is left after the sale of those properties. Or I could recommend you for a promotion, if that’s what you want.”

“All for the price of keeping silent?”

“Yes.” Slade looked over Belvedere’s shoulder again. Old Lady

Reed was hovering near the canned goods at the back of the store, eagle-eyed and eager for gossip. "But this is not the time and place for such a discussion. Meet me at Herman Cantrell's farmstead on the other side of the river. I'll be there at seven o'clock tomorrow evening."

I DID ACCOMPANY Belvedere on his journey north of the river one night later. He told me to have my revolver loaded and ready for use as I might be needed for backup. I remained in the evergreens with Colonel Herchmer, who had arrived in town under the cover of darkness. Having received my letter, he'd thought it best to proceed with Belvedere's stratagem until Slade's guilt was proven. We stood, hidden, a hundred feet away from the house, while Belvedere strode across the yard to meet the sergeant. Slade was dressed in his spotless finery, looking every inch an officer and a gentleman. The handle of his Enfield gleamed in the waning sun, his boots were polished, and his pith helmet made him seem six inches taller than he was. I leaned forward to hear their conversation.

Slade greeted Belvedere in a friendlier manner than I had seen before. "Hullo, my brother-in-arms," he said, "and thank you for taking the time to meet me here."

Belvedere shook his hand. "It was the least I could do," he said, "after your kind offer."

"Yes, well," Slade said, "do we have a deal?"

"I'd like to discuss the matter further," Belvedere replied, "before agreeing to anything."

Slade eyed him suspiciously. "What's left to discuss?"

"I want to know why you got involved with O'Rourke in the first place." Belvedere smiled. "Just for my own edification. I've spent so long trying to solve this mystery."

Slade instinctively glanced over his shoulder. Satisfied that the two of them were alone, he answered Belvedere's question. "I got involved for the same reason you will. Because the government of Canada pays its officers a pittance and expects them to risk their lives at every turn."

"And did you murder any of these men?"

"No," Slade said. "McQuaid committed all the murders. That was always the plan. He shot Chen from the hill near the police stables. He was a crack shot."

"I know."

"And then he killed McKay and Cantrell, but, from what I was told, at closer range."

"And you were to split the money from the land sales three ways?"

"We were," said Slade, "but now it's down to the two of us."

"And we'll still get paid?" Belvedere asked.

Slade nodded his head. "O'Rourke gave me a promissory note for two hundred dollars almost a year ago. I'll give you half of that."

Just then, a branch I had been leaning against snapped with a sound that was probably quite negligible, although it seemed thunderous to me at the time. A startled Slade looked in my direction. Then he peered at Belvedere as though he couldn't believe his own ears. His hand was on his revolver. "Did you bring somebody with you?"

At that moment, Colonel Herchmer stepped into the clearing. The colonel's bulky frame was shaking with anger. His moustache twitched. "He most certainly did, Sergeant Slade, and I have heard as much as I need to hear. I must ask you now to hand over your revolver and to accompany me and my loyal companions back to Prince Albert."

Slade's handgun was drawn at that moment, and he waved it indiscriminately at Belvedere and Herchmer. I stepped into the clearing with my own revolver drawn. Belvedere tried to talk him down. "The jig's up, Slade. There's no place to go from here."

"I won't be made a public disgrace," Slade said, "and paraded through the streets like a common criminal." He turned his revolver on Belvedere. Belvedere dived out of harm's way as Slade fired, landing in some tall grass near Cantrell's barn. He drew his Enfield from its holster, but not before I fired my weapon. I cannot say that I aimed the gun with the precise form I had been taught months earlier, but from my vantage point at the edge of the clearing, I had a clear shot at Slade. I straightened my arm as though the revolver was an extension of my hand. I blinked twice, held my breath, and squeezed the trigger. I heard the gun go off, and Slade clutched his chest and collapsed to the ground. My recollection is that he fell slowly, his eyes full of wonderment, a knee hitting the ground first, the handgun spiralling away, his pith helmet flying off seemingly of its own accord, a shoulder colliding with the earth, and then his head hitting the ground and recoiling, his contorted, angry, dead face partially covered by the tall, soft grass.

The reverberation of the gunshot was still in my ears, and I remained there with my arm extended for what seemed like a moment but was possibly an eternity. Colonel Herchmer was at my side. "You did what needed to be done, young man. There will be a commendation for you when you return to Battleford."

Belvedere stood up and walked over to the body, which was crumpled awkwardly on the ground. He stood there, staring at Slade, for a moment. Then he turned to me. His voice sounded like it was three hundred miles away, but I shall never forget what he said. "Jesus Christ, Montgomery, you've killed the man." I was still holding the gun, arm outstretched, and I felt my body shaking. It was the first time I had ever shot a human being. The next thing I remember is Belvedere standing beside me, wrestling the revolver out of my hand. "Let go, Montgomery," he was saying, "it's over and done with now."

I felt the sweat running down my face. "Is he dead?"

"As a fekking doornail," Belvedere said. "You shot him right through the heart."

"I should take a look."

Herchmer took me by the arm. "You need to sit down." He escorted me toward the house.

My knees were weak, quaking under me. "I'm going to be sick," I said, and I was hunched over, vomiting, even as I said it. Herchmer backed off for a moment and, when I was finished, he helped me walk a few extra feet and sat me down in the grass.

Belvedere sat down beside me. "Listen, Montgomery," he said, "what you are feeling at this moment is what every man feels when he takes a human life. It is not pleasant, I know, but rest assured that the memory of this will one day fade or you will become hardened to it."

"I should examine the man." I tried to stand up, but Belvedere clutched me by the arm and held me in a sitting position.

"The thing to remember is that he was a bad man and that he was trying to kill us."

"Nevertheless—"

Belvedere was not taking no for an answer. "You sit here," he said. "The colonel and I will attend to Slade."

I RESTED at the McLaughlin house for several days after the shooting, finding it difficult to get out of bed in the mornings. The image of Sergeant Slade grasping his chest and then tumbling to the ground kept appearing before me in my dreams, each time with a horrific variation. In one of those variations, I heard the thud of the bullet more clearly than I had heard it on the evening when I fired the shot. I heard Slade's bear-like grunt as the slug collided with his chest. In another variation, I saw his dead eyes peering at me through the tall grass at Cantrell's farm.

The other inhabitants of the house were kind to me. Mrs. McLaughlin ferried hot tea and largely inedible biscuits up the stairs every three hours or so. Belvedere left me in peace. I heard them speaking in hushed whispers outside my door on one of those mornings. Belvedere was explaining to her that I'd been through a traumatic ordeal and that I must be given time to "sleep it off."

There was concern in Mrs. McLaughlin's strained reply. "Is he going to be all right?" she asked.

Colonel Herchmer appeared in my room on the third day. I was up and about by that time, fully dressed and staring at a blank canvas on the store-bought easel in my room. Herchmer was dressed for travel in his uniform and a long coat, but he took a moment to sit in a chair beside my bed. He said nothing for a long while, and in that regard, the old colonel reminded me of how my father might have behaved, had he lived long enough to see me into maturity. Then he told me that he would be leaving on that day to accompany Sergeant Slade's body back to Battleford. Slade would be given a private funeral, he explained, and his involvement in the case would be kept out of the press. It was paramount that the good name of the North-West Mounted Police should not be sullied by the dangerous and illegal activities of one of its members. Furthermore, Herchmer said, he would be requesting a retrial of Egil Johnson and his immediate release from Stony Mountain Penitentiary, on the grounds that new information about Dan McQuaid's activities had come to light.

He finished by telling me that the police force owed me a great debt of gratitude, assuring me that a promotion was in the works. "You are like a son to me," the old man said. "I know you will come through this with flying colours. And I know you will live to serve the force with grace and dignity for many years to come." Having said those words, he got up, tapped me lightly on the shoulder, and hastened out of my room, closing the door softly behind him.

On the fourth day, Belvedere knocked gently at my bedroom door. I opened the door, and he came inside. "The tables have turned, Montgomery," he said, "and it's time for me to rally your spirits." He told me about the first man he had ever shot. He was serving under Wolseley on the Gold Coast of Africa at the time, and had fought in the third Ashanti campaign. "The blighters shot me in the hip in that warm African sun," he said. "I lay there against a rock in the battlefield for what seemed like hours, and the sun got hotter and hotter. And then I spotted a witty fellow running toward me with a spear. I shot him through the guts. I can still remember the blood-curdling scream and the way that man fell."

Then the conversation turned to the Canadian North-West and to the job at hand. Belvedere spoke about the importance of loyalty and duty and service. "It's a rough-and-tumble world out here. My own brother was killed on these plains." Finally, he looked me in the eyes. "I know I've been a right bastard and a ragtag son-of-a-bitch," he said, "and you've been a level-headed friend from the start. And now it's time to get up off your backside and help turn this godforsaken land into something that's more livable."

WE TOOK our leave from Prince Albert settlement at the end of the week. It was a bittersweet departure. Mrs. McLaughlin saw us off at the front door of her house. She presented each of us with a gift. Mine was a paintbrush and a box of watercolours. Belvedere's was a sheet of paper which he read but did not let me see. He folded it neatly and put it in his breast pocket, and then Mrs. McLaughlin petted the dog a last time and handed the animal to Belvedere.

Mrs. McLaughlin and Belvedere stared at each other for some time. "I'll miss you," Mrs. McLaughlin said.

Belvedere's eyes were glazed with laudanum, but I could see some human kindness in them still. "You'll have the house to yourself," he said, "at last."

"I will be lonely."

"You will have other boarders," he replied, "if you care to."

Mrs. McLaughlin did not say another word. She retreated not to her bedroom but to her husband's disused study, and Belvedere and I stepped out of the house into the warmth and splendour of a prairie spring day.

News of Sylvester O'Rourke's death, and the passing of Sergeant Slade, had already been eclipsed by far more resounding events elsewhere. It was rumoured that Gabriel Dumont and others from Batoche had journeyed to Montana to effect the return of Louis Riel into the territory. Townspeople were on edge with a fear of annihilation. Wedges had been created between white citizens and the Métis farmers at Prince Albert settlement. We knew that another battalion of mounted policemen was on its way to the town and that military troops would not be far behind. The fife and drum were in the distance, and the roar of the nine-pounders was nearly audible.

On the journey back to Battleford, Belvedere was even quieter than he had been the week before. He sat like a lump of clay upon his horse, peering hood-eyed at the traders' road in front of him. I reckoned that he had taken a large quantity of laudanum to dull the pain of his existence. The little dog was curled up behind the saddle's horn, and Belvedere absentmindedly stroked the mutt's fur.

I wondered about Belvedere's culpability as we rode. I knew from the previous months that he was not one to forgive, but did he have it in him to take the law into his own hands? Was he capable of becoming judge, jury, and executioner? He had denied any insinuation to that effect. And it was quite possible that O'Rourke had taken his own life or that some other anonymous enemy had aided him in his demise. Belvedere's horse picked its way along the dirt road ahead of me. From where I was sitting, the man in the saddle might have been a slouching devil or a world-weary god.

Nothing is quick on the prairies. The seasons change with a slowness that is almost imperceptible. We rode slowly, too, staying at the Buckton farm on the first night of our travels. The children had not lost their horror of Belvedere's stern face. They shrieked and howled as we entered the house, almost as though Belvedere had become the boogeyman of their nightmares.

We managed to find the McCallum homestead on the second night. I was glad we had avoided Lefreniere, who had been ungenerous on our ride to Prince Albert settlement months earlier and who was likely to be even more so now. Mr. McCallum was a kindly fellow. He fed us a lovely meal of roasted venison. Later that evening, we were treated to a concert of fiddle music as we drifted off to sleep.

WE MET a small band of Cree along the way, a few of them on scrawny horses pulling travois, most of them plodding moccasin-footed through the tall grass along the river. Dressed in rags and hand-me-downs, they appeared sullen and malnourished. The buffalo had all but vanished from these plains, and so their food supply had dwindled. I hollered a greeting as we met, but they did not respond. Like a line of weary soldiers, they trudged toward the hope of something better.

A mile or so after that, we came upon a hilly landscape that looked vaguely familiar. Belvedere reined his horse to a standstill and climbed down from the saddle. Mumbling to himself, he limped blindly toward a clump of poplars. I thought he was heading there to relieve his bladder. He bent low behind the trees and, when he reappeared a moment later, he was carrying a faded wooden box that contained the eight bottles of whisky he had confiscated from the Hudson Bay man several months earlier. Without saying a word, Belvedere transferred seven of the bottles from the wooden box to his saddlebags. The eighth bottle, he opened on the spot, taking a long, hard drink. He was unsteady, but he managed to climb back into the saddle, and he rode like that, quietly drunker with each pull of the bottle, all the way into Battleford.

THE END

ACKNOWLEDGMENTS

The author would like to thank his editor at Shadowpaw Press, Edward Willett, for his countless hours spent on this manuscript. He's indebted to Mark Eisenzimmer for his advice on police procedure. Special thanks to Ronald Gerber, literary agent at Lowenstein Associates in New York, who took the time to read an early draft of the novel and provide helpful feedback. And thank you, as always, to Beverley Brenna, my first, best reader, and to my three sons, who are always there when I need them.

ABOUT DWAYNE BRENNA

Dwayne Brenna is the award-winning author of several books of humour, poetry, and fiction. Coteau Books published his popular series of humorous vignettes, *Eddie Gustafson's Guide to Christmas,* in 2000. His two books of poetry, *Stealing Home* and *Give My Love to Rose*, were published by Hagios Press in 2012 and 2015. *Stealing Home*, a poetic celebration of the game of baseball, was shortlisted for several Saskatchewan Book Awards, including the University of Regina Book of the Year Award. His first novel, *New Albion*, about a laudanum-addicted playwright struggling to survive in London's East End during the winter of 1850-51, was published by Coteau in 2016. It won the 2017 Muslims for Peace and Justice Fiction Award at the Saskatchewan Book Awards and was one of three English-language novels shortlisted for the prestigious MM Bennetts Award for historical fiction. His baseball novel *Long Way Home* was published by Pocol Press in 2022, and his theatre history text *Nights That Shook the Stage* (McFarland Books) came out in 2023. His short stories and poems have been published in an array of journals, including *Grain*, *Nine*, *Spitball*, *The Antigonish Review*, *Intima*, and *The Cold Mountain Review*, and his short-story collection *Theories of Everything* came out from Shadowpaw Press in 2025.

ABOUT SHADOWPAW PRESS

Shadowpaw Press is a traditional publishing company, located in Regina, Saskatchewan, Canada and founded in 2018 by Edward Willett, an award-winning author of science fiction, fantasy, and non-fiction for readers of all ages. A member of Literary Press Group (Canada) and the Association of Canadian Publishers, Shadowpaw Press publishes an eclectic selection of books by both new and established authors, including adult fiction, young adult fiction, children's books, non-fiction, and anthologies, plus new editions of notable, previously published books in any genre under the Shadowpaw Press Reprise imprint.

Email: publisher@shadowpawpress.com.

 facebook.com/shadowpawpress

 x.com/shadowpawpress

 instagram.com/shadowpawpress

ALSO FROM SHADOWPAW PRESS

Literary Fiction

Theories of Everything by Dwayne Brenna

Let us be True by Erna Buffie

Hello by David Carpenter

Elephants in the Room by Betty Jane Hegerat

Dollybird by Anne Lazurko

The Lavender Child by Harriet Richards

Waiting for the Piano Tuner to Die by Harriet Richards

Small Reckonings by Karin Melberg Schwier

Thickwood by Gayle M. Smith

Poetry

First Light, Last Light by Glen Sorestad

The Door at the End of Everything by Lynda Monahan

The Glass Lodge: 20th Anniversary Edition by John Brady McDonald

Phases by Belinda Betker

Stay by Katherine Lawrence

Literary Nonfiction

Tales This Side of the Elysian Fields by Trevor W. Harrison

Cupboard Love: A Dictionary of Culinary Curiosities by Mark Morton

The Crow Who Tampered With Time by Lloyd Ratzlaff

Backwater Mystic Blues by Lloyd Ratzlaff